THE HOLIDAY
AT ARDMHOR

Lea Booth

CONTENTS

PROLOGUE

12th of April 1893

Eliza pulled her shawl tightly around her, trying in vain to keep dry. It was well after dawn, but the sky remained dark as brooding clouds tumbled their contents to the ground. Although she had dressed in her warm coat, Eliza shivered in the mist and drizzle. Her excitement had been enough to keep her warm when she'd hurried from the house, but now, as time wore on, a chill worked through her. It was a chill accompanied by a growing sense of unease. Her eyes never moved from the drive leading up to Ardmhor House. Where was he?

The cart which made deliveries to the house each morning would return down the drive soon. If he hadn't arrived by then, Eliza knew she would have to leave alone. She'd already purchased her train tickets from Inveravain, and she had to be in Manchester by Monday. It would be impossible to reach the station on time if she didn't leave with the cart.

She tried to reason with herself and quieten her mind. Surely he would come. They had been a part of each other's lives for so long that she couldn't comprehend a future without him. And he had made promises. He might not be the boldest of men, or the most self-assured, but he was nothing if not a man of his word. Also, maybe she was wrong to question his boldness. A flush stole across her face at the memory of the previous night. He'd shown a different side to himself then: a side Eliza had never seen before. For once he hadn't worried about what was proper, or what his parents might think, or what his duty was. The only thing he had thought about was being with her. That must have meant something.

The sound of the horses' hooves interrupted her thoughts. The panic that had been rising inside her threatened to swallow her whole. If he didn't appear in the next minute, she would have to leave alone. She would have to accept he had chosen Ardmhor over her. Over the last month or so, she'd tried to train herself to live with that idea. She had thought she'd almost managed it, but then last night had changed everything.

She felt for the locket that hung around her neck; he had said his heart had to be with hers, and she had believed him. Everything about him the previous night had spoken of confidence and certainty, as if he'd finally known who he wanted to be. The doubts that characterised him had been nowhere to be seen. Surely he would come. She didn't know if she could start again if he didn't.

CHAPTER ONE

A working holiday wasn't how Beth Hutton had expected to be spending her summer break. In fact, when she first saw the advert for working holidays on the Ardmhor estate, she'd been sceptical as to whether such a concept was even possible. She certainly hadn't considered that one could change her life.

She'd been sitting on the floor, like a little island surrounded by a sea of marking. It was assessment week at the secondary school where she worked, and that meant hundreds of hard to decipher answer papers to mark. Looking at the difference in size between the pile of completed marking and the pile still to do was depressing. Beth could almost picture the stacks of paper coming to life and drowning her completely. The enormity of the task seemed to leave her with only one option: temporary denial. Instead of getting on, she picked up her mum's magazine from the sofa she was leaning on. She couldn't get across the heap of marking to access anything more interesting. Such was her reluctance to work, she had now read through each of the articles and was making her way through the adverts at the back. She had spent longer than was necessary, especially for someone who didn't own their own house, considering the apparently life changing potential of a heated clothes airer, when her eye was drawn to a smaller black and white advert.

WORKING HOLIDAYS ON THE ARDMHOR ESTATE, the top line stated. Surely a contradiction in terms, Beth thought to herself. You were either working, or you were on holiday. How could you be both? The basic premise seemed to be that you would be so happy to be fed, watered, and housed with a group of like-minded individuals that you would be willing to firstly, hand over a decent amount of money and secondly, labour away for no reward on some big estate in Scotland. Beth wondered what kind of loser you would have to be to actually sign up for that.

As she was pondering the ridiculousness of the idea—she'd devoted at least 5 minutes to the clothes airer, so it was only fair the working holiday got the same consideration—her mum came in bearing refreshments. It had crossed

Beth's mind more than once that her mum's excellent snack production ratio was one reason it was taking her so long to find a home of her own. She had been back living with her parents ever since she started work, and as they charged her no rent, she had a decent wedge of savings in her bank account. The mortgage advisor she'd spoken to, after a bit of prodding from her parents, had made it clear her savings were enough for a deposit on a small house, but somehow nothing felt right. Truth be told, she liked the company of her parents each evening, and it was much easier to continue with the status quo than risk making the wrong decision.

"Have you seen this?" Beth asked, pointing out the advert to her mum. "Can you believe people actually pay to do work for someone else and then call it a holiday? Who on earth would want to do that?"

"Hang on a second," said Jean, interrupting the flow. She was well used to the fact Beth couldn't always stop once she warmed to a topic. "That name looks familiar. Let me have a closer look. Yes, that's it, Ardmhor. Don't you remember it?"

"I don't think so, should I?"

"You remember going to Scotland a few times when you were little, don't you? We stayed in that cottage with a path down to its own beach. Well, there was a big house just along the road, with a café and gardens. You loved the playground there. Anyway, Ardmhor was the name of the house."

"Oh, I remember the house with the beach, and I remember the playground, but I didn't recognise the name. Do you think it's the same place?"

"Well, Ardmhor is a fairly common name in Scotland, but it says it's near Inveravain, which was the town there, so it looks like it must be. Maybe that's what you should do this summer? It'd solve all your problems about what to do since Lucy backed out of going to Greece."

"I don't think so," Beth replied, slightly incredulous that her mum could even suggest such a thing.

It had devastated her when her best friend, Lucy, admitted she wanted to go away with her new boyfriend, Dan, instead of on their usual girly two weeks in the Greek sun. Beth didn't blame Lucy: she didn't have the amounts of holiday Beth enjoyed as a teacher, and it was only logical she'd want to spend her time off with her boyfriend. But just because her usual holiday in the sun wasn't happening, it didn't mean Beth was up for spending her precious time off with a bunch of middle-aged, waterproof wearing losers.

However, the holiday situation wasn't the only thing bothering her. All her life she'd felt like she'd been waiting for the next stage: the point where she would finally feel content. Admittedly, it wasn't great to be wishing your life away, but at least looking forward was positive. Recently though, she'd noticed she was increasingly looking backwards instead. Maybe it was normal to get nostalgic as you neared thirty? But it didn't look as if things had stalled in the same way for everyone else she knew. More and more of her friends were disappearing. They were moving away for exciting career opportunities or settling down into serious relationships. Some were even getting married. The reasons didn't really matter because the result was always the same: Beth was being left behind and alone, feeling like everyone else's worlds were opening up, whilst hers was closing in.

Her job was also getting her down. Each day, as she made her way to work, her stomach would churn with trepidation. She would look at others making their own journeys and think to herself 'I wish I was going where they're going'. It was ridiculous, but she felt convinced that each person she saw was confident, fulfilled, and happy, whereas she was dreading every lesson of the day. She imagined turning her car around and going somewhere different, but her fear of getting into trouble meant she never actually would. And anyway, what else would she do? Teaching was the only idea she'd ever had for a proper job, possibly because it was the only job she'd really experienced. Admittedly, she had never planned to become a history teacher. She had wanted to teach in a primary school, imagining adorable little children and nativity plays, but when she'd graduated with her history degree, she'd discovered that getting a place on a primary teaching course was a very competitive business. So rather than apply and fail, she didn't even try. Instead, she applied for a secondary school course because she'd heard it was much easier to get on to. She'd done a pretty good job of convincing herself that it was for the best. The kids wouldn't be so cute, but on the plus side, she'd get to focus purely on her favourite subject. However, even during training, she knew something wasn't quite right. There were too many variables beyond her control in each lesson, and she hated being observed as she taught, but she pushed on, completed the course, and got a job. She'd always been waiting. Surely, all she needed to do was wait a bit longer, and eventually it'd all be fine. But now here she was, several years down the line, still full of anxiety each day. Beth couldn't put into words what made her so worried. People always told her she was doing a great job, but it was all so overwhelming. There was always something she hadn't done, or something she could have done better. She simply never felt very good at it, and there was this gnawing fear that one day someone else would find out. But she did nothing about it—she just carried on waiting. There was no guarantee that change would make her happy. She could easily make the wrong decision again, or maybe she'd hate whatever job she did. So she took the easy option and just plodded on.

To top things off, as well as being unhappy at work, Beth was increasingly worried about her lack of a relationship. She'd always pictured herself having a family: a handsome husband and a couple of children. In her imagination, she pictured a boy and a girl. They would be cheeky and cute, but ultimately well behaved. Or, even better, they'd be identical twins; she'd dress them in matching outfits borrowed straight from the 1950s and involving knee-high socks. When she'd first got her job, she'd seen settling into a relationship as the next step, but it hadn't happened, and it was dawning on her it might not. Mr Right would not materialise out of thin air, and with her friends disappearing, how was she supposed to go out and find him? It was a depressing thought that the only relationship she'd had where she had actually wanted things to work out was way back at university. It was debatable whether what she had shared with Anthony had even been a relationship. A series of encounters might be a more accurate description. He hadn't been conventionally attractive and certainly wasn't her usual type, but he radiated self-confidence, and Beth couldn't get enough of him. He was just interested enough in her to keep her hopes up, but he always made it clear that he didn't want a girlfriend. She hadn't realised it at the time, but that was what made him perfect. She could throw herself into pursuing him, lose hours in daydreams about him, all without the fear of having to decide whether he was the right person for her. For someone who doubted every decision they made, a half relationship where there was no chance of having to make a commitment was ideal. Really, the problem wasn't meeting a man: it was that she was too insecure to commit to one. What if she made the wrong decision? Would she end up going off them and leave them feeling hurt? Would it be obvious to others that she'd picked a complete loser and make her look silly? And if she wasn't sure it was going to last forever, what was the point of bothering? So her relationships never got very far. It was much easier to pursue unobtainable, or unavailable people: like the confident but detached Anthony, or men who were already in relationships and made promises that Beth was reassured they wouldn't keep. Now it was becoming obvious that something had to change. After all, no matter how much a person enjoys their own company, or the company of their parents, having no other options is nothing to boast about.

So the abandoned Greek holiday was just the final straw, the cherry on a cake of mild disappointment. The problem was that the cake looked great from a distance, and it didn't even taste that bad as you ate it, it was only later, as it sat heavy in your stomach, that you realised just how unsatisfying it was.

CHAPTER TWO

Over the final few weeks of the summer term, Beth had taken to moping. When she wasn't delivering lessons, she moped about completing her other work tasks in a dejected and lacklustre manner. When she was at home, she moped around the house in a way that thoroughly tested the patience of her parents. However, despite all the energy that moping took, she couldn't fail to notice that her mum's magazine, open at the page of the Ardmhor advert, kept mysteriously appearing wherever she went. Not that she would admit it to her mum, but it had piqued her interest, and she did a bit of online research. There were, in fairness, aspects of the holiday that spoke to her. The accommodation looked lovely. Participants could sign up for between a week and a month's stay, and the price, considering it included all food, was surprisingly reasonable. Volunteers, as the website referred to them, had unrestricted access to the grounds of Ardmhor house and could also study the estate archives. This last snippet of information particularly appealed to Beth. It had been a long time since she'd done any historical research just because she wanted to. Nowadays, she only looked into the past to prepare lessons, and the reluctance of her teenage audience had pretty much destroyed any joy in it. The photos of the estate and surrounding area looked glorious, and they reawakened memories of those wonderful childhood holidays. However, the other photos on the website were definitely not drawing her in. The pictures of previous groups enjoying their stays confirmed Beth's initial fears: revealing plenty of middle-aged, possibly retired, people who were dressed head to toe in waterproofs. They were not the sort of people that were going to propel her to where she really wanted to be. 'Mr Right' wasn't likely to be discovered amongst them, so she dismissed the idea again.

Matters were finally taken out of Beth's hands when her parents decided a more direct approach than subtly placed magazines was necessary. They announced they had been fancying revisiting Scotland for a long time and had booked themselves a short break an hour's drive from Ardmhor. They had also booked a few nights in a luxury Scottish hotel later on in the summer. By what was apparently just a fantastic coincidence, it turned out those breaks coincided with the start and end of the month long Ardmhor holiday—the same holiday on which they happened to have reserved a place for Beth. The holiday which they could now deliver her to and return her from as they went about their travels. It was basically a fait accompli and Beth quickly realised acceptance was the only course of action. Acceptance also provided an answer to her earlier ponderings. It appeared that the type of loser spending their summer on a working holiday would be her.

When the time came to set off for Ardmhor, it was one of those rare, perfect summer days. The type you picture when you're invited to a summer event, but you know that in reality you'll probably be shivering under an umbrella. The sun was shining brightly, and the only interruption to a sea of pure blue sky was an occasional wisp of white cloud. Although he loved a decent road trip, David Hutton's demeanour wasn't quite as sunny as the weather as he wrestled everything his wife and daughter had packed into the boot of the car. Admittedly, Beth's suitcase was on the large side, but she had found packing a challenge. A month away was a long time, and her last few summer holidays had only really required bikinis and factor 50.

It felt as though she'd told everyone she'd met recently about her packing dilemma. When something was playing on her mind, no matter how trivial, Beth found it hard to stop herself from mentioning it. After much research, she had invested in the most stylish waterproofs she could find and some sturdy footwear. The rest of her case was jammed full of jeans, vests, t-shirts, and jumpers. Layering was, she had read, the key to a Scottish summer: actually, it was layering and insect repellent, which she had also packed plenty of.

The start of the journey passed without incident. They had set off mid-morning, so rush hour had long gone, and the traffic was light. The further north they travelled, the higher the hills seemed to get and the more dramatic the surrounding scenery. They stopped for lunch at a pub hidden just off the motorway. Beth's dad loved to research before travelling and had discovered this place when planning their first trip to Scotland. It had then become part of the tradition of the journey to make it their first stop.

"Don't you remember it?" Jean asked as they got out of the car. "It doesn't look as if it has changed at all."

Beth didn't think she really did. It was an old, low building, with thick stone walls and tiny windows. Despite the sunshine, the interior was cool as they stepped through the door, and the peat fire crackling in the hearth didn't seem out of place. They ate homemade burgers with the mouth-watering hand cut chips, and Beth wasn't sure whether it was memories that were emerging or just a sense of anticipation. Maybe it was the smell of the peat or the atmosphere of the old building, but she had a sudden feeling of excitement, as if something thrilling was about to happen.

"Do you feel it?" she asked, trying to explain to her mum.

"Maybe not like you," Jean replied. "I always loved this journey, but you would be totally beside yourself with excitement by the time we reached this point. That's why I'm surprised you don't remember more. You used to beg us to come back each year. But I suppose you were only little, and it is a good while ago now."

Although they could easily have done the journey in one go, they had decided to stay in a hotel about an hour from Ardmhor. That meant they could have a leisurely trip, enjoying the scenery, rather than rushing to be in time for Beth to register. As they arrived at their hotel for the night, Beth felt her nerves return, replacing the pleasant anticipation she'd felt earlier. The hotel sat on the edge of a sea loch, and the owners had added a restaurant on the back to take advantage of the views.

Their table by the window meant they could eat whilst enjoying the sight of curlews and oystercatchers exploring the shore. By the time the sun set, turning the sky a glorious shade of pink, none of them felt they could manage another mouthful. It was at this point that Beth broached the subject of cancelling Ardmhor and joining her parents at their cottage instead. It seemed, however, that their planning had pre-empted this situation. They had booked a tiny one bedroomed cottage, which definitely did not have room for another adult in it. Beth wondered if the whole 'drop off/ pick up' scenario they had engineered was just to make sure she couldn't chicken out and drive back home before she'd even signed in.

The next morning saw the three of them back in the car bright and early. Although Beth didn't need to arrive until midday, Jean and David were keen to see if things were the same as they remembered. So they decided they would aim to reach Ardmhor early, allowing them time for a trip down memory lane before they continued on their journey.

The previous day's travels had brought back some memories for Beth, but as they got closer to Ardmhor, the floodgates opened. Every mile they covered seemed to bring up a fresh recollection: mornings on the rock and shingle shore, buckets and spades out on the one tiny patch of sand, the sound of the waves through the open bedroom window, daylight still showing round the edge of the curtains, even though the clock said it was nearly midnight, afternoons watching the ferry load and unload at the pier, begging for an ice cream before fighting off the wasps, the sheer beauty of the light reflecting off the sea, and, finally, a sense of calm, of being in the right place, that Beth couldn't explain.

After a while, Jean pointed out the driveway to the house they'd stayed at all those years ago. It was only possible to make out the top of the chimneys from the road, but a bubble of excitement rose inside Beth. She couldn't wait to arrive and get out of the car.

A moment later, the entrance to Ardmhor House came into view. A long, winding approach road hid the main house from sight, but it was clear, even from the car parking area, that things had changed since their last visit. What had been a set of derelict outbuildings was now a sympathetically converted shop and café, replacing the old ones, which had been in an annexe of the big house. They unravelled themselves from the car and trooped in, enjoying the lovely gift shop smell of lavender bags, leather goods, and scented candles that drifted out of the shop door and into the hallway. The café was a few steps further along the corridor. It was like a mini baronial hall, with raised seating around the edges and enormous windows looking out over the surrounding garden, affording occasional glimpses of the sea. Beth's nerves about the holiday settled a little. Even if she had nothing in common with anyone else there, at least she would be lonely and bored in gorgeous surroundings.

Time slipped away over coffee and a vast slab of chocolate cake, and it was almost midday by the time she said goodbye to her parents. Feeling more emotional than she had expected as she watched their car disappear along the road, Beth decided she needed to get straight in there and take the plunge. So she wheeled her suitcase over to the wooden ticket hut, which served as the entrance to the main house and gardens, and looked for someone who would tell her what to do next.

It certainly wasn't what she'd been expecting for the summer, and all she could hope, given her initial thoughts on working holidays, was that she'd be proved wrong.

CHAPTER THREE

B eth hovered awkwardly in the middle of the ticket office. The man behind the desk was on the phone with his back to her. It had been several minutes since she'd entered the room and his conversation showed no sign of winding up. The frequent use of the words 'sweetheart' and 'babe', along with references to 'when I get you to myself', suggested that it either wasn't a work call or that someone might need some training on workplace harassment. Beth was unsure how to proceed. There was a bell on the counter to press for attention but, seeing as the assistant was right in front of her, using it seemed pushy. Maybe it would be better to go out and then return more noisily? But what if he turned round as she was leaving? How would she explain coming back in? She'd have to pretend she had left something outside and it might get very awkward. She retrieved her booking details from the pocket on the front of her suitcase instead. They would be needed for check-in anyway, and perhaps the noisy zip would be enough to announce her presence.

It didn't work. The assistant was still deep in conversation, but just as Beth was straightening up, a young woman with cropped pink hair and an Ardmhor branded fleece bustled through the door at the other side of the counter.

"Hi there, are you here to check in for the volunteer holiday?" she asked, quickly taking in the suitcase by Beth's feet.

"Yes, I'm Beth, Beth Hutton."

"I'm Eilidh," the young woman said with a smile, ticking something on a sheet of paper and selecting a key from behind the counter. "You're the first to arrive, so I'll take you across to your room, and you can get settled before the orientation session. I'm sorry about Calum," she continued, motioning towards the young man on the phone. "He's new, and he's in love, and I'm not sure he's realised he's here to work yet."

They made their way out of the ticket office and back across the parking area to the converted outbuildings, which Eilidh referred to as the coach house. At one side of the building, an external staircase lined with pots of flowers led to a large wooden door. Eilidh unlocked the door and led them into a corridor lit by a window at the far end, before opening a door on the left and showing Beth into a large, sunny bedroom.

Beth thought she would describe the furnishings as modern Scottish in style. Everything was wooden and traditional, but the crisp white linen on the bed stopped it from looking old fashioned. Thick tweed curtains were hanging at the windows, but they were updated by bright pinks and turquoises, instead of being the traditional browns and greens. The same colours were then picked up by the tartan cushions on the bed and the armchair in the window. Beth felt a trickle of relief flow through her. She had been sure that the reality wouldn't match the attractive rooms shown on the website and was pleased to find out she was wrong. Spotting the shiny white bathroom through a door in the corner was even more reassuring. She would be very comfortable here.

"Before you unpack, I'll just show you where you need to go for the orientation session," Eilidh said, bustling back out of the room and down the corridor in the opposite direction from the one in which they had entered. In the middle of the corridor, there was a half-glass door leading to a staircase, which ended in the hallway next to the café.

"Your key," Eilidh said, fishing the key she'd taken from behind the counter back out of her pocket and handing it over, "will open the door at the top of the stairs, the outside door, and your own door. You can use whichever entrance is easiest during the day, but at night the main entrance to the café and shop is locked, so you won't be able to get in that way." She carried on talking as she walked through another door to her right. "This is the room where we'll have the orientation session."

It was a bright room looking out onto the same garden as the café, but without such large windows. It held an array of mismatched chairs and a collection of coffee tables. In the corner, there was a little kitchenette and shelves with seemingly hundreds of mugs balanced on them.

"This is a sort of base for the volunteers over the holiday, somewhere you can relax away from the other visitors, without being stuck in your room. Hopefully, you'll all get on really well. That generally happens, and we have people coming back year after year."

"What are the other people usually like?" Beth asked, realising she'd hardly said a word. Not that Eilidh had noticed; she was bubbly enough to carry a conversation alone.

"It's impossible to say," Eilidh replied. "We get a complete mix: from pensioners, to students, to people from overseas who want to reconnect to their Scottish heritage." She paused for a second, looking Beth over discretely before she continued. "Don't worry, you'll be fine. You'll find something in common with someone."

Beth wondered if she was that easy to read.

"Do you think you can find your own way back to your room?" Eilidh continued. "I need to pop in and speak to Sally in the café. I'll see you at the meeting in an hour. There'll be food."

Beth had just about squeaked out a goodbye as the back of Eilidh's head disappeared through the café door. She made her way back to her room, wondering whether the quick dismissal meant Eilidh had confidence in her ability to look after herself or that she was already fed up with her company. Fortunately, she was thrown off this train of thought by the view from her window. The room had distracted her from looking at it earlier. Like the café, her room looked over the gardens, but being on the next floor up, the extra height meant the occasional glimpses of sea became a breath-taking vista. The Ardmhor estate sat on a mountainous peninsula jutting out into the sea. The sun sent sparkling shimmers over the water, highlighting the valleys and mountains visible across the sea loch which the peninsula formed. Her bedroom window at home enjoyed a view of the neighbour's shed roof. It was impossible to deny that this was a major improvement.

By the time Beth had unpacked her case, it was only a few minutes before the orientation session was due to begin. She gave herself a quick spray of perfume and checked her reflection. As someone on the tall side, it pleased Beth that the bedroom mirror was full length: too often she had to contort herself in order to see how she looked. Her curly red hair was by some miracle still mostly contained in its bun, although it was clear the bits around her ears were planning an escape bid. A headscarf tied in a jaunty knot solved the hair issue, and a small collection of hoop earrings up the edge of her ear made her feel a bit more confident. Beth decided the jeans and black jumper she was wearing were practical but also not totally outdoorsy. She had to concede that clothing wise a Scottish holiday could have some advantages over a Greek one. There had been no worries about getting bikini ready, and her pale skin could remain safely covered up. Giving herself a last glance, Beth was pretty happy with what she saw. Although she doubted there would be anyone she'd want to impress in the group, she still felt it was important to make as good a first impression as possible.

CHAPTER FOUR

The door to the volunteer base was open as Beth approached it. Eilidh was chatting to an older couple in the doorway and other people sat on chairs around the room. Beth hesitated slightly, feeling unsure what to do, but Eilidh had already spotted her and motioned for her to take one of the empty seats. Within a moment they were all sitting down, and Eilidh was leading the round the circle introductions that seem to be required by law at the start of any organised gathering of strangers.

Beth's eyes took in the group. It surprised her to find a full range of ages: from what looked to be a few years younger than her, right up to retirees, and they weren't all dressed entirely in outdoor gear. However, there was no time for this to please her: she was too busy trying to focus on what they were saying at the same time as panicking about how to introduce herself.

There were twelve volunteers in the room: six who would stay for the full month and six who would leave at the end of the week to be replaced by others. The first of the month-long guests to introduce themselves were Mary and Bob, a retired couple who were there for their fourth working holiday at Ardmhor. They bickered lovingly over whose turn it was to speak, before finishing each other's anecdotes, and Beth felt reassured that people had enjoyed the holiday enough to return. Next there was Steve, a university lecturer who looked to be in his fifties. He was a wildlife enthusiast and keen amateur photographer, drawn to Ardmhor by the gardens and the wildlife surrounding the house. Then there was Megan. She was an American divorcee who wanted to discover her Scottish roots. Megan looked as if she was a similar age to Steve and was so well groomed, or 'just so' as Beth's mum would say, that Beth couldn't really picture her wearing waterproofs and digging up weeds.

However, most interesting to Beth was the discovery that the other two month-long guests were her age or younger. Fraser was handsome, blonde, and the heir to his family's estate in England. He was at Ardmhor as research for starting up a similar holiday business back at home. He joked his mum had sent him away to meet a suitable young lady, as his gallivanting around London hadn't produced the right results. Beth's heart performed a little leap at this. Who'd have thought that her ticket to a different life would be on a working holiday after all? Fraser was attractive, the right sort of age, and best of all she wouldn't need to teach anymore because there was bound to be a castle, or something, on the family estate that she could take over running. Fraser was the answer to all her life concerns tied up in one handsome package.

Less appealing to Beth was the final month-long guest, Olivia. Olivia was petite and, in Beth's opinion, perfect. This meant she took an instant dislike to her. Olivia's hair was a glossy waterfall flowing down her back. Her skin didn't appear to have pores, and her nose was so dainty it was probably used as an 'after' photo in plastic surgery adverts. She had just finished her degree in environmental science and had come to Ardmhor in preparation for beginning a land management course. The worst thing about Olivia was that as well as being young, beautiful, and knowing where she was going in life, she also seemed decent and friendly. Beth practically hated her.

She was also very aware that everyone else staying for the month had a much better reason for being there than 'my parents made me come', which made introducing herself even more intimidating. As the group looked expectantly at her, she took a deep breath and said,

"I'm Beth, I'm a history teacher. I love the scenery around here, and old houses have always fascinated me."

Which was, in fairness to Beth, the truth, even if it omitted the actual reason for her booking onto the trip.

After the introductions, one of the cafe staff wheeled a buffet in and set it up at the back of the room. Beth tried to engineer a place in the buffet queue next to Fraser but found herself caught in conversation with Mary and Bob instead. They were a very entertaining couple, with their good-natured jibes and 'insider' information about Ardmhor, and Beth found herself laughing along with them. But she couldn't relax and fully enjoy herself because she was also very aware that Fraser, Olivia, and the other young people who were just staying for the week were all sitting together; it set off a familiar feeling in Beth that she had once again somehow missed out on a place in the 'in-crowd'.

After everyone had eaten their fill, Eilidh began outlining the basics they would need to know during their stay. As the forecast for the next week was good, she explained to the group that they were going to be restoring a part of the network of footpaths that crisscrossed the estate. Although all of their work would be outdoors, this job was on the higher parts of the estate, which were more exposed when the weather was poor, so it made sense to tackle it first while the pleasant weather held. There was to be no working until Monday though. Each weekend was leisure time for the volunteers to spend as they pleased.

Guests on the volunteer holiday were free to explore the estate and the grounds of Ardmhor House whenever they wanted. However, Eilidh explained they would need to be mindful of the privacy of the MacAird family, who owned the estate and lived in a wing of the house. Although Eilidh was very upbeat in her description of how the family shared their home with the staff and visitors, it was clear that gossip about the family, or unnecessary intrusion into their realm after opening hours, was frowned upon.

Access to the estate archives, which had been a selling point of the holiday for Beth, was through arrangement with Lady MacAird. After the warning not to intrude upon the family, Beth wondered whether she'd be brave enough to seek her out and make enquiries. Eilidh also informed them that, as part of the holiday, they could choose to shadow other estate workers in roles that interested them. Olivia's hand shot straight up, and she asked whether she could shadow the estate manager. It was a perfectly reasonable thing to do in the circumstances, but her calm confidence made Beth envy her even more.

Over the buffet, Bob and Mary had mentioned

to Beth that one tradition of the holiday was a Saturday night meal at the pub. The idea was to help the volunteers get to know each other, especially as more arrivals joined the group each week. Eilidh confirmed that this was the case and added that it could get messy once the Friday night farewell pub trips began as well. She laughed as she said they'd be grateful that they didn't work on Saturdays and Sundays.

By the time Eilidh had finished outlining all the information the group needed, from Wi-Fi codes to laundry facilities, it was already mid-afternoon. This left everyone with a couple of hours to spare before the trip down the road to the local pub. Beth hung back as people began to leave the room, keen to time her exit with Fraser, Olivia, and the other young members of the group. However, before she'd had a chance, Mary had grabbed her arm and told Beth she would be joining Bob, Megan, and herself on a tour of Ardmhor House. Mary said they needed someone with historical knowledge to explain it all to them. Beth didn't have the heart to say no. It was clear they were trying to make her feel needed. Maybe, she thought, it had been obvious to them over lunch she was feeling lost. Also, she didn't know if the younger group would actually want her joining them. It would be pretty embarrassing to end up left alone. So she followed Mary, Bob, and Megan up the path to the big house, fixing a smile on her face as she walked.

CHAPTER FIVE

The Ardmhor Hotel was the rather grand name for the pub just down the road from Ardmhor House. It was a long, whitewashed, one and a half storey building, which had clearly grown over the years. With its slate tiled roof and traditional white painted skews, it wouldn't have looked out of place on a tourist board poster. It seemed to Beth that she'd barely taken a breath between leaving the meeting and finding herself at the entrance to the pub. Eilidh had fallen into step beside her on the short walk there.

"I told you that you'd fit in," she said. "I saw you up at the big house this afternoon. You looked totally at home."

Eilidh was right. Beth had been having a good time, but she couldn't help thinking that perhaps Fraser and Olivia had been having an even better time elsewhere. Beth really wasn't happy with her relegation to the middle-aged and retired group, especially on her first afternoon there.

Eilidh had reserved a large table for them in a corner of the pub. Beth tried to judge her seating choice correctly this time and all but leapt into the chair at the side of Fraser. Olivia was sitting opposite him, Mary and Bob to the other side, and Megan in the space opposite Beth. The meal went well, with laughter ringing across the pub as the alcohol flowed. However, the alcohol also loosened Beth's tongue. She felt too embarrassed to even look at Fraser the next day as she remembered trying to monopolise his attention, shoehorning in questions about whether he had a girlfriend and how big his family home was. He didn't seem entirely horrified by the attention, treating her to a flirty wink when she'd asked him whether being Lord of the Manor came with any privileges, but it was pretty obvious what her intentions were.

It was also, unfortunately, obvious that others had noticed. When Beth had suggested another round of drinks, Megan had stepped in, suggesting that they walk home together instead. Beth had considered refusing, but Eilidh had joined in saying she needed to be getting home as well. Then Bob and Mary had agreed that some fresh air would be good, and pretty soon the entire group was ready to set off. The only thing tempering Beth's annoyance that she had failed in her quest for Fraser's attention was seeing Olivia caught in conversation with Steve, the wildlife enthusiast. The delectable Fraser was walking happily with Mary instead.

Back in her room, Beth was restless. She hadn't been ready for the night to end and stood gazing out of the window. Although it was long after the sun had disappeared from the sky, the view was still spectacular. There was a huge full moon reflecting on the sea, making it bright enough to pick out the hills across the water. With her alcohol induced confidence still very much in place, Beth made use of her right to roam the grounds. When she had been to look around Ardmhor House earlier, she'd walked past a viewpoint overlooking the sea, just to the side of the house. She thought to herself that it should be pretty easy to reach, even in the dark, and she hoped she might get a photo of that amazing full moon, which hung low in the sky, like a magical silver sun.

It was at the viewpoint that Beth first saw him. The moon had made it bright enough for her to follow the path without difficulty, and she felt as if she'd stepped into a new world. She could see almost as clearly as during the day, but the range of colours was totally different, with everything washed out in silvers and greys. A gentle breeze rustled through the trees behind the viewpoint, and waves broke on the rocks below, blocking out any other noise.

Beth was concentrating on trying to keep her camera steady enough to capture the scene, becoming more frustrated each time she checked the screen and found a blur rather than the beauty she could see in front of her. Finally, accepting her camera just wasn't up to the job, she slumped down onto a bench; then she almost shot straight back off it when a voice cut through the darkness.

"It's never quite the same, is it? I'm sorry if I startled you. I meant the pictures. They never seem to come out how people expect. You were so intent on getting the picture that I didn't want to interrupt you."

The voice had a hint of Scotland to it but spoke much more of an English public-school education. However, what really struck Beth was that it came from a vision of male beauty that put Fraser firmly in the shade. This man was exactly her type. The older she got, the harder Beth found it to place people's ages, but she'd have guessed he was in his late twenties or early thirties. He had dark tousled hair, a lean but athletic build, and was quirkily handsome. His nose was perhaps a little large for his face, but that somehow added to his appeal. For the second time that day, Beth felt her heart give a tell-tale quiver of excitement. She looked at him in wonder. What was this place? She'd been picturing a month of old people in waterproofs, and on the first day she'd met not one, but two gorgeous men. Ordinarily she might have felt more cautious about being alone, in a remote location, with a stranger who'd been watching her, but she'd had quite a lot to drink, so it didn't occur to her there might be anything to worry about.

"I'm Alex," he said. "The moon's amazing tonight, isn't it? I spend a lot of time out here, especially later on, when there's no one around."

"I'm Beth," she replied, realising she'd been staring at him like he was an exhibit in a zoo. "I'm on the volunteer holiday."

"Beth," he repeated slowly, as if he was putting together the pieces of a puzzle in his head. "So what are you making of it so far? The volunteers work pretty hard from what I've seen."

"We only arrived today, so it's just been getting to know people so far. We don't start work until Monday. Everyone seems nice though. I was worried whether I'd like it, but I think it might be alright."

"Well, I'm glad Ardmhor's making a good impression and that you're not too disappointed with us," Alex said, smiling.

"Oh, I didn't mean that. I already knew Ardmhor would be lovely. I've actually been here before, when I was little. It was the group holiday I wasn't sure about. I thought everyone might be total losers, you know, boring outdoor types."

"Because obviously everyone who enjoys spending time outdoors is a, how did you put it, 'total loser'?" Alex queried, with a twinkle in his eye.

The alcoholic fug cleared just enough for Beth to make the connection between the fact that she talking to a gorgeous man, who had said he frequently spent time outdoors, whilst casting aspersions on people who made similar choices.

"I didn't really mean that either," she began, trying to think how to dig herself back out of her hole. "I'd just really like to meet someone: you know, someone special."

Usually, she'd try to play it a bit cooler around a bloke she fancied. She didn't think it was a good look to come across as too needy, but once again, the alcohol wasn't doing her any favours.

"All my friends are settling down, and I'd like that too, but I can hardly plan a future with a married retiree, can I? And I thought that's what everyone on the holiday might be."

"And are they?" Alex asked, not doing too well at disguising the amusement in his voice.

"No, not at all. That's what surprised me. There is a retired couple, but they're really nice and they've taken me under their wing a bit. Then there are plenty of younger ones as well. Like there's this gorgeous bloke called Fraser, who's got his own castle or something in England."

"Wow, his own castle," Alex said, actually laughing now.

Beth wasn't alert enough to notice he was teasing her, continuing earnestly with her description of Fraser's selling points. "I know, it's amazing, isn't it? He's basically perfect. I could give up teaching and run his castle for him and we'd have loads of beautiful babies running about the place. But to be honest, I don't think it'll work out. There's also this girl called Olivia in the group, you'll definitely notice her, she's tiny and perfect: perfect hair, perfect clothes. It's already pretty obvious they'll get together, so I don't think I can plan my wedding just yet!"

Alex had stopped laughing. He'd turned, so he was looking at Beth directly, staring at her as if he was searching for something hidden in her face, something he'd been expecting to find but couldn't quite see. Beth knew there must have been plenty of other times when people had looked her in the eye, but this felt different. It was intense, and even in her inebriated state, she couldn't hold his gaze.

"Firstly," he began, "you shouldn't put yourself down. I'm sure Olivia is lovely, but that doesn't mean she's better than you. Anyone would be a fool not to see how beautiful you are."

Beth met his eyes again as he said this, grateful he couldn't see her blush in the dark and excited about where his words might lead. She felt herself slowly edging towards him.

"Secondly," he continued, "you've only met him today. You can't really know anything about him yet, so it shouldn't matter if he likes you or not. And finally, if you're unhappy at work, wouldn't it be better to do something about it yourself, rather than waiting for someone else to change your life?"

Now Beth really blushed, relieved she hadn't reached out for his hand in the way she'd been contemplating. She'd thought he'd been about to make a move on her, when actually he'd been thinking how ridiculous she was. She didn't know whether to feel angry or embarrassed. Alex was right, she didn't know Fraser, but surely it had been obvious she was just saying whatever came into her head, filling the silences as she always did when nervous. It wasn't as if Alex had seen the dodgy flirting in the pub, and the comment about running Fraser's castle had clearly been a joke: she didn't even know for certain that he had a castle. Her mind conveniently glossed over the fact that she had indeed been seriously contemplating a future with Fraser and channelled her embarrassment into anger. Even if Alex was right, where did he get off coming out with all that when they'd only known each other for two minutes?

"Well, it doesn't really matter anyway," she said eventually, attempting to move the subject on before failing miserably. "Fraser and Olivia were obviously really into each other today. In fact, they're probably getting to know each other better as we speak."

"And now you're spreading gossip about them, which really isn't right. It might seem harmless, but rumours can destroy lives."

This time, Beth didn't know how to respond at all. She felt thoroughly told off; and although she thought Alex was overreacting, she also knew that, ultimately, he was right. She had always struggled with making mistakes: not because she thought she was beyond them, but because she felt that no one else would have been so foolish. The realisation that she had gone wrong and that she'd end up spending the next few hours, possibly even days, analysing just how bad the situation was, or how silly she'd looked, always made her want to cry. Please, not that, she thought to herself as she felt tears prick at her eyelids. Don't let me make this situation even worse by blubbing all over him. She wished she could rewind time by a few minutes and start again. This is so typical, she thought. I meet a gorgeous man and then ruin it all within minutes by making the most vacuous and inane comments ever uttered. Surely I'm capable of better?

"You're right. I'm sorry," she said after a minute, aiming for that fresh start. "I don't know why I said all that. I get nervous when I first meet people. I want to seem friendly and make a good impression, so I tend to just say anything that pops into my head. I'm thinking that maybe I need to re-evaluate my strategy." She looked at him with a small smile, hoping he'd humour her.

"No, I'm sorry," he said finally. "I think it's probably me that's making a poor first impression. I must sound so pompous, telling you what you should think and what you shouldn't say."

He got up, walked a few steps away and then walked back towards her, holding his hand out in front of him.

"Why don't we start again?" he said. "I'm Alex, and I basically hang around Ardmhor."

Beth smiled at him. Maybe she hadn't totally messed things up.

"I'm Beth," she replied, accepting his proffered hand and enjoying the smoothness of his fingers around hers. "I've just arrived for the volunteer holiday."

"Well, it's a pleasure to meet you," he said with a smile. "So tell me about yourself. Where do you usually live?"

Beth relaxed then, telling him about her home, her job, and her parents. It was only when her phone suddenly picked up enough signal to deliver some earlier messages that she realised how long they'd been chatting.

"I'd better be getting back," she muttered. "I hadn't realised how late it was."

"Of course, you must be tired, with travelling up and settling in."

Once again, he looked at her intently, and Beth felt another flutter of excitement. Was he going to move in for a goodnight kiss after all? But it wasn't to be. Rising from his seat, he smoothed down his trousers and said, "I hope I'll see you out here again."

"That'd be nice," Beth replied, hoping the disappointment didn't carry in her voice.

She watched him disappear towards the house, before making her own way down the path which led to the ticket office and the coach house beyond. She'd only made it a few steps before her mind began analysing their conversation. It seemed the terrible start hadn't totally put him off, as they'd chatted for ages. However, it occurred to her she'd practically told Alex her life story, yet she had learnt very little about him. Had she just ended up prattling on again, without giving him a chance to speak? She tried to replay the conversation in her mind. No, she'd definitely asked some questions, or at least she'd tried to, but he just kept asking more and more about her. The more she thought about it, it was him that was oddly curious, rather than her who'd gone on. She let out a sigh of relief. She was much less critical of other people's social skills than her own. In fact, she preferred it when others made awkward mistakes, as it somehow took the pressure off her. And to be honest, she'd have forgiven Alex anything. He was just so beautiful. She had to admit he'd spoken a lot of sense, too. Maybe she should value herself more, rather than always worrying about what others thought.

When Beth finally fell asleep that night, she dreamt about the way Alex had looked at her: as though he was searching for something, something he hadn't seen for a long time but still hoped to find. However, in her dream, the intensity didn't feel awkward; instead it felt just how she imagined love must feel.

CHAPTER SIX

Before heading down for breakfast the next day, Beth spent a bit of time searching the internet for information about the MacAird family. Alex had been on her mind since waking, and she was hoping to find out more about him. He had spoken as if he was a part of Ardmhor and had headed off towards the big house, so her assumption was that he was part of the family. Sure enough, a quick search brought up an entry about the residents of Ardmhor House. It said that Lady Angela and Lord James MacAird, the owners of the Ardmhor estate, had two adult children, James and Alexander. They owned the estate at Ardmhor and had another home in London, which explained Alex's almost English accent. Once again, Beth felt her heart skip. Alex definitely lived here, which meant she had a very good chance of seeing him again.

However, before there was any possibility

of that happening, she needed to get through breakfast. Beth was feeling sensitive about her behaviour at the pub the previous night and tried to keep a low profile as she carried her plate over to a table in the corner, but it was only a moment before Megan joined her. Remembering Eilidh's warnings not to intrude on the family's privacy and wincing at the recollection of Alex telling her off for gossiping, Beth kept their meeting to herself when Megan asked if she'd gone straight to bed after the group returned from the pub.

There was an excursion organised for anyone that fancied it to the nearest town, Inveravain. Most of the group seemed to be going, so Beth followed the crowd. The day passed pleasantly. The sun was still shining, adding to the beauty of the scenery, and everyone enjoyed ice creams on the harbour. Beth couldn't help but notice Fraser and Olivia walking side by side. However, she tried to focus instead on the fact that she was actually enjoying herself. Mary and Bob were hilarious company, and Megan was turning out to be much more down to earth than Beth had imagined. Maybe Alex had a point, Beth thought. Maybe she should take more responsibility for herself. It might make more sense to base how happy she was on how she actually felt, rather than basing it on whether others might be happier.

Everyone decided against the pub that night,

in anticipation of hard work the next day, and Beth decided not to go out and look for Alex, either. Not that she didn't want to, she definitely did. She was both attracted to him and intrigued by him. However, the lack of a pub trip meant it was much earlier than the previous night when Beth returned to her room, and she wasn't sure he'd be out at the viewpoint. Also, after what Alex had said to her about essentially planning a new life with Fraser when she didn't even know him, she didn't want to appear too keen. So, summoning every ounce of her willpower, she tried to lose herself in a book. Much to her surprise, she was asleep within minutes.

By half nine the next morning, the group was outside the coach house wearing sensible footwear and waiting for the minibus that was going to deliver them to the far reaches of the estate. Steve's camera was clicking away nineteen to the dozen as they gradually wound their way to the top of the hill. Beth couldn't blame him, either. She'd thought the views were stunning as they'd travelled along the coast road to Inveravain the previous day, but the higher they climbed, the more spectacular the outlook became. Islets became visible at the mouths of sea lochs, and a ferry tracked through the water, setting off on its journey to distant islands. It was truly beautiful, and Beth's spirits soared at the realisation she was part of it.

The group's destination was part of the nature trails that covered not just the gardens around the house but made their way out onto the wider estate as well. The section they were to work on had partly washed away during heavy rains earlier in the year. It needed edging with stones, which were already on site, and drainage channels would have to be dug in to prevent it from washing away again. It was heavy, physical work, and Beth tried not to be jealous as she saw Fraser helping Olivia manhandle a rock into place. She tried even harder not to be jealous when Megan looked at them, nudged her, and said, "Don't they make a cute couple?" And then, by the time it got to their first break, Beth was so exhausted she didn't care.

Physical work wasn't something Beth was used to, but she knew immediately that she liked the sense of achievement it provided. It wasn't as easy to see instant change when teaching history to teenagers. While they were eating lunch, which was produced from the back of the minibus in old-fashioned wicker hampers, Beth caught sight of a figure waving from further down the hill. She could just make out that it was Alex and smiled as she remembered the sensations from her dream. As she laboured away, Beth mused on what he had said about making changes herself, instead of wanting others to make change for her.

"I'm sorry about earlier. I didn't upset you, did I?" Megan's voice cut through Beth's thoughts.

"Upset me? I don't think so, when?"

"When I made that comment about Fraser and Olivia. It was only after I said it that I remembered how keen you'd seemed on him the other night."

"Oh, right…" Beth hesitated, feeling embarrassed and wondering what the best response was. "You didn't upset me. It's fine, they do make a good couple. I was drunk the other night. Probably because of first night nerves. I feel silly about it now."

"Don't feel silly. You did nothing wrong, and I doubt anyone else noticed. I only picked up on it because it's exactly what I used to do."

"I can't imagine you ever making a fool of yourself like that, you're so…." Beth tailed off, not sure how to phrase what she meant.

Megan laughed. "I've had a long time to put this image together, and even now sometimes an image is all it is."

"What do you mean?" Beth asked, intrigued.

"Well, I was always desperate for everyone to like me, especially men. I made it my mission when I was young to find a man that was going to take care of me, so I know every trick in the book for trying to get a man's attention. And it worked, in that I got married young to a very successful man. I had everything I thought

I wanted, but I was miserable. Since we got divorced, I've been determined to do things my way, for myself. I don't want to be reliant on someone else ever again, but that doesn't come naturally to me, so I've worked hard at this poised, capable image. It doesn't always work, but gradually the image has become the real me. However, I can still spot someone doing the things I used to from a mile off."

"Like what?" Beth asked, amazed that Megan could relate to any of her insecurities.

"You know, being desperate for people to like you, changing your personality slightly to fit in with who you're speaking to, always worrying about what people think of you."

Beth blushed. She hadn't been expecting a conversation of this depth, and how obvious must she be if someone she hardly knew had noticed all this?

"I didn't mean to embarrass you. And I might be completely wrong. Maybe I'm just projecting my own thoughts onto you," Megan said, with a small shrug of her shoulders.

"No, it's fine. I definitely do too much worrying about what people think."

"And there's no easy way to stop. I don't have any solutions, I just wanted you to know it's not only you that feels like that."

"Do you still worry, then?"

"Of course, but I've learnt to deal with it

better. I feel like I lost me by trying to make myself into what other people would like. When I got married, I didn't just give up my name, I gave up my entire identity. I didn't even notice I'd done it until he wanted to divorce me for a younger replacement. Then I realised if I wasn't Mrs Bellington anymore, I wasn't anyone. I wasn't too sad about losing him. What made me sad was losing my identity again. I'd devoted my whole existence to being this perfect wife, and then suddenly I was on my own. He left me with a lovely house and plenty of money, but I had no role in life. It's taken years since then to learn who I am and what I want, and I will not let others define me again. If I ever meet someone else, it'll be on my terms. Anyway, what I'm trying to say is: I've had a long time to figure all this out. You'll get there too and probably much quicker than I did, but you won't find what you want looking for it in others."

"You probably won't believe me," Beth began, "but when you came over, I was deep in thought about how I need to sort myself out."

"Maybe that's what made me come out with it all! I promise I don't make a habit of pouring out my life story. But you don't need to sort yourself out: you just need to listen to what you want, rather than thinking what the right, or the easiest, or the most sensible thing might be. Just try to trust yourself a bit. Anyway, lecture over!

Let's get back to digging."

First Alex and now Megan, thought Beth. In the space of just a couple of days, two separate people, who were essentially strangers, had tackled her about her lack of self-belief. It bothered her she was so transparent. But what made her most uncomfortable was that they were right. She did measure her worth by what others thought of her, and she didn't know what would really make her happy. Experiencing a new style of working and finding she enjoyed it had given her a ray of hope. Maybe there could be something else out there for her. But how would she work out what that was? Listening to herself sounded simple. Beth felt she was already very much in touch with her inner voice. The problem was, it only pointed out what could go wrong and told her she couldn't do things. She had never noticed a voice that encouraged. She didn't know what it would sound like, or how to start listening to it.

By the time the volunteers arrived back at the coach house, Beth doubted that full on physical labour was for her. She could hardly move, but it was a good feeling of exhaustion all the same. Everyone decided a pub trip was necessary to celebrate their achievements, so the entire group set off along the road once they'd eaten and cleaned themselves up. This time, Beth kept her distance from Fraser's seat. Despite

Megan saying her flirting hadn't been noticeable to anyone else, Beth was eager to avoid embarrassing herself again, especially as it had become increasingly obvious that something was developing between Fraser and Olivia.

She went to the bar a couple of times, once to buy her round and once to help Mary carry a tray of drinks back. The young barman chatted to her each time and said with a smile that he was glad she was staying the full month. He was yet another handsome young man. It seemed to Beth that Ardmhor had far more than its fair share of them. His curly hair was just long enough to dip into his clear blue eyes, and his face lit up when he smiled. A bit of small-scale flirting, especially from a handsome man like this, would usually be enough to get Beth flirting in return, but she was determined to remember Alex and Megan's words. Her actions shouldn't be solely based on reacting to others around her, they should be about her own decisions instead. So she returned to the table without a backward glance. However, she knew deep down that nothing was really different. It was just she was more concerned with impressing Alex than she was with impressing the barman.

She didn't need any encouraging to leave the pub that night because, after a day's break to avoid seeming too keen, she wanted to see whether Alex might be out at the viewpoint.

They were earlier arriving back at the coach house than after the previous pub visit, probably the result of the day's hard labour, which gave Beth time to check her hair was behaving before she set out. The moon seemed just as bright when she arrived at the viewpoint, but her heart sank when she realised the space was empty. However, before she'd even had time to settle onto a bench, she heard the scrunch of gravel behind her. Her heart gave a brief flutter of excitement as she turned and saw Alex approaching.

"I hoped you'd be out here again," he said, coming to a halt in front of her.

A smile played on Beth's lips as her insides danced with happiness. He had hoped she'd be here, which meant he'd been thinking about her.

"I saw you busy working a few times today," he continued, "but you were so engrossed you only noticed me once. You looked like you were having a great time."

"I'm surprised at how much I enjoyed it," she replied. "It was really satisfying seeing the progress we made. I don't think I could do it permanently though. I ache all over!"

"I'm sure you'd get used to it, eventually. Not that I'd know, I don't exactly do much hard labour myself."

Beth had wanted to ask him what it was he did, but she didn't know if that would sound too pushy. Or worse, what if he thought she was fishing to see if he was so wealthy he didn't need to work and was trying to figure out if she could run his house for him? Like she'd stupidly said about Fraser.

"I was right about Fraser and Olivia," was what she said instead. "They are definitely becoming close."

"I saw them," Alex replied. "It was easy to work out who they were from your descriptions, and you're right, they seem to fit well together." He paused before continuing. "You don't need to worry about chasing relationships though, Beth. The right person for you will think you're the right person for them, and then it should all seem easy."

"Is that how it's been for you? You're very sensible for one so young," she said, in what she hoped was a light-hearted tone.

"Well, maybe easy wasn't the right word, and I definitely don't feel young," he replied, leaving Beth desperate to know more, but again feeling unsure whether it was appropriate to ask.

They chatted for a while about nothing of consequence, relaxing into each other's company, when Alex brought up the subject of Olivia and Fraser again.

"I'm glad you're not upset about Fraser though. You seemed really keen on him the other night."

"I can see he's more suited to Olivia than to me, and like you said, I don't even really know him. Anyway, the barman at the Ardmhor Hotel said he was glad I'm staying the whole month, so I might have already found an alternative!"

As the words came out of her mouth, Beth wished the ground could swallow her up. What had possessed her to add that last bit about the barman? After sounding about as deep as a puddle the other night, what on earth was she thinking? But if she was being honest, she knew the answer to that before she'd finished asking herself the question. Old habits die hard, and she'd wanted Alex to know that someone else considered her attractive—that he might have competition on his hands if he didn't act.

"Of course the barman likes you," Alex replied, fixing her directly with his gaze again, back to stern, serious mode. "You're beautiful. Who wouldn't? What you need to decide is whether you're happy with someone who likes you based purely on how you look? You need to remember he doesn't actually know you, Beth. So when he's flirting with you, it isn't telling you anything about yourself, apart from the fact you look great. You need to decide if that's good enough for you."

After he'd finished speaking, he continued looking at her so intently, so closely, that she wondered if he was going to kiss her. It wouldn't really make sense based on the content of his little speech, but she knew that if he did, she'd respond. Despite how Alex might feel about flirting based purely on physical attraction, Beth knew she didn't care if he was only interested in her looks. In fact, that would have been more than good enough for her at that moment. His proximity was turning the butterflies she'd felt earlier into a swarm. But there was no kiss to come. Instead, Alex looked away and got to his feet.

"Anyway Beth," he said, "it's time you got yourself tucked up in bed. You've got another busy day tomorrow."

And with that he was off, leaving her totally confused about whether he liked her, or thought she was a shallow, man-obsessed waste of space. Initially, he'd seemed pleased to see her and interested in what she had to say, but then he'd practically dismissed her before he left. However, there was no confusion over how Beth felt about him. He was confident, self-assured, and possibly not that interested in her. When you threw the fact he was also drop dead gorgeous into the mix, Beth just knew she'd finally met Mr Right.

CHAPTER SEVEN

The first week continued in a blur of path building and pub visits, culminating in the 'welcome meal' on Saturday, when new recruits to the group arrived. Beth tried her best not to flirt with the friendly barman, who she now knew was called Andrew, but Eilidh tested her willpower by constantly telling her what a great bloke he was. What tested Beth's resolve even further was not going down to the viewpoint. She desperately wanted to see Alex again, but she didn't want to mess things up. The connection she felt to him had an intensity that she'd never experienced before, and she really wanted him to feel the same. She was determined to become the woman that Alex thought she should be, a woman who was happy with herself, rather than one who worried about what others thought. That in trying to become this she was once again changing to suit others somehow didn't register. And if she couldn't change, she at least wanted to give the impression of being a strong, confident woman. So for over a week, she'd stayed away, but she'd wandered down to the viewpoint in her dreams just about every night.

The intensive path repairs had left little opportunity to sort out exploring the Ardmhor archives, but Beth had spent plenty of time thinking about what she really wanted to do with her life. She wasn't sure if she was listening to herself in the way Megan meant, but she had been constantly asking herself what she enjoyed. The thought she kept coming back to was that time had always flown when she was lost in the past, reading and researching. However, teaching history daily to a pretty resistant audience had gradually sucked out all the enjoyment. She hoped that spending time in the archives, looking through documents for no reason other than her own pleasure, might rekindle the spark. Beth had brought going to explore the archives together up with Mary, basically hoping that Mary might sort it all out for her, but she came away disappointed. Mary had said that she'd looked at the old photo albums a few times, but she wasn't particularly interested in the rest of it. She did, however, add that Lady Angela was very friendly and was sure to be happy to sort out access. It sounded simple, but after Eilidh's warning about intruding, Beth was worried about going about it in the wrong way. The fact she was harbouring dreams of one day being introduced to Lady Angela as a potential daughter-in-law made her especially concerned about making a good first impression. She decided to ask Eilidh's advice. Maybe she would set things up? Or, as they were going to be working in the main gardens now, perhaps she would finally meet Lady Angela in person and be able to make a casual enquiry.

The main project for the volunteers that summer was creating a new play area. There was already an impressive adventure playground for older children, which Beth remembered fondly from her childhood holidays, but this was going to be for the really little ones. The plan was that over three weeks they would clear the site, help to install the new equipment, and have everything ready to go. It was a big job for an inexperienced group, and Beth felt quite daunted looking at the overgrown patch of land in front of them. The focus of the first week was clearing the ground. The work was just as hard as repairing the paths, especially as the weather had now turned to four seasons in one day instead of the non-stop sunshine they'd enjoyed at the start, but the volunteers appreciated the novelty of seeing the visitors to the house. They had been removed from that side of things when they were working up at the top of the grounds, but now they saw why the MacAird family was keen for privacy after visiting hours ended. The stream of people was constant. Despite the weather and the distractions, work started well, and it looked like they would be on target to have the ground cleared by the end of the week.

Over the course of the holiday, it had become clear that Fraser and Olivia were officially a couple, but Beth no longer felt any jealousy towards them; she could see how well suited they were to each other, and, if she was honest with herself, she knew she would never have been happy with Fraser. He had a very boyish sense of humour and was constantly playing practical jokes. Whilst the silliness was initially somewhat endearing, the novelty quickly wore off, and Beth thought you would need the patience of a saint to live with him. Besides, her daydreams were all of Alex now.

Despite her initial concerns about being left out, or stuck with the older folk, there didn't actually seem to be any divisions within the group. In fact, there was a genuine camaraderie, with lots of laughter and good-natured teasing. For the first time in her life, Beth felt like she was really part of something, rather than hovering on the outside of the group. She wondered if she'd ever admit to her parents that they had been totally right to force her to come.

It was while Beth was making her way towards the bonfire, struggling under an awkward pile of branches, that Mary called across to her.

"Beth, there's Lady A. Go over and introduce yourself and ask about the archive."

But before Beth disentangled herself from her load, a smartly dressed man approached Lady Angela and they disappeared together into the house. There was no time to be upset about the missed opportunity, though, as at the same moment, she spotted Alex crossing the lawn. He didn't come over, but he smiled as he continued walking, and all thoughts of archives disappeared from Beth's mind.

As well as not speaking to Lady Angela, Beth hadn't found much time to speak to her mum. Since Jean had returned from Scotland, she'd been busy helping her own mother prepare for a move into sheltered accommodation. Although Beth's gran was totally together in her mind and her activity levels sometimes put Beth to shame, she was in her nineties, and after a couple of small falls, she wanted the security of knowing help was at hand if something more serious happened. Beth had sent her mum a few messages, and they had chatted briefly, but Jean had been too busy to talk for long. As a result, Beth was a little worried when she received a text asking her to phone home as soon as she got the chance. It was just after the group's evening meal, so Beth hurried up to her room to make the call.

"I'm sorry I scared you; I didn't think," Jean said, after registering the panic in Beth's voice. "I was just really excited to tell you what we found at Gran's today. You'll not believe it. It's such a strange coincidence."

Beth could hear her gran in the background, urging her mum to get to the point. Jean explained that in a box of things belonging to Beth's great-grandmother, they had found a framed picture of Ardmhor. Jean had realised it was a postcard she had sent from their first holiday there, and she'd taken it out of the frame, curious to see what she'd written on it. As expected, there were a few words describing what a great time they'd been having, but what she hadn't expected to see were the words Beth's great-grandmother had added. Scribbled at the bottom it said, 'I think this is where Mum lived—look for diary, to show Jean.'

The first time Beth's family went to Ardmhor had only been a month before her great-grandma died. She was already in her late nineties and quite forgetful by then, so scribbled notes to herself weren't uncommon. However, it seemed she hadn't acted on this note. She'd never mentioned a connection to Ardmhor to anyone, and she hadn't shown Beth's mum a diary.

"What? So my great-great-grandmother lived here? Really? Do you know where the diary is?"

Beth asked.

"Yes, it was in the box too, but Gran had never opened it because she'd thought it was her mum's diary and that it wasn't her place to read it. After seeing the note, she let me open it to check what it actually was. Anyway, the first page says, as clear as can be, 'Elizabeth Ruth Turner – Ardmhor'. Gran wouldn't let me read further than that, even though your great-grandmother's note said I was the one supposed to see it. She's insisted on me posting it straight to you because she wants you to read it at Ardmhor. We've sent it recorded delivery, so it should be with you tomorrow. You know your name comes from her, don't you?" Jean continued. "I mean, I know we never actually call you Elizabeth, but it's because of her it's on your birth certificate. She was the most confident and determined lady I'd ever met, and that's how I wanted you to be. It's crazy that you're there, and she lived there, and we never knew."

"I'm not sure the name passed on the confidence and determination," Beth replied, "but you're right about how strange it is, especially finding out now."

The two of them chatted a while longer, with Jean recalling all she could about Beth's great-great-grandmother, Elizabeth. She was never known as Elizabeth, only Eliza, and had lived to the impressive age of one hundred, so although she had died before Beth was born, Jean had known her until her late teens. Jean couldn't recall any family connection to Scotland, but Eliza had already lived longer than most people's lifetimes when Jean entered the world, so Jean supposed there were many things Eliza simply never had time to mention. As well as being the source of Beth's name, Eliza was also apparently the source of her red curls. Family legend said that she was determined and let nothing defeat her. If she wanted something, she worked out how to achieve it, and woe betide you if you got in her way. It seemed to Beth that their names and hair were perhaps the limit of their shared features, but she couldn't wait to read the diary.

She decided she would go out to the viewpoint that night. It had been over a week since her last visit, and Alex had smiled at her from the lawn the other day. It would surely look friendly, rather than keen, if she went out there tonight. Also, she was desperate to tell him about her mum's discovery. Maybe their ancestors had known each other? She couldn't help wondering if he would sort out access to the archives for her as well. She was even more intrigued about viewing them now, knowing that they might include her own flesh and blood.

She waited until a similar time to her previous visits, but as the cycle of the moon had moved on, it was much darker. It occurred to Beth that the darkness would make it obvious that she was looking for Alex, rather than admiring the view, but at least there was just enough light to see the path. The viewpoint was empty again, but Beth was hopeful as she sat down. After a few minutes, she heard the scrunch of gravel she'd been hoping for and turned to see Alex emerging from the darkness.

"I've missed you," he said. "I didn't know if I'd upset you with what I said the last time we met. I wondered if that was why you hadn't been out."

Beth could have leapt for joy at the fact he'd said he'd missed her, but she attempted to play it cool. "I've just been pretty busy."

"I'm so glad that's all it is," he replied. "Tell me what you've been up to then. It looks like you've almost finished clearing the spot for the playground."

"We have. It's going really well, and I think we're pretty much on target. It's hard work though. I've got muscles aching that I didn't even know I had!"

"Well, the hard work seems to suit you," Alex said, as he looked her up and down with that strange intensity of his. "You seem really happy. Maybe your mum and dad knew what they were doing by sending you here."

"I was thinking the same thing earlier, but don't ever tell them that!" Beth said, laughing. "Anyway, there's something I wanted to tell you about. I spoke to my mum today. Apparently, she's found a diary that my great-great-grandmother wrote, but the crazy thing is, she was living here at Ardmhor when she wrote it."

Alex seemed as surprised as Beth had been. He sat silently for a moment, as if working out how to respond.

"Really?" he said, eventually. "So your holidays aren't your only connection to Ardmhor. Your great-great-grandmother actually lived here. Do you know any details yet?"

"No, my gran made my mum post the diary straight to me, so it should arrive tomorrow. I can't wait to read it. Imagine if our ancestors knew each other. Do you think they might have sat right here, like we're doing now? Maybe my great-great-grandma was in love with one of your relatives!"

Alex smiled slowly and Beth felt her heart race a little.

"That would be quite something, wouldn't it?" he said.

"It totally would," Beth replied excitedly. "None of us knew she'd even been to Scotland, never mind lived here. It's just such a bizarre coincidence. It's made me really keen to look in the Ardmhor archives and see if I can find any records of her." She paused before continuing more cautiously, wondering whether she'd sound silly. "Do you think you could sort it out for me?"

Alex fixed her with that direct gaze, which, although more familiar, had become no less unsettling. The familiarity certainly hadn't reduced its impact on Beth's heart rate.

"No, Beth. I can't," he said after a moment. "It'd be much better coming from you. I know you get nervous about going about things the wrong way, but each time you chase after something you want for yourself, you'll see a little more of what you're capable of. You're so like... But you're... No, it doesn't matter."

He stopped and looked away for a while, gazing out toward the waves they could hear gently scouring the shore below them. Beth wondered how he'd been able to know what was worrying her and also what he'd been trying to say. She was so like what? But when he spoke again, the seriousness was gone.

"I know there won't be a problem when you finally ask. Lady A loves showing off the archives. You just need to gather your courage and speak to her."

And with that, he leaned in and placed a kiss on Beth's cheek before he set off up the path. She felt a warmth spread through her, but it wasn't like the desire she'd experienced in the past when she really wanted someone. It wasn't lust from the physical touch of his lips to her skin. After all, it had only been the most fleeting of kisses.

No, this was something else. She'd never felt anything like it before. She didn't really know how to describe it, but when he'd kissed her, she'd felt like they were connected, and more than anything, she wanted to feel it again.

So for once, she left the viewpoint certain of something. She knew that tomorrow she would have to be brave and ask Lady Angela about the archives. What she wished she knew was how to make Alex want her as much as she wanted him.

CHAPTER EIGHT

Beth was glad it was Saturday and there was no work to be done because the diary had arrived. The dark leather cover contrasted vividly with the bright plastic it was so carefully wrapped in, and the pages inside had a satisfying crinkle, each one lovingly filled by hand. Fortunately, the ink was still bright, and although it was of that looping, old-fashioned style, Eliza's handwriting was easy to follow. Beth settled into the armchair and began to read.

Elizabeth Ruth Turner - Ardmhor

21st of May 1891

It seems appropriate to start this new diary today because it's like I'm starting a new life. I'm not Eliza Turner with a home and a mother and a father anymore. I'm Eliza Turner living at Ardmhor House, with no control over my own life. I feel completely lost, possibly the most miserable I've ever felt. But then maybe I'm being too dramatic. I suppose that being told I have to live in a luxurious house is hardly comparable to the deaths of my parents. It's just that until now, I always had my own place in the world. I was loved by two parents and living far away from here. Then I was a dutiful daughter, supporting my father in building a new life. Now, I'm an outsider in another family's home, and I'm stuck in a place I've never really wanted to be.

I don't know why all of this wasn't discussed before Father died. We knew what was happening and had plenty of time to prepare. Although I suppose he was discussing it, it just wasn't with me, which makes me so angry. And then, of course, I end up feeling guilty. When it became obvious that Father would not recover, I'd assumed that eventually I would return to England. Both Mother and Father still have some family there, even if they haven't maintained contact. I was hoping I'd move back to England and contribute to my upkeep by assisting someone in their business, in the same way that I'd helped Father. I'd hoped that eventually I could attend a university. I know it would be unusual for a woman, but it's not completely unheard of now, and just imagine— with a university education, I could be in control of my own life.

But instead, I find myself here. Father had nothing to leave behind when he died. Our house came with the job of factor for the Ardmhor estate and had to be vacated ready for his replacement. There was no money. Every penny had been used to pay off the debts left by Mother's long illness and then to pay for Father's medical bills. Essentially, I was penniless and alone. So out of respect for my father, as Lady MacAird put it, they had decided between them that I would move into Ardmhor House. Lord MacAird would act as my guardian, and I would be a companion to their daughter, Flora. When I asked whether it might be better for me to return to family in England instead, Lady MacAird said that I shouldn't be questioning my father's decisions. She also implied that I was being extremely ungrateful, which I suppose I am. The MacAird family has no obligation to me, after all.

It could be argued that they have been more than generous to my family. Father and Lord MacAird studied together in England and had remained friends and correspondents since. Mother's long, drawn out illness had seen the collapse of Father's law practice, and Father struggled greatly after her death. We could easily have found ourselves destitute if Lord MacAird hadn't stepped in with the offer of a fresh start on his Scottish estate. Mind you, it wasn't all a big favour for Father. There had been issues at Ardmhor. Father's predecessor as factor was unpopular. He was heavy-handed in his duties and this, coupled with the fact that the local population was unwilling to forget the evictions his father had overseen, had led to some trouble. Lord MacAird had essentially ended up paying him to move away, so it was to his advantage that my father, a man he had trusted for years and who had the necessary skills to manage the estate, was now without employment or direction. It wasn't all a case of them saving us out of the goodness of their hearts.

However, it means that after over 10 years in this desolate place, I am now here alone. I am to share a room with Flora, which I think is supposed to be seen as an honour, but much as I love her, I won't have my own space. And even though I think I trust Flora completely—I still feel I need to keep this diary hidden.

I find it difficult to understand Lady MacAird, or Lady Constance, as I am to call her now. She came into our room when I had finished arranging my belongings and picked up Mother and Father's wedding portrait, which I'd placed on the small dresser next to my bed. She studied it for ages looking quite sad, and I thought she might understand how lost and alone I felt, but then she suddenly put it face down on the dresser and said I should keep it somewhere out of sight, as it did no good to dwell on the past. I put it straight into a drawer in order to please her, but it made it clear to me that my security depends on the whims of others. Just a moment or two after this, she suggested I should call her mother, as I am now a part of the family. Then, with the next breath, she announced that would be wrong, as my mother couldn't be replaced. Finally, she decided I should call her Lady Constance. I just don't know quite where I am with her. I can hear the gong sounding for dinner now, and I've done nothing to get myself ready, so I suppose I need to stop scribbling and collect my thoughts.

28th of June 1891

I can't say I feel totally at home here yet, although Flora tells me frequently how much better her life is with me close to her. Lord MacAird and James barely seem to have noticed that I am here, and Lady Constance veers between reminding me I should be grateful for my place here and smothering me with motherly affection. However, I must admit that I am enjoying studying alongside Flora. Flora hates most of her lessons, which is probably part of the reason I'm here. I overheard our tutor and Lady Constance discussing how much calmer Flora is, now that I provide an example for her. We don't cover all the things I'd like to learn, apparently if a girl knows too much no one will want to marry her, and it's no secret that Flora is supposed to make a good marriage. However, studying with an actual teacher again is so fulfilling.

Our days have fallen into a sort of routine now, and it makes me feel more at ease. After breakfast with Lady Constance and Lord MacAird, Flora and I are expected to help Lady Constance with any necessary household organisation. Lady Constance says it is vital we understand the challenges of running a household. We then take a turn in the gardens, where Flora makes us wander until we spot Angus, the youngest of the team of gardeners. Then she teases him mercilessly until I drag her away. This is probably another thing Lady Constance is hoping I'll put an end to, although I can't claim I'm being very successful yet. If I tell Flora her mother will be angry, she simply says 'well make sure she doesn't find out then!' She really can be quite exasperating. I look across the sea to the distant hills at the times when she is testing my patience and imagine myself far, far away.

After the garden, we have a light meal with Lady Constance before our tutor arrives in the afternoon. Then, once our lessons are over, I like to continue to study, and Flora likes to distract me. We eat dinner with whichever members of the family are around. Sometimes the minister will join us, only from the Church of Scotland though, the MacAirds are not supporters of the

Free Church. They say it gives people ideas above their station; I think they just don't like their lack of control over who is in charge. After dinner, sometimes we ladies end up talking over coffee in the drawing room, while the men end up in the billiards room. Other days, we all sit together, and Flora and I entertain with the piano and a song.

It means the days are full and pass quickly, but I often find myself stood in the main hall at the foot of the grand staircase, watching the light from the huge stained-glass window playing across the floor. As I stand there, my mind always wanders. I think about what would happen if instead of following the plan, I took myself off. What would happen if I slipped out between those beautiful columns and disappeared through the huge front door, off to do whatever I wanted?

19th of July 1891

Finally, exciting news. Alexander is coming home. It has been decided that Alexander is to take over the day to day running of the estate here. Lord MacAird has not been happy with Father's replacement, and as the second son, Alexander won't have anything better to do. James, as the heir, is far too important to act as factor, and he'll be occupied elsewhere as the family wealth and interests in London expand.

That's why Alexander hasn't been around. He has been away studying in England, as all the males in the family do. He still has more studying ahead of him, but his classes conclude for the summer this week and he will be coming home. I'm really looking forward to his return because when we first moved here, after Mother's death, Alexander was the only person who seemed to notice how hard I was finding everything. I don't think every young boy would comfort an even younger girl when he saw her being left out of the other children's games. I think he recognised me as a fellow outsider. He's never had the confidence enjoyed by his siblings, and I've always wanted to be somewhere else. Anyway, he's looked out for me ever since. He always wants to know how I am, or what I think of various bits of news, so I am overjoyed to think of him back here, another friend at the dinner table.

CHAPTER NINE

Beth was desperate to learn more about Eliza's life at Ardmhor. She could hardly believe that her grandmother's grandmother had lived in the big house, and it appeared she'd lived there with an Alexander as well. Had he looked like 'her' Alex, Beth wondered? There were so many questions in her mind. Which had been Eliza's bedroom? Where did she and Flora take their lessons? Did the hallway still look the same as it did when Eliza stood daydreaming at the foot of the stairs? Although she'd visited the house with Mary, Bob, and Megan on their first day at Ardmhor, she'd been so overwhelmed by meeting everyone and trying to fit in that she hadn't really paid attention to what she saw. Beth knew that she finally had to take the bull by the horns and sort out access to the archives. She put down the diary, realising that a couple of hours had passed since she'd picked it up, and although sorely tempted to just continue reading, she resolved to set off up to the house to speak to Lady Angela.

Ardmhor House was open for tours every day in the summer. The tours took in the main reception rooms on the ground floor and some bedrooms on the first floor. This gave visitors a chance to appreciate the scale of the house, to walk up the grand staircase and see the amazing views from the bedrooms, whilst allowing the MacAird family privacy in the rest of the house, which could be kept completely self-contained from the public areas.

Beth stood in front of the main entrance, looking at the house. It had a long frontage which had grown over time, leaving a mishmash of styles. The first section was turreted, its appearance like an illustration from a childhood fairy-tale. This was the wing of the house where the rooms open to visitors were located. The tall middle section of the house stood stark and plain, the crenelated top lending it the impression of a castle. The oldest section was different again, looking as if someone had tacked a small, whitewashed house onto the end of a much grander building. Beth said hello to the house guide, Kath, who was manning the entrance and instructing visitors on where to go. She had met most of the staff who worked in the house, shop, and café over the past couple of weeks, knowing them by sight, if not by name.

Taking a deep breath, Beth enquired whether Lady Angela was around.

"She's not, I'm afraid. She's popped down the road to Inveravain," Kath explained. "Do you want to leave a message, or is there anything I can help with?"

"I was hoping to have a look at the archives. Eilidh said we needed to arrange it with Lady Angela."

"Lady A does usually sort it all because the archive room isn't accessible from the public areas, so she likes to know who's coming and going, but it'll be no bother. She'll want to show you what's what, but then she'll probably leave you to it. I'll let her know you've asked. In fact, leave me your mobile number and then she can ring you when she gets back and sort it out."

"Oh, she doesn't need to do that," Beth replied, backing away slightly. "I can just call back up another time."

Kath pushed a pen and paper into Beth's hand.

"Don't be daft! You could keep missing each other for days. Stick your number on here and then go and have a good nosy around the house."

Beth did as she was told, smiling to herself over how easy it had been against the ordeal she had pictured in her head. A group of visitors came in, taking Kath's attention, and Beth drifted away towards the centre of the magnificent entrance hall. Her gaze moved to the staircase at the far end of the room, partially separated from her by a series of slender columns that soared up to the ornate ceiling, exactly as Eliza had described in her diary.

She walked over to the foot of the stairs. A large gong stood to one side of them, surely the same one that Eliza had heard calling her to dinner. The huge stained-glass window, rising from the height of the half landing, illuminated the hallway below with shafts of coloured light, and Beth marvelled at the fact she was standing in the same spot her great-great-grandmother had all those years ago. That her own flesh and blood had been a member of this household gave a surreal quality to Beth's experience as she climbed the stairs.

At the half landing, the stairs branched off into two; both sides led to the same place, but they were now used to filter visitors either up or down as they travelled between the floors. Beth walked into the first of the two bedrooms open to the public. It was a large room with windows to the front and side, taking in views of the sea and the gardens. The laminated information sheets said the furniture was original to the time this part of the house was built, although the fabrics had been updated at various points since the 1850s. The other bedroom was similar, but it had twin beds instead of a double and looked over the gardens to the rear of the house.

Between the two rooms was a bathroom, which must have seemed the height of luxury when it was installed. There was a toilet, with its cistern high above it and colourful painted flowers around its base. The enormous bath was stained at the end, where over a century of peaty water had dripped from its huge taps. The information sheet said this room was Victorian and had been one of the earliest installed in a Scottish house. Victorian covered a long timeframe and meant it could easily have been installed by the time Eliza moved in, Beth thought to herself. It was becoming clear that Eliza's description of the house as luxurious was true. Beth wondered if either of the bedrooms was the one occupied by Flora and Eliza and whether there would be a way of finding out.

Making her way back downstairs, Beth wandered through the billiard room, dining room, and drawing room. She listened as a guide answered the questions of a group of visitors, explaining that, just like upstairs, everything was original to the 1850s when this wing was built. She tried to picture Eliza, Flora, and Lady Constance sat chatting on the elegant sofas, or Eliza and Flora at the grand piano entertaining the others. Beth realised she was picturing Eliza as herself. The only photograph she had ever seen of her great-great-grandmother was of her as an old woman, so she didn't really know whether they shared any similarities beyond their hair, but without a more accurate image to base her daydreams on it was easy to let the fantasy take flight.

The sun was shining as she wandered back out onto the front lawn. Enticed by the shimmering sea in front of her, Beth made her way across the grass and onto the path that led to the viewpoint. It was the first time Beth had been there during opening hours since meeting Alex, and it was almost a shock to find it bustling with visitors, each bench occupied. Although the view was still stunning, more so really because the sunlight picked out previously hidden detail on the distant hills, it didn't hold the same attraction for Beth without Alex there, so she made her way along the path leading further into the woodland rather than lingering. As she ambled through the soaring trees, enjoying the dappled sunlight playing across the ground, her phone buzzed in her pocket. A message was displayed on the screen.

'Hi Beth, Kath said you wanted to see the archives. Are you free at 2:00? Let me know if you are, Lady A.'

A glance at the time told her it was now 1 o'clock, so she'd just have time to nip down to the café, grab a snack, and make it back up to the house.

Beth sent a quick text agreeing as she walked in the direction of the café.

She hadn't even made it out of the woods before a reply pinged back. 'Excellent! I'll meet you at the main entrance. I can't wait to show you everything!'

Beth smiled as she hurried her pace back across the grass. She was going to see the archive, and maybe she'd be able to put a face to the young Eliza as well.

CHAPTER TEN

Although according to Beth's phone it was only five to two, Lady Angela was already stood waiting by the door as she approached the house.

"Hi, I'm Beth," she began, wondering if she ought to offer her hand to shake but thinking better of it. "I'm sorry if I'm late. The time on my phone must be out."

"Don't panic, you're not late. It's me that's early. I get really excited about showing off the archives. I'm Angela, but I've been known as Lady A since the day I arrived here, so feel free to use either."

Angela led the way from the main entrance, round the front of the house to a side door. She unlocked it, and they made their way through a couple of slightly musty smelling rooms into a dark corridor.

"Did the café used to be in there?" Beth asked.

"It did," Angela said, surprised. "Have you been here before?"

"We stayed in a house nearby a few times when I was little. We used to come up here to use the playground and have cake. That's partly what tempted me to come on the volunteer holiday."

"I like that. You used to play in the playground, and now you're helping build the new one. I love little connections like that. I think something about Ardmhor encourages them. Anyway, we moved the café and shop out to the coach house about 10 years ago. This section of the house is the oldest part, and it needed some repairs, which would have left the café and shop out of action for quite some time. So we decided to invest in the coach house, as then the café could still operate from here until the new one was ready. Also, having a café and shop visible from the road has really increased our trade."

"I remember what the coach house was like before. The transformation is amazing. The rooms are beautiful."

"Thanks," Angela smiled. "We're all thrilled with it, but the idea was always that once we made the repairs here, we would look at developing this into a sort of museum. We did the repairs, but the museum always ends up behind something else on the list of priorities."

Angela unlocked another door and led them

into a room lined with chests and bookcases. She crossed the room and pulled up the blinds, allowing the light in.

"This used to be the estate office, but they moved into a new, purpose-built space a few years back. The house is only a small part of the estate really, so the separate office is much more convenient. A lot of these," she said, sweeping her arm over the chests and bookcases, "have been housing the same papers for well over a hundred years. That's another reason the office needed to move. There was no space for modern business alongside the old, and it seemed easier to move the office than to move the history. The stuff in the files is official records, who held the land, who worked in the house, even inventories of the food that was ordered in. I've been trying to add in the more personal side, photo albums and family letters and so on. There are drawers and cupboards in parts of this house that probably haven't been opened in a century, so things turn up all the time."

"This is amazing," said Beth, gazing around in wonder at the sheer amount of history in one room, some of it connected to her.

"I know," Angela said with pride. "I love it. I'm not originally from a background like this, so that sense of continuity never ceases to impress me."

"I've just found out," Beth began, "that my

great-great-grandmother lived here, in Ardmhor House. My mum found her diary last week and posted it up to me. I've started reading it today. We had no idea, so it's such a strange coincidence finding out while I'm here."

"Wow, when did she live here?" asked Angela. "There might be photos."

"The diary starts in 1891. I've only read the first couple of months so far. There's a lot more to look through."

"We definitely have some albums from the late 1800s," Angela mused, walking towards a cupboard in the far corner of the room. "I just love this, another Ardmhor connection."

Beth stood thinking about how daft she had been, all that worry about asking to see this, when Angela couldn't be nicer and more welcoming. She watched as Angela walked back to the central table and placed a couple of old-fashioned albums in front of her.

"We've got this album, with photos dated up to 1878, and this one starting in 1900, but I can't see anything from the 1890s. There must be some though, if there are photos from before and after. I thought you might like a look at these, anyway."

The two of them chatted easily as they looked through the albums, commenting on the styles of the dresses and noticing how small the trees were in some photos of the woodland. Beth talked about what she had learned so far from the diary. On hearing that Eliza's father had worked as the factor for the estate, Angela pulled out some old ledgers. They found records of a Joseph Turner who had been employed as factor from October 1880 until May 1891, which was the time Eliza moved into the house. Although Beth hadn't known his name, Eliza gave her surname as Turner, and the dates fitted, so it had to be him. It sent a shiver of excitement through her, seeing her ancestor's name there in black and white—her own official connection to Ardmhor.

Angela then pulled out some books on the history of the Scottish Highlands and soon they were absorbed in accounts of the Clearances. Beth could now understand why the previous factor Eliza mentioned in her diary had been so disliked. The Clearances had been brutal, as people were forced off land their families had worked for generations, in order to make way for sheep. Many had been left with no option but to start new lives overseas, some being physically forced onto boats that would take them to unknown lands. Although acting on the instructions of the landowners, it was the factors who enforced these actions that took most of the blame in the eyes of the people. By the time Eliza's father took on the role, in the 1880s, it had been over twenty years since the last Clearances on Ardmhor land, but it was easy to see why tensions still ran high and why it could have seemed preferable to employ someone with no previous history in the area. Glancing at the time, Beth realised it was half past four. They had been in the old office for well over two hours! Panicking that she had taken up too much of Angela's time, Beth thanked her profusely, while hastily standing to leave. Sensing the reason for Beth's discomfort, Angela was quick to reassure her she couldn't think of a nicer way to spend the afternoon and promised to look for the missing photo albums, insisting Beth was to phone her whenever she wanted to look at more of the Ardmhor records.

Although she had found no mention of Eliza, Beth was buoyed up by how much she had enjoyed her morning reading the diary and her afternoon in the archives. It was a relief to realise that losing herself in the past still made her happy, and Lady Angela's mention of a museum had slowly started some cogs turning in the back of her mind. Beth had always seen her obsession with reading and the past, along with her somewhat solitary nature, as a problem, as if it was a way of hiding from the real world, but maybe she'd been wrong. What if being a little solitary was actually just different from needing to socialise all the time, rather than being lesser than? Was this what Alex and Megan meant by trying to decide what she wanted for herself, rather than basing decisions on what others would do? Was this the positive inner voice she was supposed to be listening to? It was certainly different from the one she usually heard.

She chatted happily in the pub that evening as she got to know the new recruits and even accepted Eilidh's proposal of a night out in Inveravain later in the week. It would be Eilidh, her boyfriend, Rich, Andrew the barman, and Beth. It did sound a little too like a double date for Beth's comfort, after all she only had eyes for Alex now, but Eilidh assured her they would be meeting up with others.

As she walked back from the pub alongside Mary and Bob, Beth noticed a for sale sign at the side of the road. She couldn't see much of the property it belonged to. The dark stone building stood sideways on to the road, hiding in a tangle of vegetation. It made Beth's thoughts turn to living at Ardmhor. She was feeling so happy, so much more positive about her future, but she was always aware it was just a holiday, not real life. Was she wrong though? Could she actually make a future here? A little seed of possibility was sowing itself deep down inside her.

Before they'd made it back to the coach house, Beth had decided she was going to the viewpoint to look for Alex. It was much darker than even the previous night, but with the help of the torch on her phone she could easily make out the path. There was absolutely no clinging to the pretence of the view now, but she reasoned with herself that if Alex was there, he couldn't use that excuse either. That thought, along with the memory of his fleeting kiss, gave her the motivation to keep going.

As she reached the viewpoint, Alex appeared from the other path. They arrived at the benches together, smiling at each other as they took a seat.

"Did the diary arrive? What have you found out? I want you to tell me everything."

"Well, my great-great-grandmother was called Eliza, and she lived here in the 1890s. Her dad had been the factor, but he died, and she moved into the house as a companion for the owner's daughter. Eliza's dad was a friend of the then Lord and Lady MacAird, so there was already a connection. It's funny because my full name is Elizabeth, in honour of her, and in the diary, she talks about James and Alexander being the sons of the house, like you and your brother."

Beth stopped there, realising she couldn't remember if Alex had ever mentioned his brother's name, or if she just knew it from her internet enquiries. She didn't want to end up looking like a stalker.

"It's not actually that strange," said Alex eventually. "If you look at the MacAird family tree, everyone seems to be called James or Alexander. It's like the family never realised other names had been invented. So, did you manage to arrange looking in the archive?"

"I did," Beth replied, feeling proud of herself. "I spent the afternoon there, and there was so much fascinating stuff. There were no photos from Eliza's time, although your mum is convinced there are some, so she's going to have a search."

"Was Lady A excited to show everything off, like I said she'd be?"

"Totally! I can't believe I made such a big deal out of approaching her. I should have listened to everyone else from the start."

"No, you did things your way, in your own time. That is absolutely fine." He looked at her with a smile and they sat in silence for a moment.

"What have you been up to anyway?" Beth asked. "I feel like we're always talking about me."

"That's because I have nothing exciting to tell you. I'm just hanging around, really. Are you feeling settled with the other volunteers now? Are you feeling happy?"

"Yes, yes I am." Beth thought how nice it was to say that and mean it. "Everyone's lovely and I actually feel like a proper part of the group. Also, Eilidh's asked me to go for a night out in Inveravain in the week."

"Be careful!" Alex laughed. "It'll seem like the bright lights after two weeks of the Ardmhor

Hotel."

Beth considered asking whether he might want to join them, but she wasn't sure what the relationship was between the boys from the big house, with their English education and their other home in London, and the locals who often worked for their family. She wondered about asking Eilidh, but that would mean revealing her meetings with Alex, and as everything that happened here seemed to get back to him, would he see that as gossip?

"I saw a house for sale on the way back from the pub. It made me wonder what it would be like to live here," Beth said, changing the subject slightly.

"Was it on the left as you're heading back here? That's the old factor's house. Eliza would have lived there before her father died. It hasn't been occupied for years now."

"Really?" said Beth, smiling at the thought. "It feels like everything keeps ending up being connected to me today. It's a nice feeling."

"Maybe it's meant to be," Alex said quietly, the gap between them seeming to almost imperceptibly close. "It'd be nice if you did live here."

"It would," Beth replied, her voice little more than a whisper.

She was almost holding her breath. She so wanted to kiss him. She gazed directly at him, the increased darkness making her feel much bolder. He really was beautiful. For once, she knew exactly what she wanted; she wanted him, but she didn't want to risk pushing things. She wanted this to be something that he wanted as well. So she didn't make a move. She just sat there looking at him. They were both completely still, holding the contact between each other's eyes. It felt as if even the air surrounding them had ceased moving. Other sounds seemed to disappear, leaving Beth and Alex somehow separate from the rest of the world. Beth willed him to move closer to her, and if the power of thought was actually enough to make things happen, he would definitely have reached his hand gently to her cheek and moved his lips to meet hers. But he didn't. He remained totally still, just looking at her, as though he was absorbing her into him. Eventually, Beth dragged her gaze from his and stood up.

"It's late, I should get back," she mumbled as she turned and walked down the path. She was hoping she might hear footsteps behind her; that she'd feel his hand on her shoulder, turning her round and pulling her into his arms. But there was no sound other than her own feet disturbing the gravel. She felt a sense of satisfaction alongside her disappointment though. She was being patient, she wasn't trying to force a relationship, and she was imagining a different future. Maybe her life did still have as much potential as anyone else's.

CHAPTER
ELEVEN

26th of July 1891

Alexander is back. Lady Constance drove us all to distraction as she prepared for his arrival. The staff had to try hard not to show their irritation as they were sent on more and more errands, to source his favourite foods, or to make sure his favourite part of the garden was looking its best. Although I wouldn't have gone quite so overboard with the preparations, I must admit that it is lovely having him here. I've always felt like he understood me. Despite there being two years between us and him being away at school so frequently, he has always made the effort to seek me out, writing to me occasionally, asking me questions about what I am reading, and even lending me some of his own books. I feel much more part of the family when Alexander catches my eye over dinner, winking as his father starts another of his monologues!

30th of July 1891

Just in from a long ramble around the estate. Hopefully, I'll have time to describe it all before dressing for dinner. Flora persuaded Lady Constance that we should be allowed to take a picnic with us, and she also persuaded the gardeners to spare Angus so that he could help carry our provisions. Lady Constance said that Alexander would have to accompany us if we were going beyond the main gardens, which had the happy effect of giving me a distraction from Flora's teasing of Angus. Obviously, there could never be a relationship between Flora and a gardener, which is why she finds it so hilarious to watch Angus try to think of appropriate responses to her quite inappropriate behaviour.

Having Alexander with us made it a splendid afternoon. The weather has been unusually warm, so we walked up the hills behind the house for a while and then set up our picnic, enjoying the cool breeze and the view over the sea. Angus relaxed a bit, once we were away from the prying eyes of the house, and Flora took him off, making him name every plant she saw. That left Alexander and I chatting on the picnic rug. It was the most wonderful hour. He has picked up some fascinating ideas at university. His plans for the estate could make a real difference for everyone living here, if his father will accept them. I can tell he is worried that his father will be reluctant, and he is already concerned about whether he will be able to persuade him. He was keen to talk about me as well, quizzing me on what I have learnt with Flora's tutor. I don't think anyone else ever wants to know my thoughts. Well, other than Flora wanting an opinion on the latest young man she has taken a fancy to or whether a dress suits her.

Anyway, then Flora appeared back, teasing Alexander about how boring he is and how his head has grown unusually large, in order to fit in his huge brain. Dark clouds were gathering over the hill and there was an ominous rumble of thunder, so we packed up quickly and moved as fast as we could, considering everything we had to carry. We didn't quite make it, though, arriving back at the house out of breath, soaked through, and a little giddy. Lady Constance was not impressed. She said she expected better of Alexander and me. Flora says she doesn't know whether to be insulted her mother didn't expect better from her or relieved she missed out on the telling off!

10th of August 1891

I am 20 years old today. Only one more year until I will be considered an adult by anyone's standards. I wonder what I will have achieved by then. I've been enjoying life here so much more over the last few weeks. I've hardly thought about wanting to return to England. Alexander gave me a book by an author I had once told him I enjoyed. I am flattered that he remembered and took the trouble to think of such a thoughtful gift. I find myself thinking much more carefully about what to wear for dinner since his return.

14th of August 1891

I am in love with Alexander. I suppose it should have been obvious to me, as I've barely written about anything else in here since he came home, but I've always preferred him to any other boy, so I hadn't really thought about how the feeling has changed. The house is in chaos as Lady Constance is organising a party. The purpose of which is mainly to introduce both Alexander and Flora to suitable marriage partners. James is back at the London house now and already has a fiancée. Anyway, the thought of Alexander getting married filled me with anger. I suddenly realised that the only person I'd be happy for him to marry was me. I wonder what Lady Constance would make of that idea! But it is such a lovely daydream. Alexander and I walking out of the church down the road, then setting off to start a new life together. A life where we just read books and learn all day. I can't believe it has taken me so long to realise how I feel because now I can't imagine feeling any other way.

15th of August 1891

I have completely lost the ability to have a sensible conversation with Alexander. He asked me whether I was enjoying the book he gave me for my birthday, and all I squeaked out was 'yes' before the power of speech left me completely. I was just stood there in the hall, staring at my shoes as if they were the most fascinating things I'd seen in my life. How can it be fair that realising how much I care for him means I'll end up losing him? It's bound to happen now that I am incapable of saying anything intelligent to him.

16th of August 1891

I don't know how I'll cope at the party tomorrow. All these girls Lady Constance is inviting are bound to be prettier, better dressed, much richer, and definitely more suitable than me. More importantly, they will probably be able to form actual sentences when talking to Alexander. I can't think about anything other than his smile and his gentle voice. I can hardly concentrate to read, and I can barely eat. I don't feel like myself at all. Flora, on the other hand, doesn't seem the least bit bothered by the party. I feel as if we have somehow switched personalities.

17th of August 1891

I don't know if I can explain the events of the party adequately. Flora is asleep on her bed, and I suppose I should really date this entry as the 18th of August, as it is already long past midnight, but the most wonderful thing has happened. I think Alexander feels the same for me as I feel for him, and I can scarcely believe it!

I was full of nerves as the party began. Lady Constance was ever so kind. She could see I was feeling lost, so she kept making sure I had partners to dance with. Anyway, despite the distractions of dancing, I couldn't turn my attention away from Alexander, and I found myself constantly searching the room for him. Occasionally, I would see him whirl past, with yet another girl in his arms, but he never caught my eye and I felt quite distraught.

I think anyone would agree that the party was a success. The music moved from swift to slow at exactly the right moments. The flowers looked beautiful, scenting the air with their petals. The food was not too heavy, but also not too light, and the drinks were passed round readily, leaving no one with a chance of developing a thirst. I think every guest would have described it as perfect, but the perfect moment for me came as it was over, as the last guests had gone, and we were retiring for the night. Alexander walked over to me as I was making my way to the stairs and asked me whether I had enjoyed the party. I replied I had and asked him the same question. I can remember his reply word for word, and I think I always will. He said, 'The only thing wrong with the party was that I didn't get to dance with the girl I admire the most. The only girl I've ever wanted is standing right in front of me now, and I wondered when I saw her watching me tonight if perhaps she felt the same.' I could barely breathe, and I doubt I could have found the words to reply adequately, but my heart was soaring.

Fortunately, Flora bounded up and saved me from ruining that perfect moment. She gave her brother a playful shove and dragged me up the stairs so she could give me a full account of her evening. I must admit I could barely focus on anything she said. My mind was just repeating, 'he likes you too, he likes you too'. I don't know how I shall sleep tonight.

24th of August 1891

This has been the most perfect week. Alex and I (he says I should always call him Alex now, Alexander for everyone else and Alex just for me) have happened to take a walk in the gardens at the same time as each other every day. And by coincidence, each day we have arrived together at the clearing overlooking the sea. The little arched gate, leading to the path through the rhododendrons, is in distant view of the house, but the clearing is just out of sight and sound, hidden by the new woodland.

Our meetings, of course, haven't really happened by chance. Alex carefully slipped a note, asking me to meet him, into my hand the morning after the party. I'm so glad he took control, as I'd hardly been able to look in his direction over breakfast. I just didn't know the correct way to react to his revelation of the previous night.

Alex says that we should wait before telling anyone else how we feel. He wants to finish his studies so that when he returns home next year, he can ask me to marry him. He thinks his mother and father will be more accepting of the idea if he is already working here and contributing to the estate. I think he is probably right. I am sure that Lady Constance likes me, although she confuses me at times, veering from affectionate to cross. However, I do not bring any of the connections, or money, to the family that they might have hoped for, so Alex proving he can make other contributions might soften that blow.

It is quite exciting to have such a life-changing secret. We have talked and talked, constantly marvelling at the fact we have felt a connection since the moment we met, yet it took us ten years to understand it. Alex has a book that he had altered so that he could hide secrets in the back. Apparently, one of his university friends had one, so Alex took a book from the library, one that it was unlikely anyone would miss and had it converted in the same way. He has left me a note in the hidden compartment each day. Reading his words makes me so happy, I can no longer understand how I ever felt miserable here. I love reading, but even I could not have predicted that a book on clan history could fill me with such joy. The only shadow on the horizon is knowing that he must leave soon, in order to return to England and his studies.

12th of December 1891

We have just heard that Alex will not be returning home for Christmas. Heavy snow means the trains can't run, and it will take too long to make the journey in any other way. It makes far more sense for him to remain at the London house over the holiday. I remember how long the journey took when Father and I travelled here before they completed the railway, so I know there is no other way he can make it, but I don't know if my heart can bear it. I have only had two letters from him since he left Ardmhor in late August. I am lucky really; if he hadn't already been in the habit of corresponding with me, we would have felt letters were too obvious and he couldn't have written at all. But our old rate of correspondence doesn't match our new desire for knowledge of each other, so I feel I am constantly waiting.

I don't like to admit it, but I had been counting down the days until his return at Christmas. I felt I could make it until his permanent return if we were to have this time together. Now that won't happen, I feel quite desolate, and I can't even confide why to anyone. I had imagined gazing at him over the table. I saw us sneaking off to hidden corners, for whispered conversations I could replay in my mind after he was gone. I'd thought of the notes I'd be able to add to my collection when the history book returned to its place on the unnoticed shelf. And I can hardly write this, but I'd wondered if I would be brave enough to persuade him to kiss me in the way he sometimes does in my dreams, the dreams that cause me to wake feeling flustered and hoping Flora hasn't noticed. I know those things shouldn't happen until after a marriage, and I know it would be most unladylike for me to make a suggestion like that, but I liked the idea that I could. Now he will not be here, and all I can do is dream. I don't know if I have ever felt worse.

7th of May 1892

Flora is to be married! Incredibly, she has found a match that both she and her parents agree on. His good looks and his wit impressed

Flora. She feels he is the first man she hasn't been able to run rings round. Then, his fortune impressed her parents! Fortunately, he is just as impressed with Flora as the MacAirds are with him, so it seems an advantageous match all round. They aren't due to marry for quite some time, so perhaps there is nothing to be concerned about, but as happy as I am for Flora, I can't help thinking, where does this leave me? I can't be a companion to her at Ardmhor if she no longer lives here. Would they expect me to go with her to her new home? What if she leaves before Alex feels it is time to tell his parents? I've been wishing for change, for something to break up the monotony of life, but now I'm wishing it hadn't come.

16th of June 1892

The house is a flurry of activity to prepare for the return of Alex. This time I know I am far more excited than Lady Constance, but I am doing my best to keep my feelings hidden. I'm sure everyone is noticing the spring in my step though. It has been so long since I last saw him, and I can scarcely believe he will soon be here. I find myself on unnecessary errands, errands that just happen to take me past the photograph of him in the hall. My feelings have only grown stronger, and from Alex's last letter, I feel confident it is the same for him. Flora is constantly talking of her plans and her dreams of what married life will be like. I hope that once Alex is back, it won't be too long before I can talk freely about my own dreams.

CHAPTER TWELVE

S o, Beth thought to herself, her great-great-grandmother had been in love with an Alex of her own. Surely this was a sign that something was supposed to happen between herself and the modern-day version. Maybe that was why she felt such a connection to him. It was also reassuring that despite all the stories of Eliza's confidence and determination, she hadn't been above panicking over a man. Although in fairness to Eliza, she had known him for 10 years by that point, so she could hardly be accused of rushing into something.

Beth had started reading the moment she came back from the viewpoint, intending to just spend an hour looking through the pages before going to sleep. A glance at the clock told her that two hours had gone by in what seemed like minutes. Eliza didn't write entries every day, and some of the contents were just lists of activities, so Beth had homed in on Eliza's discussions of her feelings and on any mentions of her relationship with Alexander, but all the details of day-to-day life at Ardmhor fascinated her. When she finally fell asleep, Beth dreamt of living in the big house. The twin-bedded room she'd wandered through earlier in the day was hers, and she was carefully hiding the diary under the edge of the mattress.

When she woke the next morning, Beth was gripped with excitement over what more she could learn about Eliza, but she went for breakfast before starting to read again. She was too hungry to risk getting lost in the diary before food. She was just carrying her used pots back to the counter when Sally, the café manager, called to her from the kitchen.

"Beth, I know this is your day off, and it's not your responsibility at all, but do you think you could help me out?"

"What do you need doing?" Beth asked as she looked around her, hoping to spot some other more capable staff member so that she could pass the situation over to them.

"A supplier has let us down, and we'll not have a lot of the stock we need for the rush later on. I need to get over to Inveravain and see what I can buy to make up for what we're missing. I can't send anyone else because without knowing what's available, it's too complicated to work out the best things to buy, but if I go, I'll be leaving the café short staffed. Do you think you could help with the orders and taking food to tables? Just for an hour or so? I know it's not your job, but I'd be so grateful."

"It's no problem. Take as long as you need," Beth responded. Although she wanted to, she couldn't say no: she always felt obliged to agree to any favour asked of her, even though she'd be terrified about getting it all wrong. "I've never waitressed before, but I'm sure someone can tell me what to do."

"You'll be grand, Beth, and I should be back before it gets too busy." Sally then called over her shoulder to Katie, who ran the kitchen with her, "Beth's going to help out. Will you show her how to work the till while there are no customers in? I'll be back as fast as I can."

With a vague idea of how to work the till and what the different cakes on offer were, Beth stood nervously behind the counter, praying that no customers would arrive. Katie was busy in the kitchen, working on preparations for 12 o'clock, when they started serving from the main menu. Beth checked the time: quarter past ten. 'Please let Sally be back by 12,' she muttered under her breath, as if by saying it she could make it happen. Cakes, she thought to herself, she could maybe handle, but she knew a full lunchtime service would be beyond her.

As it happened, Beth hardly noticed when Sally swept back in through the door at five to twelve. She had been rushed off her feet. At first, she had taken orders at the counter, then she had delivered food to the tables once Katie took over at the till, but she had done it with no mishaps. As Sally thanked her profusely, Beth felt as if she might be visibly glowing. She knew others probably wouldn't consider it a big deal; after all, putting some orders into a till and carrying cakes to tables was hardly rocket science, but to Beth, it felt huge. She was always so wary of getting things wrong she found it hard to step out of her comfort zone and try new things. In situations needing volunteers, Beth would always hang back, assuming that someone else would do things better than her. To have stepped in successfully, to help with something she had no experience of, felt like an achievement in line with climbing Everest.

Back in her room, Beth intended to settle down with the diary, but her phone rang the moment she shut the door, so instead she chatted to her mum about what she had read so far. She had been fairly certain that there were no MacAirds in her family tree. There was certainly none of the MacAird money. However, she asked her mum anyway, just to be certain. Jean told her that Eliza's husband, and the father of her two children, was a man called William Burton, so Beth had to assume that Eliza and Alexander's relationship did not have the happy ending she was dreaming of. Beth updated her mum on the progress with the playground and told her how settled she was feeling, although she still stopped short of saying that her mum had been right about the trip. Jean then filled Beth in on how well her gran was settling into her new sheltered accommodation. They had chatted for almost an hour and were in the middle of the drawn-out process of saying goodbye when there was a knock at Beth's door.

Mary, Megan, and Olivia stood in the doorway and announced they were heading out for ice cream at the end of the pier. Beth loved the pier: the bustle and excitement of people boarding and leaving the ferry, the seals basking on the rocks, and the little gift shops selling things you didn't need but still really wanted. She said a final goodbye to her mum, grabbed her coat, and followed the others. On the walk to the pier, Beth noticed the for sale sign she had seen the night before. She could see the stone building more clearly in the daylight. It was bigger and grander than the standard croft houses dotted around the area, with two full storeys and glass panels in the roof, suggesting an attic hidden within. The house stood sideways on to the road and was in a total state of disrepair. Glass was missing from the windows, and slates were missing from the roof. It was so overgrown you could barely see the bay windows on the ground floor, but it was clear the old factor's house had once been an imposing building. Beth made a mental note of the estate agent's name so she could look it up online later. The house was yet another place she now knew she had a personal connection to.

The pier was busy when they arrived. Several coaches were waiting to board the next ferry, and the passengers from them milled around. There were no seats outside the little café at the end of the pier, so the four of them drifted around the gift shops, chatting comfortably. Just as they were leaving one of the shops, each of them with at least a couple of unnecessary purchases tucked away, Mary spotted a group about to vacate one of the tables. The rest of them laughed as she sprinted over to avoid missing it and then tried to look as if she had been casually standing there all along. Over ice cream, Olivia told them that Fraser had asked her to go back to his family home with him when their month at Ardmhor finished. He wanted to introduce her to his family before she returned to university. Beth was relieved to discover that she didn't feel any jealousy at all, instead she felt genuinely pleased for Olivia. She decided not to dwell on how uncharitable her thoughts had been towards her when they'd first met and tried to focus on this new, happier version of herself instead.

By the time she had returned from the pier, enjoyed an evening meal with the group, and then been persuaded along for a quick drink in the pub, it was getting pretty late. Beth had already decided to go out to the viewpoint and look for Alex again, but she thought she would just have time to look up the details of the factor's house first.

There weren't too many houses listed on the estate agent's website, so it only took a minute to find what she was looking for. The house looked different with the photos taken from the front, but it was definitely the right one. Beth couldn't get over the asking price. It was less than half the price of the small semi-detached houses she'd been looking at back at home. In fact, as she had saved so much while living with her parents, she could almost afford to buy it outright. However, it did say that it required total renovation and that caution would need to be exercised when viewing, so Beth reasoned it would probably cost far more than the asking price to make it liveable.

It was the darkest Beth had ever seen it when she arrived at the viewpoint. It felt much lonelier surrounded by blackness, and she was relieved to hear Alex calling out to her.

"I'm glad you're here Beth. I was worried the darkness might put you off, and I'm desperate to know if you've read any more of the diary.

Although I hear you've been pretty busy today, so I suppose you mightn't have had time."

"Do you always know about everything?" Beth said, laughing.

"Well, not everything, but it's a small place, so it's hard to avoid finding things out. Sally was really grateful for your help in the café. You'll have to watch out though or people might forget you're only here as a volunteer."

"I really enjoyed myself. It was nice to feel helpful. I don't like putting myself forward for things like that because I'm always worried I'll somehow make things worse, so it was good to be forced into it."

"Have you ever noticed that even when you're being given a compliment, you put yourself down, Beth? I wish you could see yourself how others see you. Everyone here thinks you're great."

Beth wanted to ask if that was what he thought as well, but she couldn't bring herself to say the words. Instead, they chatted about her afternoon and the other volunteers.

"I know you didn't really want to spend the summer here at Ardmhor, but are you glad you did?" Alex asked after a while.

"I am," she said, meeting his gaze. "There's so much that I love about being here. I really didn't expect to feel so at home."

Alex was still looking directly at her, but he

didn't speak, so she pressed on.

"I saw the house that's for sale again today, the one you said was the factor's house. I looked it up online and it's so cheap. It's less than half the price of the houses I've been looking at back home. But obviously it'd cost a lot more than I can afford to make it liveable, and it'd probably be a bit too far to get to work each day!"

"Not if you worked here though," Alex stated simply.

Beth felt that flutter of butterflies inside her again. This was the second time he'd made suggestions about her staying. Maybe he did feel a little of what she felt for him.

"I've read a bit more of the diary," she said, changing the subject. "It turns out Eliza was in love with Alexander. They'd been friends since they were children, but they realised they'd fallen for each other. It says they used to meet at the front of the new woodland, overlooking the sea. Do you think that's here? She's struggling in the bit I'm up to at the moment because Alexander, although she calls him Alex now, is finishing his studies in England, and she's missing him and panicking about their future. He didn't want to tell his parents about them yet, and she's worried about how it will all work out."

It was a while before Alex spoke. "It would have been here, where they met. The woods behind us were planted in the late 1800s, so it would have been new woodland then."

"I can't get over the idea of someone related to you and someone related to me, sitting in this same spot all that time ago," said Beth. "It's crazy, isn't it? Maybe that's why I feel so at home here…" She paused as she thought. "But then again, I suppose it might not feel strange to you at all. You've grown up in the mansion your ancestors built, whereas I don't even know who lived in our house before my mum and dad bought it."

"I suppose I am more used to it than most people," he responded absently. "I just keep thinking how hard it must have been for Eliza. Alexander would have held all the cards, and she'd have had no control over anything. You don't always think about how hard it is to put that trust in another person."

"I've never had a relationship like that, where it meant everything," Beth admitted.

"I have," Alex said sadly, "but it didn't work out."

Alex looked so distraught that Beth ached for him, even though she hated the thought that his heart might already belong elsewhere.

"Anytime I've started seeing someone," Beth began, trying to find the words to explain why her relationships never worked, "I always decide there must be something wrong with them if they seem to like me, then I start finding faults with them and end everything, so I've never

119

had a relationship that lasted long. I can only imagine how hard it must be when you actually love someone and it doesn't work out."

"It was a long time ago now," Alex said quietly, still looking away, offering no further details.

Beth decided not to push him, sensing the memories were painful. "We should be ready to install the equipment in the new play area this week," she said, steering them onto safer ground. "I loved the playground here when I was little. I like the thought that I'm contributing to a new one."

"I'm sure the little ones are going to love it," Alex replied, seeming to shake off his earlier tension as he spoke. "What time do you have to start work?"

"Nine," said Beth, "which I suppose means I should get going. It's been a busy day, and it's getting late."

"Will I see you tomorrow?" Alex asked, his expression making it clear he wanted her answer to be yes.

"Definitely," she replied.

She couldn't contain her smile as she walked away. Alex's question had finally made something clear: it wasn't only her that their meetings mattered to.

CHAPTER THIRTEEN

Beth's muscles ached, and she was soaked to the skin, but she felt immensely satisfied as she looked around her. It had rained non-stop throughout the day, and the group had needed to draw on every ounce of energy they possessed to keep going. The ground beneath their feet had turned into a muddy quagmire, and they hadn't been able to install any equipment, but they had moved forward with the site preparations, so they were still on track. As Beth surveyed her surroundings, the sun finally broke through the clouds. A shaft of light lit up the front of Ardmhor House, and Beth could just make out the familiar shape of Alex as he passed the front door. He seemed to sense her presence and looked across to the playground site, smiling as he saw her. The sunlight created a glow around him, like the golden halos Beth had seen painted on religious icons in Greek gift shops. It was a beautiful image, and she tried to fix it in her mind so that she'd be able to replay it when she was back at home, back at work, and far from this place that had become so special to her.

As she made her way back to the coach house to clean up, she pondered on the fact that maybe it wasn't just the sunshine, maybe *she* was attributing a sort of godlike status to Alex. He was pretty perfect, definitely the most attractive man she had ever met, and there was a connection between them she'd never experienced before. He seemed somehow to understand her, even though they had only really met a few times. However, she had to remind herself that he wasn't actually perfect. Firstly, he lived a few hundred miles away from her job and home. Secondly, he was clearly still hung up on a previous broken relationship. Finally, if he really was interested in her, surely he'd have made a move by now? There had been ample opportunity during all those intense moments staring deep into each other's eyes. Maybe she needed to accept things for what they were. She had made a good friend in a beautiful place, and that was that. Beth resolved to enjoy the time they had left together, without over analysing it. Maybe she'd ask him to join the trip to Inveravain after all. However, not over analysing was a resolution she couldn't keep. Before she'd even reached the ticket office, her mind was busy replaying each conversation they'd had, looking for hidden meanings once again.

Eilidh was rearranging information on the notice board when Beth walked through the main entrance to the coach house.

"Come and have a look at this, Beth," she called, removing the drawing pins from a notice and holding it out to her.

Beth scanned the headlines. 'Ardmhor Estate, full-time staff wanted, variety of roles, temporary and permanent opportunities, potential for development.'

"So," said Eilidh. "What about it? What about staying?"

"I don't know. I've loved it here, but I live hundreds of miles away, and I'm expected back at work in a few weeks."

"But you've told me loads of times that you hate your job and you're not happy, so why not start again?"

It sounded so easy the way Eilidh said it, but Beth couldn't imagine it was really possible.

"I know nothing about working here for real though, and where would I live? And I don't even know if I can leave my job at this point. I think you have to resign in May to leave before

September."

"I don't know anything about the last bit, so you could be right," Eilidh conceded, "but you do know about working here. We need staff for all roles and you've been doing some of them already. We always end up having to hire throughout the season, as lots of temporary staff move on unexpectedly. For some reason, this year has been worse than others and we've ended up quite short staffed, as you've noticed in the café. We have staff accommodation if it's needed. It's not as nice as the coach house, but it's fine. Why don't you have a look at all the details on the website? And then you can ask me any questions when we go to Inveravain tomorrow night."

Beth logged onto the Ardmhor website the moment she stepped into her room. As Eilidh had said, they were looking to cover many roles, from within the cafe and shop, right through to working in the grounds. The advert also made a lot of the fact that they liked to offer staff the opportunity to progress, stating that several of their long-term and senior staff had created their own roles by putting forward development ideas that utilised their skills. Beth thought again about Lady Angela mentioning her desire to set up a museum, something that had been popping into her thoughts ever since their afternoon in the archives. Maybe that was a niche she could use her skills as a historian to develop. Perhaps she could make a proper life for herself here.

Her mum's phone rang for a while before Jean answered.

"Hi sweetheart, are you ok? I'm just at Gran's."

"I'm fine. I just fancied a chat. How's Gran? Have you two made any more big discoveries?"

There were only muffled noises from the other end of the phone for a moment, and Beth could just make out the sound of her mum speaking to her gran.

"She says she's fine, and as it happens, we have made another discovery. We found Eliza and William's wedding photo yesterday. I've had copies made and posted one up to you."

"Oh, that's really exciting. I was trying to picture her when I walked around the house, but I only know what she looked like when she was old."

"Well, you'll be able to see young Eliza for yourself in a day or two. How's everything else? Are you still enjoying yourself?"

"I am. I've just seen an advert for a permanent job here." She tailed off, leaving the statement hanging there.

"Are you thinking about applying?" Jean asked.

"What would you think if I did?" Beth countered.

"I really don't know, love. I think it'd be an

amazing place to live, but it's a long way from home, and you worked so hard to get your teaching qualifications."

"I know, and I don't even know if I can leave work until October. I think it's too late to resign now."

"But you could cross that bridge when you come to it. If we're being honest, you haven't seemed too happy recently, so if you fancy trying something different, why not apply?"

"But it's not like a proper career, is it? I could just be serving in the gift shop, and I'd miss all of you."

"It is a long way," Jean agreed, "but we'll always be on the end of the phone, and it'd be a good excuse for us to spend more time in Scotland. Also, you don't know how a job can grow, they all have to start somewhere, and I happen to know you've always fancied working in a shop."

"I have, but what was the point of university if I'm not going to use my degree? And it's not very sensible to take such a massive pay cut, is it? But the advert does say there's potential to develop roles, so maybe you're right that it could lead somewhere else. I know Lady Angela has been wanting to set up a museum."

"Lady Angela!" Jean said, in her special voice reserved for teasing. "Name dropping the big wigs now, eh?"

"I am," Beth said, laughing. "We chatted quite a lot when she showed me the archives on Saturday, and she said she's been wanting to set up a museum since they moved the café to the coach house, but it always ends up at the bottom of the list of priorities."

"Well, that would be right up your street, wouldn't it? I can just see you planning it all out and showing people round. Which means the only problem would be finding somewhere to live."

"Actually, that would probably be the easy part as they have staff accommodation available. And houses seem cheaper up here, so maybe I could still use my savings to buy something, even though I wouldn't be earning as much."

"Well, there's no harm filling in an application, is there? And you know that we'll be happy as long as you're happy."

By the time Beth hung up, she was feeling excited. This could be exactly what she needed, instead of plodding along in a job that filled her with anxiety. She was also excited because she was meeting Alex later, and for the first time ever, it was an agreement, rather than a chance meeting. Everything was looking good.

Approximately six hours later, as Beth climbed into bed, all of her excitement had evaporated. Her meeting with Alex hadn't gone at all as she had expected. Yes, he had been kind and polite as usual, giving the expected responses to her news about Eliza's photo and her thoughts about applying for a job at Ardmhor, but there had been none of the enthusiasm she was used to from him. After he'd briefly mentioned his failed relationship when they'd last met, Beth had hoped that he was on the verge of opening up about himself, instead of always deflecting with questions about her, but that hadn't happened. Instead, he'd seemed quite withdrawn. All his usual self-assurance was gone. He never once met her eye, and he definitely didn't pick up on her hints about joining the night out to Inveravain. It was as if she'd imagined any connection between them.

The idea of applying for a job at Ardmhor had enthused her, but now she felt disillusioned and unsure. Could she only picture herself leaving everything behind because she was imagining she'd be with Alex? If there was nothing between them, did she really want to stay? When it came down to it, many of the friends that had made this experience special would leave in a couple of weeks. Would she even like it here without them? All of her earlier certainty had disappeared, and doubts crowded her mind. Sleep offered no solace, either, eluding her until dawn touched the sky.

The next day brought little improvement. Beth overheard Eilidh and Sally discussing a problem with staffing in the café just as she was finishing her lunch. After her successful stint working there the other day, Beth was quick to volunteer to help. The rain was pouring down again, so there wasn't a lot the volunteers could do at the playground site.

"Are you sure, Beth?" Sally asked. "It'll be a bit more complicated than Sunday morning because the full menu will be running."

"I think I can do it," Beth replied. She'd managed it once, so surely she could do it again.

"Well, it'd be a massive help. If you can do the till, Katie can get the orders ready for you."

Once again, the time in the café passed in a blur. Beth keyed orders into the till, just as Katie had shown her to on Sunday. Items like cake, or soup, were simple enough for her to plate straight up and hand to the customers. More complex orders, she noted down and rushed out to the tables as soon as Katie had prepared them. After a couple of hours, the issue had been resolved, and Sally was able to get back to the café.

"Thank you so much, Beth," she said as she took the apron from her and logged back into the till. "I'll be so happy when these new positions are filled. Two staff just aren't enough for the café, especially when one of them is constantly being called away."

Helping out had lifted Beth's mood, and she sang along to the radio as she got ready for the night out in Inveravain. She could worry about whether applying for the job was the right thing tomorrow. Tonight, was about having fun. She had only brought jeans with her, but she swapped her sturdy boots for her trainers, put on her favourite t-shirt—the one that always seemed to fit just right—and added a bit more jewellery. She'd washed her hair after finishing in the café and although her red curls were so thick they hadn't quite had time to dry, they looked pretty good, so she left them down for once. The previous day's good mood was almost fully restored as she bumped into Sally on her way to meet Eilidh.

"Beth, I'm glad I've caught you. Have you got a minute to spare? I couldn't work something out when I was cashing up and I thought you might be able to help."

"Of course," said Beth with a sinking feeling in her stomach, knowing instantly that she must have done something wrong.

"Can you remember which meal people had ordered when you typed meal 3 into the till?"

"Yes," said Beth, peering at the list at the side of the till. "It was the special, the stew."

As she said it, she looked at the list more closely and realised that the stew was actually meal 2. Meal 3 was the light sandwich, and there was a significant price difference between them.

"I'm so sorry," Beth began, realising her mistake. She'd only been charging for the cheaper meal each time she'd taken an order for stew. So essentially, she'd been costing the café money. "I'll pay you back whatever you've lost."

"Don't be daft, Beth," Sally responded quickly. "You were doing me a favour, and it's a really easy mistake. I should have told you to include the number on the order slip as well. There were only a couple of them, so it's not a problem. I just couldn't work out why it didn't add up."

Despite Sally's many reassurances, Beth felt close to tears as she left the café. She had been overconfident. Sally had told her it would be more difficult, but she hadn't listened, and she'd made a really stupid mistake. Her usual inner voice was back in an instant, telling her she wasn't good enough, that she was useless. Her mind started running away with itself. Her mistake was another reason why she should just go home at the end of the holiday. She was probably useless at teaching as well, but at least she was used to it. Fortunately, there was no time for her to slide further down into her pit of despair, as a car screeched to a halt in front of her. Eilidh bobbed out, her pink hair glowing in the evening light.

"Rich is going to drive us in, then we'll leave the car there and get a taxi back. He can get a lift to work tomorrow and collect it after."

Beth climbed in the back next to Andrew and let the conversation distract her. Apparently, nights out often ended up on random weeknights as lots of their friends worked in hospitality, and time off varied. After a drink in the first pub, Beth felt much more relaxed, and as the night wore on, she felt some of her happiness return. She had confided in Eilidh about the mistake in the café, and Eilidh had reassured her by telling numerous stories of things she'd got wrong during her time at Ardmhor. It really helped Beth to hear mistakes weren't just something she made. As they moved to another bar, she found herself walking next to Andrew.

"You look amazing tonight," he said, slowing down and widening the gap between them and the others. "I love your hair; you should wear it like that more often."

"It has a bit of a mind of its own," Beth said as a sudden gust of wind whipped her curls around her face. "It's been quite well behaved so far tonight, but I'm already struggling to see where I'm going without it tied back."

Andrew stopped and gently brushed the hair back from her face.

"Is that better?" he asked, standing incredibly

close.

As he leaned into her, it suddenly became clear to Beth where this was heading, and she made a split-second decision to go with the moment. Sure, she'd prefer it to be Alex kissing her, but he hadn't turned up, despite her making it very clear he'd be welcome, so maybe she should just try to enjoy herself.

Andrew's kiss was soft, but insistent, and Beth had to admit that the sensation was definitely enjoyable, but she didn't feel any sparks, and it occurred to her that nice as it was, she'd rather be in the pub talking to the others. She took his hand and pulled him in the direction the others had headed.

"Come on," she said, laughing to lighten the mood. "This seems a somewhat elaborate plan just to avoid getting the next round in."

Beth was glad the taxi windows were open as they travelled back to Ardmhor. Everything was spinning, and the fresh air seemed to help. The taxi dropped her in front of the coach house before continuing to take the others home. She decided not to go into her room yet, instead she turned on the torch on her phone and set off to the viewpoint, a slight wobble to her step.

Although she was hoping to see Alex, Beth hadn't really expected him to be there. It was much later than usual, so it was a surprise when he appeared, walking towards the bench where she was sitting.

"You're out late," he said, sitting down. "Your hair looks lovely. It suits you like that."

"I went to Inveravain, and you didn't come," Beth replied. There was a harder edge to her voice than normal. The alcohol had left her feeling confrontational. "I kissed Andrew, the barman."

"You didn't invite me, Beth. I knew you were going, but you never actually said you wanted me to come. And you can kiss whoever you like."

"I know I can, I'm just telling you in case you thought I was bothered about you. I'm not, and I'm not applying for the job here either because I've got a perfectly good job at home, and I don't care if you like my hair."

Even in her inebriated state, Beth was aware she wasn't making much sense.

"You sound a bit drunk, Beth. You might be better off in bed."

"I don't want to go to bed, and I'm allowed to get drunk if I want to. You could hardly be bothered to look at me last night, so you've no right to tell me what to do."

He sat there for a while, not responding to her outburst. Then eventually he turned, so he was looking directly at her, as he had first done on the night they met.

"You're right. I was totally caught up in myself

last night, and I didn't listen properly. I feel terrible that I've disappointed you. It was the last thing I wanted to do. But please don't let me put you off doing what's right for you. Why not just fill in the application, Beth? What is there to lose?"

His voice was gentle and kind as always, but she turned away from him, trying to fight the growing sense of irritation. What did he know? No one else ever seemed to experience the level of fear and anxiety she felt over seemingly simple things. Alex could never understand what it was like for her. He'd been born here, so he'd always known there would be a job and a home for him. No wonder he was so bloody sure of himself all the time. He couldn't know what it meant to take a real risk. For her, giving up a career to take on a job that didn't even require any qualifications, well, it just didn't seem like something she could do. It wasn't a sensible option, and she didn't think she could live with making that big a mistake.

But at the same time, Alex obviously meant well, and he seemed to think she could do it. More importantly, he seemed to be saying he wanted her to stay. Maybe it was more of a risk to just go back home. What if she got to the end of her life and realised her biggest mistake had been not taking any chances?

"Maybe," she answered, speaking quietly now

the anger had gone. Maybe she could do this, maybe she could be brave enough to try.

Alex rose from the bench. His tall frame looming over her.

"Maybe isn't good enough, Beth. Maybe means you're not committed, that you won't actually do it, and do you know what that means?" Now he was the one sounding angry, something Beth had never heard from him before. "It means missing out on the life you're supposed to have because you're too scared to take a chance, and it means other people missing out on that life with you. Maybe you should be more scared of that." And with that, he walked away, leaving Beth shocked and alone.

CHAPTER FOURTEEN

24th of June 1892

I cannot describe adequately how wonderful it is to have Alex back here. All my worries just seemed to float away the moment he walked into the house. I know, with more certainty than I have ever known anything, that we belong together. The entire household had rushed into the hall to greet him. My heart was beating so fast, I was worried it might give up before he appeared. Then he was there, right in front of me, smiling at me, and I knew everything was going to be alright. I could tell in that very second that his feelings had not changed. Lady Constance had arranged for tea in the drawing room as soon as he arrived. It was agony to finally be so near him but be unable to do anything more than smile politely and listen to him tell his mother about his journey. At last Alex excused himself, saying he needed some fresh air after his travels, and everyone drifted off to various other occupations. I quickly took the chance for a stroll to the little clearing where we always met. I was sure I would find him there, and he didn't let me down. We sat together, and he discreetly took hold of my hand. I honestly cannot explain the pleasure I felt at his touch. We gazed into each other's eyes and hardly needed to speak. We already knew that we were both feeling the same thing. It was a feeling of joy that we were together and that we would never need to endure such a long separation again.

1st of July 1892

It's as if we exist in our own little world. I hardly notice the comings and goings of the house, or the time passing each day. I live solely for our moments together, out in the garden, away from prying eyes and ears. Alex's book is back on the library shelf. I check its contents every day, and every day I find another token of his love. With the help of our little system, it is easy for us to chance upon each other in a quiet corner of the woodland, or in a hidden nook in the gardens. The moments when it is just the two of us are so special: we talk, and he holds my hand, and he kisses me. He is far too much of a gentleman to kiss me in the way he does in the dreams I can't control, but even the gentlest of kisses from Alex, just a whisper of his lips against my cheek, well, those kisses spark feelings in me far harder to control than the frantic kisses in the depth of my sleep. If only we could be open with everyone about how we feel. How wonderful it would be if every moment could be like the moments when we are alone.

2nd August 1892

Alex says we must wait another few months before revealing our feelings. He thinks it will take at least that long for him to have made enough progress in his work. He wants his parents to have faith in his ability to make sound decisions, so they will have no reason to question his choice. I trust him completely, and I know his reasons make sense. But it seems so far away. Sometimes, I can't help but wonder if waiting is the right thing to do. Maybe they would be happy to accept me as Alex's wife right now. They were happy enough to accept me into their home. But I suppose that was as a companion to Flora, not as a member of the family. I need to remember that I am not of the same social standing as the MacAird family, and that Alex knows them far better than I do.

10th of August 1892

Today is my birthday. In some ways I feel surprised that I have reached the age of twenty-one, Flora and I are still very much treated as the children of the house, but in other ways I feel

every bit an adult, especially when I think of my
feelings for Alex. How different things were this
time last year. I hadn't realised the extent of my
feelings for him then, and I certainly couldn't
have imagined that he would feel the same. He
gave me another book as my birthday gift this
year. The cover said that it was a novel, written
by the same author as the book he gave me on my
last birthday. However, when I looked inside, it
was actually a book of love poems hidden within.
It is the perfect gift. A book like us, where the
true feelings have to be hidden inside. It has been
a happy day, with lots of fuss made of me. Lady
Constance organised a dinner in my honour and
gave me a beautiful brooch, a cameo of a mother
and child. She said that she knows she can never
replace my mother, but she hopes I know that
she loves me just as much as a mother would.
She explained the brooch has been passed down
through her family and is precious to her. I
pinned it straight onto my dress. The sentiment
moved me so much I almost cried, and I'm not
really the crying type. I think it gave me hope
that she might accept me as a suitable wife
for Alex. Amongst all the other lovely events, a
birthday greeting came from Edward Hardwick.
He trained with Father, and they worked
together before Father established his own firm.
He apologised for his lack of contact recently,
saying he wanted me to know how highly he had
regarded my parents and that I am often in his

thoughts. His words touched me almost as much as Lady Constance's gesture. It is reassuring to know that there is someone outside of Ardmhor who remembers my existence and cares about my fate.

11th of September 1892

Algernon Rutherford, Flora's intended, came to visit today. They make a very handsome couple. Flora is so dainty and doll like she seems somehow to fit naturally at the side of Algernon, with his much more solid build. We all took a turn around the gardens, and Algernon constantly had his arm supporting Flora's hand. I am so jealous that they can walk around however they please. Everyone was so happy for them, but all I could think about is whether they would be equally happy for me.

I've tried to press Alex on when we can tell everyone, but he insists we must wait. I don't doubt his love at all. He is so constant in his affection. He is definitely not one of those men that they warn young ladies about. The sort that will take advantage of a girl and then move on. He abhors that kind of behaviour. In fact, it is I that sometimes wishes he would be less of a gentleman. When he kisses me and those sensations spread through my body, I would happily abandon all restraint. The only thing I doubt is whether he will ever be ready to tell his parents about us. He has honoured every request from them and struggles each day to fulfil their expectations. He knows that marrying me was never part of their plans for him. How can I expect him to defy his nature and anger them by revealing our relationship?

Lady Constance now tells me frequently that she loves me as a daughter, and over time her actions suggest that this is true. There are no longer the inconsistencies and extremes that she used to display towards me. So I have every reason to think that she could accept me as Alex's wife. However, it's possible that I am being naive. She may simply be clinging to me as a replacement for Flora. She might have very different ideas about who Alex should marry. I don't know. Perhaps they will accept our feelings and be happy for us, perhaps they won't. But if we are never to tell them, I know there is no hope.

Seeing Flora and Algernon together today has brought it all back to me. Eventually Flora will leave, and if Alex still feels he cannot declare our love, what does that mean for me? Does Lady Constance really love me enough to allow me to remain here without Flora? And would I be happy here without her, if all I have is the promise of a future with Alex and no certainty of it actually happening?

16th of October 1892

Alex's time is increasingly taken up with his estate duties. It is much harder for him to find the time to meet me during the day, and as the nights draw in, it is difficult to find excuses to leave the house later on. Whether or not we have the opportunity to meet, Alex never fails to leave some loving words within our secret book. I tell myself to be grateful. This is nothing like the agony I endured last year, when I couldn't see him across the table each night at dinner and I had to wait weeks, or even months, between letters. I also remind myself that if he is busy, he is proving his worth and his parents will be far more likely to trust his judgment. Perhaps he will even begin to trust himself. But I miss him.

20th of October 1892

I overheard Lady Constance telling her good friend Lady Irvine that she is relieved Alex has no intention of marrying. She said that she is happy, as it means he will always be here, solely dedicated to the running of the estate. I am ashamed to say that my eavesdropping led to the first disagreement Alex and I have ever suffered. I confronted him about how his mother had arrived at this idea. He replied, totally calmly, that he had told her he did not intend to marry. I was incensed. It felt like a complete denial of our relationship, even if it is a relationship that no one else knows the existence of. Alex tried to reassure me that his mother had been talking about organising another party, hoping to find him a suitable wife, and he was simply trying to dissuade her. I tried to explain that not only was I angry that he could so easily deny his desire to marry, as that meant he was denying me, but I was also worried by how happy his mother seemed about the idea. Alex then sounded angry that I could doubt him so easily. The hurt in his eyes quickly turned my anger to tears. My sadness then seemed to have the same effect on him, and within seconds, we were tightly clasped in each other's arms, promising never to disagree again. I need to be more patient and be grateful for what I have. I know that my restlessness is a flaw I have to work on. Despite seeing the beauty of Ardmhor, I have always yearned to leave, to return to the bustle of the city where I began my life. My feelings for Alex have quelled that desire, but my impatience for us to become husband and wife shows that the restlessness still lurks in different ways.

7th of November 1892

A dressmaker has been visiting us to make the final preparations for Flora's trousseau. Lady Constance became quite emotional about Flora's impending departure from Ardmhor. Flora laughed at her, in her usual good-natured way.

Their loving and uncomplicated relationship sometimes makes me melancholy, as I think of what I have missed out on because of my mother's untimely death. But then Flora made a remark that has stuck with me throughout the day. It was just a little joke. Flora said it was a good job that Lady Constance had brought me in as her replacement because otherwise she might have been kept prisoner at Ardmhor forever. Lady Constance tutted and told her off for being silly in front of the dressmaker, but her face betrayed she felt nothing but admiration for Flora's quick wit and ability to make light of anything. It was just a silly remark, but it reminded me of how I felt when I first moved into Ardmhor House. Back then, I felt like a prisoner because it seemed I had no choices and no control. I dreamed constantly of moving back to England and the life I had once known there. I suddenly felt a hint of panic, what if that sense of being trapped here returns? What if Alex finally tells his parents, and they accept our marriage, but my need to escape Ardmhor comes back? What if it only left because my desire to marry Alex has become a greater focus? What if once I get my now greatest desire, the other older desires resurface? I'm probably being silly. It's probably just too little time with Alex making me anxious.

21st of November 1892

Today was Flora's wedding day. It has been so beautiful and full of love and hope. There was frost on the lawn when we woke this morning, an unusual sight here where the climate is so wet and mild. The sun never stopped shining, and it made everything look magical, highlighting the brilliant white of the frost and adding sparkle to the sea. The dress created for Flora was divine, but that wasn't what made her look so spectacular, she was just radiating happiness and appeared to have no nerves at all. Algernon looked quite moved as she walked into the church. He really seems a sweet man and completely in love with Flora. The guests were packed into all corners of the church. Lady Constance had suggested that a wedding in a large church near the house in London might be more convenient, but Flora was adamant that she wanted to be married at Ardmhor, in the church her ancestors had built. She told me that although she is excited about her new life with Algernon, she wanted to enjoy every moment left at Ardmhor. There was much cheering as the newlyweds left the church for the short carriage ride back to Ardmhor House. Most of the other guests walked the short distance, enjoying the warmth of the winter sunshine on their backs and stretching their legs after the cramped conditions of the church. I found myself walking next to Alex. We talked of nothing of consequence, aware of the surrounding crowd, but just walking beside him after the emotion of the ceremony felt special. Then, looking around to check no one could hear, he whispered that we would be next. This evening, after all the farewells, Alex found me alone in the hall. He said that he thinks we should tell his parents about our intentions soon. Finally, he believes his father to be sufficiently impressed with his work, and he thinks, as I have suspected, that after losing Flora, his mother will welcome me as an official member of the family. He thinks we could be married by spring. Oh, how my heart swelled to hear this. I can bear anything, knowing that we will soon be husband and wife. I have struggled to feel secure since Father died, but tonight I feel safer and more loved than ever before.

CHAPTER FIFTEEN

Beth lay sprawled across the bed, with her head tilted at an awkward angle and the diary still clasped in her hand. Soft light had gradually filled the room from behind the edges of the curtains, stirring her from her uncomfortable sleep. She tentatively shifted position, putting the diary carefully to the side and trying to ease her aching neck.

After Alex's harsh words, Beth had sat alone at the viewpoint for quite some time. The emotional numbing provided by the alcohol had quickly vanished with the combination of fresh air and Alex's anger. Then she had wished she didn't feel as sober. Actually, the return of the spinning sensation would have been welcome, if it had meant she would be incapable of thinking. Beth didn't know who to feel most angry with: herself, for always being ready to give up at the slightest hint of an obstacle, or Alex, for not understanding how difficult those obstacles could be. Eventually, she settled on being angry with Alex. How dare he judge her? She had said maybe she'd apply, and he should have believed her. She didn't need him to tell her that she might regret not taking chances. That was something she already knew but knowing it didn't make taking those risks any easier. And, she thought to herself, even if she didn't apply, he had no right to be angry with her. Wasn't he always saying decisions needed to be hers and hers alone?

After walking back to her room, Beth had climbed straight into bed, trying to be sensible. It was very late, and the next day was a working one. However, her mind was too busy replaying the evening's events to comply, so she had sat up, reached for the diary and begun reading. She had hoped that she would lose herself in Eliza's world and drift off to sleep. Although her plan had technically worked, it had also resulted in her waking, still clutching the diary, with a very sore neck. A glance at the clock told her it was only half an hour before her alarm was due to go off, so finding it impossible to get comfortable, she gave up on sleep and set off to the bathroom in search of painkillers.

The return of the sun, after two days of almost constant rain, meant a very busy day for the volunteers. The play equipment company provided their own experts to ensure everything was fitted safely, but the heavy work fell to Beth and the group. It felt like they had dug enough holes and secured enough supports for a hundred playgrounds, never mind a small toddler one, and this was only the start. It would take days to complete the installation. Although she was busy, Beth's mind constantly worked over whether to apply for the job. It was a tight turn around, the deadline for applications was on Friday, and the interviews were scheduled for the following week, so she really needed to decide. She ran through scenario after scenario in her head, but one thing kept pushing its way to the front of her thoughts. Eliza felt she had no control over her life, and she was right. She had no money and no way of earning any, and she had no way of forcing Alexander to stand up to his parents and marry her. Essentially, she was dependent on the MacAird family, for both her financial security and her personal happiness. She was so determined, but she couldn't control her own future. Beth couldn't escape the thought that Eliza would have loved to be in a position like hers. There was no one, apart from herself, stopping her from doing whatever she wanted. Maybe she owed it to Eliza to take this opportunity. What she now knew of her great-

great-grandmother meant it felt wrong to carry on being a bit fed up with life, but not doing anything to change it. She finally knew what she had to do. She had to at least apply for the job.

Reaching a decision meant a need for rapid action. It was already Wednesday, and applications needed to be in by Friday lunchtime. Beth knew if she was going to do this, she wanted to do it well. Her fear of failure ensured that she always prepared thoroughly, and as they cleared up after the day's work in the playground, she made a list in her head of all that she needed to do. Her first task was to find Eilidh, and she soon tracked her down in the ticket office.

"Would I be able to shadow one of the house guides tomorrow? Or is that too late notice? Will it be alright to miss a day working on the playground?"

"Hello to you too, Beth," Eilidh answered with a smile. "Any more questions you'd like to fire at me before giving me a chance to answer?"

"Sorry! I've finally decided about the job application, and I've got loads to sort out if I'm going to get it in on time. So what do you think?"

"Firstly, I think it's amazing that you are going to apply. I would love it if you were to stay. Secondly, the playground will be fine. We always build in plenty of contingency for bad weather and stuff, plus you are a volunteer, so you don't have to do anything. Finally, why do you need to shadow a house guide? You'll get all the training you need when you get the job."

Beth paused. Did she look silly wanting to experience other roles so she could write a better application? Would people think she was over keen for what was really an entry-level job? Even worse, what if she didn't get it after people knew she'd made lots of effort? Would everyone be laughing at her? She was too busy panicking to notice Eilidh's use of 'when' you get the job, rather than 'if'.

"I just thought it would be interesting to find out more about the house, and I thought it wouldn't hurt to know more about the other roles here."

"That makes sense. You can spend the day imagining you're Eliza, wandering around thinking about when you'll get married."

Beth had filled Eilidh in at some length on her great-great-grandmother's story.

"It'll be absolutely no bother to sort out," Eilidh continued. "I'll just pop up and tell Kath you'll be with her tomorrow. You can man the ticket desk for me while I go. We're closed to new entries now, so in 10 minutes you just need to lock both doors here and then open the main gate on the drive a little. That way, any stragglers will realise they can still get out. I'll get the keys back off you later." Eilidh indicated to the keys, hanging from a little hook attached to the side of the till. Then she set off out of the door, calling over her shoulder with a wink, "this'll be another role to add to your application."

Beth laughed and went back to her mental checklist. She was sorted for getting some experience in the house tomorrow. She already knew plenty about outdoor work on the estate, and despite her earlier mistake, she felt she knew what to do in the café now. In fact, the mistake had firmly stuck the correct way to do things in her head. So she knew she had plenty of suitable experiences to include on her application. She was planning to use her teaching experience and history qualifications to illustrate that she was good at dealing with people and to show that she was thinking ahead and would have relevant skills to lend to the development of a museum. If she planned some of it out tonight, there would be time to fine tune her application on Thursday evening and email it on Friday morning. So she could put that to one side for now.

Next on the list was finding out whether she could actually leave her job at this point. Really, it would have made more sense for that to be first on the list, but she was putting it off. Looking online had told her that to leave her job at the end of the summer term, she should have resigned by the end of May. Resigning at this point should mean leaving her position in October, which would clearly be too late for the

Ardmhor job. She needed to find out if there was a way she could still leave and whether this would leave people in the lurch. Beth knew that her Head of Department could tell her the answers, but she really didn't want to make the call. She hated making phone calls unless they were to her mum. She always agonised over whether it would be a bad time for the person she was calling, and without visual clues, she found it hard to judge how long to speak for. Text messages were her saviour, but they weren't going to do this situation justice.

Douglas, Beth's Head of Department, was one of her favourite people. He had an incredibly dry sense of humour, which had caused some confusion initially, but over the years they had worked together she had got used to it, and he had become sillier and sillier. The daft situations he engineered to make her laugh were the things that got her through each day. Although he had worked at the school for many years and was clearly going to stay there until he retired, he would happily while away time chatting to Beth about the different businesses they would set up together when they escaped teaching. The plan always involved her doing something creative and him being her delivery driver. But although they were close in many ways, they would never think of phoning each other for a chat, and Beth knew that this conversation could put Douglas in a difficult position. She got his number ready on her phone several times, before actually committing to making the call.

As it was, it turned out to be another of those situations where she shouldn't have worried so much. Unfortunately, no matter how many times this happened, she never seemed to learn. Douglas had been surprised to hear from her and as soon as she mentioned resignation timings, he'd worked out where the conversation was heading. He reassured her that no one had ever been forced to work their resignation period, so although it was frowned upon, if she resigned now, all that would happen was that her wages would stop with her August pay packet. She also didn't need to worry about leaving the school in the lurch, as Douglas had recently heard from the student teacher who had been placed with them earlier in the year. There had been an issue with the job they had been offered in London and they were desperately looking for work closer to home instead. If Beth got the job at Ardmhor, it seemed that she wouldn't be letting anyone down. In fact, she could actually be helping someone out. She felt sad at the idea of no longer working with Douglas; he had put a lot of effort into building her confidence at work and sounded as if he would genuinely miss her, but he also sounded excited for her and impressed that she was actually going to take a step into the unknown. With the problem of leaving her job ticked off the list, Beth dedicated the rest of the evening to her application form.

The day spent working as a house guide was a revelation to Beth. She loved every minute of it. During the morning, she just followed some of the other guides around, listening to the stories they told, but by the afternoon, she was able to answer some of the visitor's queries for herself. It was like the best bits of teaching, explaining things to an audience who actually wanted to listen, but not having to tell anybody off. As she walked back to the coach house, she was buzzing, thinking of several ideas to further improve her application. She worked solidly, only stopping briefly to eat with the other volunteers and realised it was almost dark as she finished tweaking the last paragraph. She emailed a copy to her long-suffering parents, who had agreed to proofread it for her, and took a deep breath. Barring any corrections she'd need to make in the morning, she had done all she could.

CHAPTER
SIXTEEN

The sea lapped gently against the edge of the rock Beth perched on. The morning was unusually still, and the surface of the sea lay flat as a millpond. Although it was early, the air was warm, the slanting rays of the sun promising heat to come. Beth watched transfixed as a dark head appeared in the water, trailing a v-shaped ripple in its wake. She stayed motionless as it got closer and closer, staring in fascination as an otter slipped smoothly out of the water before proceeding to devour a fish. She was close enough to see the way its fur had been slicked together by the water, and she hardly dared breathe in case she alerted it to her presence, scaring it away. A sight like this, before the day had really begun, wasn't something that happened in Beth's normal life, and she took it as a sign that she was doing the right thing by trying to stay at Ardmhor.

The morning had seen Beth awake early. She'd wanted time to give her application one last check through before emailing it in. Once she'd completed her task, there was still an hour before breakfast, and the surge of adrenaline she'd felt on pressing send meant there was no hope of going back to sleep. Besides, the sun shone far too invitingly, so she had dressed quickly and made her way out of the coach house, slipping through the gap in the wall and emerging on the rocky shore. As the otter slid back into the water, Beth stretched and made her way on to her feet. In that moment, she knew there was nowhere she'd rather be. Now she just had to hope she got the job.

The volunteers felt they were definitely earning their keep that day. The sun beat down continuously and there was no breeze, not the typical conditions at Ardmhor. They took frequent breaks and were constantly plied with drinks, but it was a relief to everyone when they finally packed up for the day. Beth had found it hard to concentrate on the job in hand. Her mind was full of applications and interviews, so she'd been grateful the day's tasks required more brute strength than mental prowess. She was also grateful when she heard Eilidh calling to the group from across the lawn. Anything to distract her from her thoughts was a good thing.

Eilidh was busy in front of the gazebo that stood on a corner of the main lawn. Its edges were lined with benches and its usual function was to provide visitors with an escape from sudden deluges of rain. Today, however, it offered shelter from the sun's rays. She had set up a table inside, which held snacks and ice buckets full of drinks, and was now arranging picnic blankets outside for those who preferred to be in the sun. The thirsty volunteers made their way over, and the space filled quickly as the house guides finished their tours and other staff came to join them. There were bodies lying across the blankets, enjoying the warmth of the sun, while others sought shade on the benches inside. Beth smiled as she noticed Steve and Megan slipping quietly off towards the woods. She wondered if something might be happening between the two of them. Now that she thought about it, they were often together, and Steve was at his most animated when Megan was nearby.

"You look deep in thought," Eilidh said, arranging herself on the blanket next to Beth and taking a sip from an icy bottle of beer.

"I just saw Megan and Steve sneaking off into the woods. If they get together, I'll be the only single person left around here."

"You didn't look that single when we were walking between pubs in Inveravain," Eilidh replied, giving Beth a playful nudge.

Beth blushed, her cheeks toning with her hair. "I didn't know anyone had seen."

"Actually, I didn't," Eilidh confessed. "I just saw you walking together. Andrew told Rich about it later."

"That's even worse! What did he say?"

"I think he just mentioned that you'd kissed, but you didn't seem that bothered."

"I do like him. There just wasn't really any spark. He wasn't upset, was he?"

Eilidh laughed. "It'd take more than that to upset Andrew. He's a great bloke, but there's never a shortage of women around him. If I had to choose which one of you was more likely to end up hurt if you got together, let's just say I think I'd be more concerned about you."

"Well, you don't need to worry there. I like him, but I don't think he's the one for me," Beth replied, picking at the label on her bottle of cider.

"Does that mean you already think someone else is? Come on, you know you can trust me!"

Beth was sorely tempted to tell Eilidh about her meetings with Alex. She'd been dying to confide in someone, but the thought of Alex finding out and thinking badly of her for it had been enough to put her off. She wasn't above a bit of gossip. She knew it wasn't a good thing, but that didn't stop her from enjoying it. However, as Alex had already pulled her up on it things seemed different. Even though she was still slightly angry after their confrontation the other night, with hindsight, she could see there was a lot of truth in what he had said. Without his harsh words, she would most likely have just given up and walked away from here. So, with things already strained between them, it seemed all the more important that she caused no more damage to their relationship, and as a result, she decided that keeping quiet was the only option.

"No, there's no exciting news. I just know that we're not meant to be."

"Alright, so you're not going to marry Andrew, but does that mean no more snogging either?"

"Well, the snogging wasn't bad actually," Beth laughed. "So never say never!"

Lady Angela had been walking across the lawn from the house and at that moment appeared right in front of them. Beth really hoped she hadn't overheard their conversation. It wasn't quite the impression she wanted Alex's mum, and hopefully her future boss, to have of her.

"Beth! Just the person I wanted to see," Angela called out.

It didn't seem like she'd heard, and Beth breathed a sigh of relief.

"I've found some more photo albums, and they definitely cover the time Eliza would have lived here. I wondered if you wanted to come and look at them tomorrow."

"I'd love to. What time?"

"Would about four suit you? I've got a few things on earlier in the day."

"That'd be great. Shall I come to the side door?"

"Perfect. Right, I've just seen Kath and I need a quick word, so I'll leave you girls to it."

As Lady Angela walked away, Eilidh asked whether Beth had any other plans for the next day.

"No, not really. I got too caught up with the application to think about it. I suppose I'll just see what everyone else is up to. How about you?"

"I'm going over to my parents' for lunch. My mum wondered if you might like to join us."

Beth's internal alarms sounded. For reasons she didn't fully understand, she found going to other people's houses awkward. She never knew quite where to put herself and struggled to work out whether she was leaving too soon or outstaying her welcome. With a liberal use of excuses, she usually managed to avoid the situation, but today she'd made an error. She'd already revealed that she didn't have any plans, so had trapped herself in a dead end, where the only polite way out was to agree to go. Beth thought about all the things she'd worried about recently that had turned out alright and told herself sternly that it'd be fine once she got there.

"That sounds lovely," was her reply to Eilidh.

Sunlight poured into her room by the time Beth woke the next day. She was hot and clammy and pushed the covers away in an attempt to cool down. Turning onto her side to check the time, she was surprised to find it was already well past breakfast. The drinks on the lawn had turned into drinks at the coach house and then finally drinks at the pub. No one had wanted to waste the opportunity to sit outside drinking on a rare night warm enough to do so, especially one that led into a weekend. Beth felt confident she wasn't the only person in the building feeling worse for wear that morning. She reached for the glass of water next to her and planned to settle back to sleep. She had nowhere she urgently needed to be.

It was then she noticed that someone had pushed an envelope under her door. Curiosity overcame her need to remain lying flat, and she crawled out of bed to investigate. She opened the envelope and immediately saw the Ardmhor branding on the paper. Her heart beat a little faster, 'please let me have an interview, please let me have an interview', she repeated like a prayer. She read the contents with an eye half shut, as if to protect herself from bad news, like a poor version of watching a horror film from behind a cushion. Then she saw the words she wanted to see, 'we would like to invite you for an interview'. She had made it past the first hurdle. All traces of headache and tiredness vanished as she performed a celebratory air punch. She forgot the idea of going back to bed and headed for the shower instead. It looked like another beautiful day, and it seemed a shame to waste it.

Feeling refreshed after her shower, Beth tamed her hair into a high ponytail and then twisted it into a bun, teasing a few pieces out to soften the effect. She knotted a headscarf at the front to control the frizz and set off to the café. Her stomach was protesting that it was a long time since it had last been fed. The previous night had focused more on liquid than food. As breakfast had long since finished, Beth settled for the healthy option of chocolate cake and a can of diet cola. She spotted Mary and Bob sat in the corner and made her way over to join them.

"I didn't expect to see you surfacing for a while yet, Beth," Mary began as Beth placed her tray down on the table. "Bob and I were just discussing who might be in the worst state today. My money is on Steve. He's not usually a big drinker, but he certainly came out of his shell last night."

"I think Fraser," interjected Bob. "I know he's used to putting a few away, but he had some sort of bet with one of the lads who's going home today and ended up stripping off and running around outside the pub starkers! I don't think Olivia knew where to put herself. If his head isn't hurting from the booze, I think it'll be hurting from the ear bashing she's going to give him!"

"I always miss everything!" Beth said, laughing. "I didn't even realise you were still there when I left."

"Face it, Beth, you young ones just can't keep · up with the likes of us. It's rare for anyone to outpace me and the missus!"

"Talking of young ones," Mary took over. "Did you notice anything going on between Megan and Steve last night?"

Beth smiled at the idea of Megan and Steve being considered young. She didn't even consider herself young and Megan and Steve had about twenty years on her, but she supposed it was all relative, really.

"I noticed them disappearing into the woods when we were out on the lawn after work, and they do always seem very comfortable together."

"See, I told you," Mary said, turning to Bob with a look of triumph. "I'm never wrong about these things. Mark my words, there'll be wedding bells before too long."

"I don't know," Beth began. "From what Megan says, she won't be rushing into marriage again."

"Beth, Beth, Beth," said Bob. "You're lovely, but you're young, so I'm going to let you in on a little secret." He paused for dramatic effect. "Only ever agree with Mary. It's not worth doing anything else."

Mary rolled her eyes at him and gave him a playful tap on the arm, while Beth laughed at the pair of them. Sally had just come over to clear the table and smiled.

"What have I missed?"

"Beth has just been learning that no one should ever question Mary," Bob said with a wink.

"Oh, I learnt that the first time I met her," Sally replied, knowing the regular joke. "I didn't see you come in, Beth. Calum from the ticket desk was looking for you earlier. Something about a parcel, I think."

There was still an hour before Eilidh was due to collect her, so Beth set straight off in the direction of the ticket hut. Calum explained a parcel had arrived for her a couple of days ago, but it had been buried in a pile of post and overlooked. At first, Beth couldn't think of anything she was expecting, but as Calum handed over the small package, she remembered the copy of Eliza's wedding picture that her mum had sent up. She'd completely forgotten about it amongst all the indecision over the job application. Beth hurried outside to find a seat in the shade, desperate for her first glimpse of the young Eliza.

Inside the package was a small cardboard

folder. Beth opened it slowly and found a serious young couple looking back at her. The black and white image was nothing like the relaxed pictures Beth was used to seeing after friends' weddings. This was definitely not a beaming couple jumping in the air, with the bride holding her bouquet aloft, or a couple walking off hand in hand, throwing a smile back to the photographer over their shoulders. This wedding portrait was a very different affair. Eliza would only have been twenty-one, so a good few years younger than Beth, but the sombreness of the image made her look somehow older. Eliza was seated on a chair, wearing a long, high-collared lace dress. Beth guessed the dress was white, but really it could have been any light colour, and the black and white image wouldn't allow her to know for certain. William stood behind the chair, slightly to the side of her, one hand resting on Eliza's shoulder, the other by his side. Eliza's hands were occupied by the enormous arrangement of flowers she held in front of her. It was impossible to tell how the young couple felt. The stillness necessary for Victorian photography had robbed their faces of the joy, or hope, or possibly uncertainty they might have been displaying in the moments either side of the image being captured.

The thing that struck Beth most about the picture was how familiar Eliza was. It wasn't like those moments you read about in books, or see in films, where someone comes across an ancestor's portrait that literally is them but dressed in the fashions of a previous century. Beth didn't think anyone would mistake this photograph for a picture of her, but there was definitely something of her in the image. None of Eliza's features had made it down the generations untouched to Beth, but enough remained similar to make someone take a second look. The photo couldn't show their shared hair colour either, which was perhaps the thing most likely to lead someone to confuse the pair. However, even though Eliza's hair was twisted up behind her head, Beth could see enough to tell that the elaborate floral headdress was performing the same frizz flattening role as her own headscarf. Looking at the familiar young woman in front of her, just beginning a marriage that was to last over fifty years, Beth felt a powerful connection to her. She wished she could step into the picture and ask Eliza the many questions she had. How had it come to be that less than a year on from being so happy with Alexander, she was posing for a marriage portrait with another man? She was desperate to read more of the diary and find some answers, but a glance at her watch told her that Eilidh would arrive shortly. Unfortunately, answers would have to wait.

The sun sparkled on the sea as they drove along the coast road. Eilidh's car was too old for air conditioning, so they had the windows down, and Beth was glad of the headscarf as the breeze whipped through the car, pulling at the flyaway hairs that constantly plagued her. Although Rich and Eilidh lived together in Ardmhor, he was away for the weekend, so it was just Beth accompanying Eilidh to her parent's house in a village further along the road from Inveravain. The two of them made the most of the journey, singing along to the radio at full volume and laughing when a car they passed gave them a round of applause. Each time Beth made the journey to Inveravain, she saw something new. Today, the sunlight shone off the windows of a croft house she hadn't noticed before. It stood on the hillside next to a small clump of pine trees, looking out to sea. Beth imagined walking out of its door in the morning, inhaling the scent of pine and taking in the view. Would this constant sense of wonder change if she got the job here and this road became part of her everyday life?

The village of Strathglen nestled at the foot of a smooth, rounded mountain, just as its slopes gave way to a wide, open bay. Eilidh's family home sat right at the water's edge.

"This is amazing!" Beth gasped as she closed the car door.

They had parked the car at the top of a set of

steps, which led down to the house. The tide was at its highest and the sea seemed to surround the house on the other three sides. Eilidh's mum, Claire, met them at the door, pulling Eilidh into a tight hug and greeting Beth warmly. From the front door, they could see straight through the hall, into the kitchen and out of the floor to ceiling windows at the back of the house. The water looked so close Beth thought it must be like living on a boat. Claire led them off to the side, through a dining area, into a living room, where the wall comprised yet more vast windows.

"I thought we'd eat out in the garden seeing as the weather is so lovely," Claire said, opening a patio door onto a lawn at the side of the house.

Eilidh's dad, Alan, was already sitting at the garden table and jumped straight up to say hello. Beth decided Eilidh took after her mum more than her dad. They were both very petite with delicate features, whereas her dad was a gigantic bear of a man. Eilidh and Alan began discussing the newspaper article he had just been reading about proposed sites for a new local hospital, and Beth felt herself relax. The water lapped gently against the sea wall, only a short distance from where they sat. A heron balanced on the tip of a rock, a little way out to sea, and some cormorants skimmed along the surface. A gentle breeze ruffled the sea grasses growing in the rockery to the side of the table, releasing the scent of the flowers surrounding them. Beth tried to imagine what it would be like to live there. Although the house was on the main road through the village, and it seemed to be a bustling place, with shops, a school, and plenty of places to eat, while sat here in the garden, they could have been in the middle of nowhere. Looking out across the bay, over the islands that were dotted across it, there was a feeling of so much space. Beth couldn't think when she'd ever been somewhere more lovely.

"It didn't look quite so good when we bought it," Claire said, as they tucked into a delicious lemon meringue pie. They'd just polished off a squat lobster salad and were chatting about the house. "Well, actually, that's not quite true. When we bought it, it looked as if it just needed redecorating, but as soon as we started work on it, we realised there were lots of problems. Basically, it's a good job Alan's a builder, or it would have cost us a fortune."

"I love all the windows. It must be amazing to see all of this whichever way you look." Beth waved her arms around her as she spoke.

"It really is. We've been here for over ten years now, but I never get bored with the view. It changes constantly, depending on the tide or the weather. We're very lucky. Although I hear you're going to stay, so maybe you'll end up somewhere even lovelier."

"I don't think I'll manage better than this, and I haven't got the job yet, but fingers crossed."

"Moving up here was the best thing that I ever did," Claire announced.

"Apart from marrying me, of course," interrupted Alan.

"Or giving birth to me," piped up Eilidh.

Claire rolled her eyes at them.

"I'd assumed you had always lived around here," Beth said, surprised.

"No, I grew up in Glasgow, but I met Alan and followed him up here."

"Wouldn't leave me alone," Alan said with a wink. "She just kept following me around until I gave in and married her!"

"That's exactly how it happened," Claire agreed, with another roll of her eyes.

They were like a younger version of Mary and Bob, thought Beth, all banter, but clearly so much in love. She was starting to see the similarities between Eilidh and Alan, too. They might look completely different, but their personalities were very alike.

"I hope I do get the job and that it all works out," Beth said. "I've enjoyed being here so much, and I'd been pretty miserable at home, so it'd be the perfect fresh start. I'm just worried in case I don't get the job or in case I get it and realise I've made a mistake."

"Eilidh says you're a teacher," Alan began. "I imagine that's quite a well-paid job to be giving up to start at the bottom, so I don't think you're being daft to worry, but there's no point being sensible and miserable. Sometimes you have to take a chance."

Alan looked across at Claire as he finished speaking, and Beth wondered if he was thinking of the chance she had taken, moving up here to be with him. That was the way she wanted someone to look at her, and she tried to think whether it was the same expression Alex used when he really held her gaze.

"Where are you thinking of living?" Alan asked, interrupting her thoughts.

"If I get the job, I'd need to live in the staff accommodation to start with, but if things work out, I'd like to buy somewhere. I've been saving to buy a place back at home, so hopefully I'll be able to afford something."

"There are definitely some bargains around here, if you don't mind a bit of work. There's a few I've kept an eye on, thinking they'd make great renovation projects to do up and sell on, but to be honest, I always end up too busy working on other people's houses to get round to it."

"There's a beautiful old place for sale just by Ardmhor House," said Beth. "Well, it doesn't look beautiful now, but you can tell it would be. The asking price is next to nothing, but I suppose it'd cost twice that again to sort it out."

"That'll be the old factor's house," said Alan, "and actually it might not be as bad as it looks. It's a pretty sturdy building, so depending on what someone was planning, it might not cost as much as you'd think to make it liveable. If you're interested, I'd be happy to come and view it with you. In fact, I'd love the excuse."

"I think it's probably a bit beyond my savings, but I'd be happy to be your excuse," Beth replied, not taking his offer too seriously. The afternoon passed quickly. It was so warm they'd had to put up a sunshade, which was not something that happened often. Beth could quite happily have stayed all day, but she was meeting Lady Angela at four to look through the photo albums, and Eilidh was also ready to get back. As they said their goodbyes, Beth thought to herself that this had been yet another situation she had wanted to avoid, which had turned out to be fine—actually, not fine, really enjoyable. How many great things had she missed out on in the past because of her worrying? But then again, it wasn't like this was a new realisation. It was one thing knowing it, the harder part was acting on it.

Lady Angela was already waiting at the side door as Beth approached a while later.

"I know. I'm early again," she called out. "I just can't help myself when it comes to showing off our history."

Beth laughed and followed her through to the old office. The albums were already spread out on the table.

"My mum sent me a copy of Eliza's wedding portrait," Beth said as she fished the folder out of her bag. "She married not long after leaving Ardmhor, so we'll be able to recognise her if she's in any of the photos."

"Quite a lot of them are labelled, so we should be alright," said Angela, "but I'd love to see it, anyway."

Beth placed the picture on the table and they both stared at it.

"She's beautiful, Beth, and so young. These old photos can be quite hard to relate to though, can't they? It's difficult to believe they would have felt the same as us when the pictures are so removed from what we're used to."

"That's pretty much what I thought when I first saw it this morning."

"Even so, you can tell you're from the same family. There's a real look of you in that picture."

"Do you think so? It's hard to tell yourself, isn't it?"

"Definitely," said Angela. "Now let's see if we can find her anywhere in these."

Lady Angela picked up an album with the dates 1890-1895 written inside the cover.

"Imagine fitting five years' worth of photos into one book nowadays!"

"That's if you actually get round to printing any," remarked Beth.

There was a sense of anticipation as they began turning the pages of the album. If Eliza's picture was going to be anywhere at Ardmhor, it had to be in here. There were quite a few pictures of groups on the lawn outside the house, but none of them seemed to include Eliza. There were some showing extremely well-dressed guests at a party. One of the pictures was labelled 'Flora' and showed a delicate young woman, who was dwarfed by one of the most extravagant floral arrangements Beth had ever seen.

"Eliza wrote in her diary about the amazing flowers Lady Constance arranged for a party she hosted. It was when she wanted to find suitable partners for Flora and Alexander to marry. I wonder if these pictures were taken at that party."

"It's a definite possibility. Let's make sure we look through the backgrounds carefully. Eliza could well be there."

But no matter how thoroughly they looked, there didn't appear to be any sign of her. There were pictures from Flora's wedding. She looked just as stunning as Eliza had described, wearing a long silky dress that pooled out behind her. However, Eliza didn't appear in any of the pictures of guests, not even in the background. Beth had expected there to be at least one photograph of Eliza and Flora together. She was, after all, supposed to be her close companion, and Lady Constance kept telling her she was part of the family, but there was nothing. There was even a picture of all the gardening staff, with Angus clearly labelled on the front row. It didn't surprise Beth that Flora used to single him out—he was gorgeous. He stared directly into the camera, looking somehow more modern than the other gardeners gathered around him. But despite all the fascinating images, Eliza was nowhere to be seen.

What was even more disappointing than the lack of pictures of Eliza, was the fact that there weren't any photographs of Alexander. Beth knew what Eliza looked like now and could picture her here, even without a physical image to look at. Alexander, however, was still a mystery. There were quite a lot of gaps in the album, though, empty spaces where photographs had clearly been removed.

"Isn't that a bit odd?" asked Beth

"Not necessarily. There are gaps in quite a few of the albums, and sometimes the photos reappear in frames or stuffed in drawers elsewhere. It makes sense that people might take out a picture they really like, so they can keep it somewhere close to hand. Although, there are more gaps in here than in any of the other albums I've looked through."

"Do you think maybe Eliza took them? So she could remember here when she left?"

"It's possible. Perhaps you could ask your mum to have a look, and I'll keep searching here."

"Thanks, I'll probably speak to her later on, so I'll ask."

They slowly turned each page of the album again, just in case there was anything they'd overlooked.

"Are you missing your mum?" Angela asked after a while. "You still live at home, don't you?"

"I do, and it seems ages since I've seen her, but I've been too busy to notice, really."

"So, how do they feel about you applying for the job here? It's a long way from home."

"They were really encouraging, actually. They're probably desperate to get rid of me, to be honest."

"No, I bet they feel lucky that you still enjoy being around them. I know I love it when my boys are home."

Beth felt herself blushing at the mention of Lady Angela's sons. She looked down, hoping

Angela wouldn't notice, but Angela spotted the movement straight away and misinterpreted its meaning, thinking she had somehow upset Beth.

"But your parents will be even happier knowing you're doing something you really want to, so don't worry about that," Angela said kindly.

"I might not even get the job, anyway. Interviews have never been my strong point."

"Just be yourself, Beth. I've really enjoyed all our chats so far, so I'm sure your interview skills will be fine. I know Sally has been really grateful for your help in the café, and Kath thought you had a real flair for explaining things to visitors. Also, I don't think we've ever had such a detailed application sent in. Just have a bit of faith in yourself and you'll not go wrong."

It took Beth a moment to respond. She had never quite mastered the art of handling compliments. Standard ones, such as, 'I like your dress' or 'your hair looks nice', she could pretty much deal with. She had learnt a quick reply about where the dress was from, or the fact it had pockets, or how her hair was behaving for once, worked nicely. But heartfelt and personal praise felt more difficult. She wanted to show she appreciated the kind words, but didn't want to sound full of herself, or even worse, accidentally cry. She took an internal deep breath before responding.

"Thank you. I'll definitely try my best. I'd love to stay here."

Beth didn't know if the conversation with Lady Angela had made her feel better, or even more nervous. It was lovely how encouraging everyone had been about her application, but now it felt like she wouldn't just be letting herself down if she messed up. She tried to talk herself round as she walked to the pub. Tonight was the welcome celebration for the last group of volunteers. Regardless of whether she got the job, there was only one week left with all the friends she had made, and she needed to try to make the most of it.

By the time the evening drew to a close, Beth was feeling much more relaxed, and she decided to try to find Alex. She'd been avoiding him for a few days. At first, it was because she was annoyed with him for judging her, and then, once she'd had time to think, it was because she was annoyed with herself. Now she'd calmed down, it was clear he'd been right. She would have just given up and gone back home because it was easier than trying something new. Now that she'd filled in the application and got the interview, she felt able to face him again.

It was brighter on the path to the viewpoint. Although the moon was nothing like the silver sun of her first night at Ardmhor, it was regaining its power. As she stepped into the clearing, Beth immediately spotted Alex approaching from the other direction. He started speaking before they'd even sat down.

"I'm so glad you're here, Beth. I went too far the other night, and I've been worried ever since that you wouldn't come out here again."

"No, you were right. I wouldn't have applied for the job. I'd already decided it was too risky and that I'd be silly to give up a career for what's usually temporary work. So actually, I should say thank you. I needed someone to give me a push, and you did it"

"But that's not what I meant to do. I didn't want you to apply because I pushed you. I wanted you to apply because you knew it was what you really wanted. I don't want to force you into things. I just don't want you to end up with the same regrets as me."

Beth wondered if he was referring to the failed relationship that had obviously hurt him so much. Was there something he had been too scared to do that he now regretted? She looked at him more closely, but he seemed so calm and capable that she just couldn't imagine him scared. However, he didn't seem keen to elaborate.

"I really do want to work here," Beth replied, once it was clear Alex wasn't going to reveal anything else about his regrets. "So I'm glad you pushed me. Otherwise, I think I'd always have wondered what might have been."

"And that's what I wouldn't want you to live with. It's not a nice way to exist. Anyway, let's talk about something else."

So, Beth filled him in on her trip to Eilidh's and what else she'd learnt from the diary. He seemed quite moved as she explained how happy Eliza was now that Alexander had told her their wedding should be happening soon. She wondered again if he was thinking about his own relationship. It was then that she remembered the wedding portrait in her bag.

"What I really want to know is how she got from being so happy with Alexander to marrying someone else in England."

Alex moved closer to her, looking at the picture in her hand.

"She was so beautiful," he whispered. "I wonder how she felt."

"I know. It's impossible to tell from the photo, isn't it? But she was married to William for over fifty years, and my mum says she talked about him really fondly, so there must have been some love there. I just don't know what went wrong with Alexander. She sounds so in love with him, but within a year she's married to William."

"You'll let me know what you find out, won't you?" Alex asked.

"Of course, but I should spend some time practising interview questions, rather than just reading the diary. I'm rubbish at answering things like 'what do you think your biggest weakness is?' or 'what's your best quality?' I go blank every time, so I want to have some appropriate answers planned out."

"That sounds sensible. I think you'll be great, but it doesn't hurt to be prepared. When is the interview?"

"It's on Tuesday. Eilidh says she's taking me to the pub that night, whatever happens. So I'll be at the Ardmhor Hotel, either crying into my pint or celebrating." She hesitated before continuing, "You could come too. We don't always have to meet here."

"Maybe," he replied.

"Maybe isn't good enough, remember?" she said with a smile. "I can't think who told me that, but apparently he's always right."

"I'll do my best," Alex said, smiling back at her as he stood up.

"That's much better," laughed Beth, joining him on her feet.

"Night, Beth," he said, turning to go.

"Night, Alex," she replied.

She was still none the wiser as to whether he shared her feelings. It seemed he was too caught up in his last relationship to be thinking about moving on. But at least they were on good terms again. Maybe they could still get back to the intense connection she'd felt when they'd first met.

CHAPTER SEVENTEEN

27th of December 1892

We are about to reach the start of another year, but I am still not engaged. Since Alex promised we could soon tell his parents of our intentions, I feel as though all I have written of is disappointment. At each suggestion the time is right, there then comes a reason it isn't. I know I should try to remember the good things and hold on to the hope that we will soon be together properly, but I am finding it so hard. Christmas was rather subdued again this year. Last year, Alex was missing, and this year Flora was. I hadn't realised how much I would miss her silliness. But this was her first Christmas as mistress of her own house, and I wouldn't have wanted to give that up either. How nice it must be to be in charge. We are to travel to Flora's new home to welcome in the New Year, which I am very much looking forward to.

Ardmhor House has been beautifully

decorated, with foliage, berries, ribbons, and an enormous tree in the hall. We have exchanged gifts and eaten splendid feasts. Really, I suppose it has all been very festive. It is just my mood that hasn't fitted the season. I received another greeting from Mr Hardwick, my father's former partner. He has moved to Manchester, in order to fulfil his wife's desire to be closer to her family. He writes of the difficulties he has had finding reliable staff for his offices, and it has made me think about whether I could be of use. If Alex can never bring himself to acknowledge our relationship, maybe I need to go back to my old dream of returning to England? What would make me happiest is for us to leave here together. However, I know that will never happen. I don't want to leave Alex and he would never want to leave Ardmhor, but I need to have some sort of plan in mind. I can't continue with this uncertainty forever. I think I am going to write to Mr Hardwick, not asking for a job, but just subtly seeing how things lie. Perhaps I can live with Alex's inaction if I am taking some action of my own.

28th of December 1892

I can't believe how different things feel today. Perhaps it is down to writing the letter to Mr Hardwick. I certainly feel a little more in control, although I doubt anything will come of it. It could also be because we take the train to stay with Flora tomorrow, and I think a change of scenery will do me good. But really, I think it is because Lord and Lady MacAird were both out visiting today, leaving Alex and me to spend time alone for what feels like the first time in months. Our meetings have been brief for so long that our time together had started to follow a miserable pattern. I would beg him to move forward with telling his parents. He would give reasons why he couldn't. I would then become upset, and he would comfort me, or he would become upset, and we would comfort each other. Then we would quickly need to go our separate ways again. Although we both still felt the same love for each other, I think we had forgotten we could just be happy in each other's company.

Today was so different. All the staff were busy with preparations for the journey tomorrow, so no one was even slightly interested in how we spent the day. It was easy to meet each other in the woods and disappear for a long walk. We talked about books, like we used to, before we even understood our feelings for each other. We dreamed of setting up our own home in the factor's house and having a room entirely lined with books, thousands of them, which we would choose together and discuss at length. Holding hands and clasping each other tightly for warmth, we kissed so deeply and for so long that I wondered if even Alex might forget himself. He is far too much of a gentleman for that, but I can't help imagining exactly what it might have felt like if he wasn't. Flora hasn't gone into any details in her letters, even she is too discrete for that, but what she has said makes it sound like that aspect of married life is something to look forward to, rather than something to dread. Lady Constance had a very uncomfortable talk with Flora before her wedding, where she said some things had to be endured, but would improve. Flora had laughed afterwards, repeating Lady Constance's words in an excellent imitation of her voice. Flora said that she couldn't imagine ever having to endure anything with Algernon, and her letters sound as if, thankfully, she was right. The feelings I have when I am alone with Alex suggest nothing upsetting could come from anything we were to do together. Maybe it is different if you have to enter a marriage to please your parents, as I suspect Lady Constance did, rather than marrying for love as I plan to. Flora was lucky enough to do both.

I feel a little foolish for writing to Mr Hardwick now. How could I have doubted Alex and the plans we have made? Building our life here is all I could want, and telling his parents at the right time is the only way to achieve that. At least I did not mention my line of thinking explicitly in my letter. Mr Hardwick should only see it as a friendly reply to his enquiries.

5th of January 1893

We are safely back at Ardmhor, and I feel as if the time away has done us all good. Flora has adapted to her new role as splendidly as I imagined she would. The staff were so eager to please her, and Algernon's devotion to her seems only to have increased. Flora and I had both heard stories of men that seemed to care until the moment they became a husband, only then to become indifferent, or outright cruel. It seems we are both lucky, as nothing of the sort has befallen Flora, and I know Alex would never treat me in such a way.

Flora's new home, Banshire Castle, surpasses Ardmhor House in terms of grandeur. It has developed from an older building in much the same way Ardmhor has, but that original building was a much larger defensive structure, a true castle, I suppose. Over the years, much more elegant and comfortable wings have been added, giving the effect that if you approach from the west, it seems you are arriving at an ancient castle, where sleeping beauty could be about to awake, but if you approach from the east, you are arriving at a fashionable country mansion. The interiors are very tasteful, and it is equipped with every modern convenience you could imagine. It has filled Lady Constance with ideas for improvements at Ardmhor, and she talked of little else throughout our return journey.

Alex was free from his responsibilities to the estate during our stay, and his old carefree nature seemed to return. I felt quite guilty, as it was only seeing him relax that made me realise how worried he had become. I had been so caught up in my own fears and troubles that I hadn't appreciated how much he was struggling. As the decisions over our future lie with him, I'd thought he had the reassurance of being in control, something that I so desperately crave. I feel ashamed that I hadn't considered how heavily that responsibility weighs on him.

There was a ball to welcome in the New Year, and it was wonderful to dance with Alex. To be openly in his arms made up for all the disappointments of the last few months. Every member of the household seems in much higher spirits than they were when we set out on our journey. I hope this bodes well for the news Alex and I plan to share with them soon.

12th of January 1893

It seems I may have unwittingly caused an enormous setback in mine and Alex's plans. Really, I feel the blame lies with Lady Constance. In fact, if she wasn't so caught up in her ideas of duty and respectability, we could have been open about our feelings from the very beginning. Although, I suppose perhaps it's the

THE HOLIDAY AT ARDMHOR

whole of society to blame for that and that she is just behaving as anyone in her position would. However, in this instance, I really do feel the blame lies entirely with her. Opening letters addressed to me seems inexcusable, but I doubt anyone else will be concerned about that. Mr Hardwick had replied to my letter enquiring about his family and his new business in Manchester. He mentioned that there would always be a place for me with his family and within his business. He knows from my father's letters that I was invaluable in assisting him with his work. Mr Hardwick's words weren't written as a reply to a request for employment. Indeed, I had asked no such thing in my letter to him. To my eyes, his words were purely a reassurance that I would always have somewhere to turn if necessary. A sentiment that I am holding very dear to me at present. However, Lady Constance has interpreted them completely differently.

Before I had even seen Mr Hardwick's letter, before I even knew he had replied to me, Lady Constance appeared in front of me in the library. She was in a state of complete rage. I had never seen her so angry. Even after terrible mistakes by the staff she always maintains a calm facade, so I could not comprehend what might have happened. She shouted I was ungrateful, and that I didn't love her, and that I was throwing her love back in her face. The behaviour she was showing was of the type she would condemn in others, and I struggled to understand what she was trying to say. My first thought was that Alex had finally told them about our relationship and that the result had been far worse than we expected, but even within the moment, I knew that was unlikely. Alex would never have gone ahead with that without preparing me first, and he definitely would not have left me to face her wrath alone. Then I saw the paper in her hand. She thrust it at me as she collapsed into a chair. Only quiet sobs escaped her now, the ranting and raving having drawn to a close. I read the contents as quickly as I could, but I struggled to see what within them had upset her so greatly. I placed my arms around her, pleading with her to tell me what I had done. At first there were just more and more sobs, and then eventually she shook me off and pulled herself upright.

Then she spoke, very calmly, as if the previous few minutes had not taken place, "You want to leave me. You have only pretended to love me. I've taken you in as a daughter, yet you've been plotting behind my back to leave. You wanted to go back to England as soon as your father died, and despite everything I have given you, you are still trying to go."

She stared beyond me into the distance, her manner icy cold. I tried to reassure her that I appreciated everything she had done for me. I told her I hadn't known a mother's love for a long time and that I could never be ungrateful for the way she had opened her heart to me. I tried to reason with her that the letter was simply Mr Hardwick's way of showing his affection for my father and that I had no intention of leaving. I even said that I'd been worried about whether I still had a place at Ardmhor now that Flora had left. However, whichever route I took, Lady Constance seemed just as angry. But now, it was a controlled anger, which in its own way was more frightening than the earlier rage.

As I was still pleading with her to understand, both Lord MacAird and Alex appeared. They had been working in the office and had been alerted to the commotion by the staff. Lady Constance's demeanour changed again as she dissolved against her husband, sniffing and holding down little sobs between words. She repeated her accusations that I was ungrateful and trying to leave her. I tried to explain what had happened, but Lord MacAird just put up his hand and told me to go to my room. I turned to Alex, but he didn't say a word. He just looked at me, and I found I couldn't read his expression. It seemed the only thing to do was to follow Lord MacAird's instruction and leave.

I've been sitting here ever since, thinking it all over. I feel terrible that Lady Constance is upset, especially as we have grown much closer since Flora's departure. However, the rapid changes between sadness and anger, then calmness and rage, were unsettling. It seems a disproportionate reaction to the contents of the letter. That Lady Constance thought it acceptable to open my post is also worrying. But my main concern is how much this sets back our plans. How can we expect a calm acceptance of our intention to marry after this? I already knew that Lady Constance would like Alex to remain an unmarried son, devoted to the estate. I can now see that I have been cast as a replacement daughter. Today's events have given me no confidence she would want that son and daughter joined in a way that would exclude her.

Morag came to see if I needed any help to prepare for dinner. I rarely make use of a maid to dress. Flora and Lady Constance do, but it isn't something I've ever been used to. I assume they sent her to make it clear my presence will be required at the dinner table, regardless of what transpired earlier.

14th of January 1893

On the surface, all has been calm since the outburst of two days ago, but the atmosphere has not lightened at all. Dinner was awkward that night. Lady Constance was not present—apparently she had been taken ill. I tried to enquire whether she was alright, and tentatively explain the contents of the letter, but Lord MacAird quickly silenced me by moving the conversation to other topics. It appeared we were to pretend that nothing out of the ordinary had taken place. When we finished eating, Lord MacAird stated we should all retire immediately to our own rooms because of the trying nature of the day. That was his only reference to the earlier events, and it prevented any chance for me to discuss what had happened with Alex.

Lady Constance was also absent from breakfast yesterday, but she reappeared at dinner. I tried to be as attentive to her as possible; although I was still annoyed that she had read my letter, I felt terrible that I had caused such upset. However, she would not meet my eye at all and only responded to questions asked by Lord MacAird or Alex. It was as if she could not even see me at the table. The worst part is that Lord MacAird's behaviour towards me suggests he too thinks I am responsible for the upset of the past few days.

I overheard Alex talking with his mother, reassuring her I regard her most highly and that he is certain I am hugely grateful to her, but also reminding her I have no official place with them and that I must be free to make my own decisions. I caught him briefly in the hall, to question him over his meaning, but it could only be a short, whispered conversation. There was no hope of escaping outside for a proper discussion of events, as it has poured with rain all day. Alex said that as well as trying to placate her, he was trying to remind her I am not her daughter. He does not want her to cast us further into a sibling role. Although I can see what he was trying to achieve, I can only focus on the fact he said I have no official place here. My position depends on the whims of Lady Constance. I serve no useful purpose here for Lord MacAird, and much as my affection for Lady Constance has grown, I can't escape the knowledge that she is highly strung, with emotions that change by the minute. If she decided to throw me out, where would I go? No matter how much I love Alex, I can't exist with such uncertainty, and I can't wait until he feels the time is right to act. Who knows how much longer he feels that will need to be, especially after this latest setback? I love him, but living like this is not the life I want.

I am going to write to Mr Hardwick again and see if his kind suggestion could actually be a reality. Also, I want to enquire whether his business needs other partners; after all, Alex has studied law. I need to know what all the possibilities are so that I can make my own plans. I can no longer leave all responsibility for my future with Alex. I realise now that isn't fair to either of us. I just need to be very careful that Lady Constance does not intercept my post.

CHAPTER
EIGHTEEN

It was the morning of her interview, and Beth was thinking about the strange parallel between events in her life and events in Eliza's diary. Just as Beth was finally taking control by doing all she could to stay at Ardmhor, Eliza was taking control by looking for a way to leave. Although their plans were moving in opposite directions, Beth finally felt she might measure up to her determined namesake. She had been worrying that she had more in common with the dithering Alexander, than with her own great-great-grandmother. Beth took a sip of her drink and tried to focus on breathing slowly. She had hardly slept due to her nerves and didn't want anxiety to get the better of her. She wondered if she might have

been better working at the playground. Eilidh
had encouraged her to take the morning off, so
that she could prepare, but she just seemed to be
making herself more nervous.

Putting down her notes, Beth walked over to
the wardrobe. She'd had a major panic, just as she
was getting into bed on Saturday night, when it
occurred to her she had nothing suitable to wear
for the interview. The only footwear she had
with her were trainers and walking boots, both
of which felt completely wrong for an interview.
She had stayed up into the early hours trawling
the internet with no success: if a suitable shoe
was available in her size, it wasn't available for
rapid delivery or vice versa.

Fortunately, Megan had come to the rescue the
next morning. She looked over the invitation to
interview and pointed out that it said business
dress was not required. Then she asked Beth's
shoe size. Although Beth was a good few inches
taller than Megan, it turned out they both wore a
size seven.

"Right, you're coming up to my room now,"
Megan announced. "Between my wardrobe and
yours, we'll get this sorted. You've got black
trousers, haven't you?"

"I've got black jeans. Do you think they'll do?"

"With the right shoes and a nice top, I think
they'll be perfect. I'm so proud of you for getting
this far, Beth. I wouldn't have imagined the girl

I spoke to in those first few days completely shaking her life up, so I'm not going to let something as simple as clothes stand in your way!"

Megan was as good as her word and produced a gorgeous pair of black suede ankle boots, which had just enough heel to transform the look of Beth's jeans while still being comfortable. She then handed over a selection of black tops for her to take away and try.

Beth opened the wardrobe door and took out the two tops she had narrowed the selection down to, holding each one in front of her as she stood before the mirror. There was a black shirt, which looked very business-like, but the sleeves were just a touch on the short side, not quite reaching her wrists. Then there was a more informal top that Megan sometimes wore to the pub. It was very simple with a high, round neckline, but it was made from a sheer material that draped beautifully. The body was lined, but the sleeves remained transparent, their voluminous shape gathering back in at the cuff. When Megan wore it, the sleeves pooled dramatically at the bottom of her arms. They didn't have quite the same effect on Beth, but they did at least reach comfortably down to her hands. Beth switched the two tops back and forth in front of her and then phoned her mum for advice. The overriding opinion from both of her parents was to wear whichever was most comfortable, or she'd end up distracted. She decided they were right and that constantly tugging down the sleeves of the shirt would take away from the formal effect. So that left the sheer top. She tried the full outfit on again and was pleasantly surprised by what she saw. Not only did she look smart and presentable, but the combination of clothes also made her feel relaxed and confident. She had to concede that her usual interview attire would have looked totally out of place here. Carefully, she hung everything back up and returned to the chair in the window.

Over the course of the volunteers work the previous day, just about every member of the group had offered Beth some advice for her interview, and she had added their ideas to the stock of answers in her notes. The playground was coming together nicely, the final piece of equipment was being installed that day, meaning that there would only be some surfacing and planting to finish over the rest of the week. The site already looked far removed from the overgrown wasteland it had been. It now joined seamlessly to the other play area, so that parents could watch their older children while they played with their little ones. Once the planting was complete and the new picnic benches were in place, it would be a lovely place to sit, sheltered by the surrounding trees, with a glorious view out to sea.

As everything was going well, there had been plenty of time for the volunteers to chat. Steve talked to Beth about his experiences interviewing prospective candidates for the university where he worked. He mentioned several times that it wasn't always the most confident candidates that caught his attention, and Beth was touched he had noticed the thing that worried her the most. The overriding message from the advice seemed to be that she just needed to be herself. She knew that made sense; it was just unfortunate that being herself had never come easily.

As she sat staring out of the window, Beth realised that a full ten minutes had passed. She turned back to the notes in her hand, but the words seemed to swim before her eyes. The clock told her she had almost two hours before the interview, so she decided to go for a walk instead. There would still be plenty of time to change and get ready, and hopefully the fresh air would clear her head. The walk helped. The cool breeze off the sea and the magnificence of the mountains put things back into perspective. Beth could see that she was over preparing for a role that was expected to be temporary. As everyone had been so supportive, she had got herself worked up about not wanting to disappoint anyone. Her mum had told her to just do her best, and

Beth knew she had definitely done that with her preparations. Now she needed to keep calm so that she could do the same in the interview.

As Beth left the estate office three hours later, she felt like she was walking on air. From her perspective, the interview couldn't have gone better. She was happy with how she looked in her interview outfit and had actually felt confident as she walked into the room. There were three people on the interview panel. Duncan Matthews, the estate manager for Ardmhor, was the lead interviewer. Although Beth hadn't met him before, she realised he was the smartly dressed man she'd seen going into the house with Lady Angela previously. Lady Angela herself was the second member of the panel, sitting to his right. The third interviewer, a member of the Ardmhor Trust board, was on his left. All of them had welcomed her with broad smiles and she had felt they were on her side. It was as if they had written the questions specifically for her. Everything they asked was something she had prepared a response for, so she could articulate herself confidently. Lady Angela was particularly interested in Beth's ideas for a museum, nodding enthusiastically as she outlined her vision. For once, Beth didn't leave the room feeling she had sold herself short or agonising over whether she had explained herself clearly. She felt she could honestly tell her mum that she had done her best—and not just her best in the circumstances, when she was nervous and unsure, but her actual, absolute best.

Beth's spirits were still high as she walked to the pub. Her plans had started out simply as a drink with Eilidh to celebrate the interview being over but had somehow ended up with the entire volunteer group making their way along the road. Beth couldn't keep the smile off her face. It felt good being surrounded by people who were happy for her. Every member of the group seemed invested in Beth getting the job, as if her remaining at Ardmhor somehow left a piece of them there as well.

Andrew wasn't behind the bar, as it was his night off, but he soon arrived at the pub anyway, along with Eilidh's boyfriend Rich, and the pair made their way over. As they chatted, Beth realised she didn't actually know that much about Andrew. Their relationship so far had essentially been quick fire banter while he manned the bar or cleared up in the pub. Even when they were in Inveravain, they had mainly interacted as part of a bigger group, so there hadn't been much chance to learn any personal details. As they talked, Beth saw that although they were very different, they also had a lot in common. Andrew loved to travel, and he meant proper travel, with hostels and backpacks, rather than the two weeks on a beach that

Beth preferred. However, between adventures, he lived at home in order to save up and pay for it all, so he could relate to feeling less of an adult because you still lived with your parents. And while he wasn't planning to settle down just yet, he could also relate to Beth's feeling that change was needed. He was an attentive listener, and Beth enjoyed their conversation. For once, her nagging worry that she was boring, and that whoever ended up sat with her was trying to escape, didn't surface.

The only cloud on her horizon was that Alex hadn't appeared. She tried not to let it bother her. He hadn't said he could definitely come. In fact, he had been the uncertain one for once. That he wasn't there didn't necessarily have anything to do with her. Something else could have come up, or maybe he didn't feel comfortable at the pub. After all, a lot of the pub regulars were employees of his family. Once again, she was desperate to ask Eilidh what she knew about him, but there was no way of doing that which couldn't be construed as gossiping, and Alex had made his feelings on gossip clear the first time they met. Beth knew she couldn't risk him finding out she was discussing him with others. So she tried her best to focus on the people that were present instead.

She was slightly behind the others as they left the pub. She'd had to go back in to retrieve her coat, which was hanging forgotten on the stand in the entrance. As she came back out, Andrew was waiting by the door.

"Can I walk you home?" he asked. "You don't need to. I think I'm probably safe enough with all that lot up ahead, but you're welcome to walk with me if you want to."

"I do want to," he replied, taking hold of her hand.

It surprised Beth that she didn't feel awkward. Instead, her hand fitted snugly into his. It was a clear night, and as they walked, Andrew pointed out the names of constellations of stars. She wondered how many times he'd done that with different girls around the world, but she didn't mind. Actually, it made her feel better. She didn't want anything serious from him and was relieved he wouldn't want that either. They stopped as they reached the coach house, and he pulled her into the shadow of the doorway. He moved closer to her, and Beth reached her hand to his cheek as his mouth brushed hers. This time, she didn't immediately feel she'd rather be with a group of others, instead she let herself be swept along with the movement of his lips and the feeling of his hand on the back of her neck. His skills befitted his reputation, and Beth felt herself responding as he moved closer still, his body pinning her against the wall. The kiss deepened, and hands wandered until Andrew muttered breathlessly,

"Should we go inside?"

Should we, Beth thought to herself? She really wanted to, her body definitely wanted to, but the interruption to the kiss had somehow brought her thoughts back to Alex. Did she really want to spend the night with Andrew when she'd spent the whole evening hoping Alex would appear? Would she wake up full of regret? Was it fair to sleep with Andrew when she knew it was Alex she really wanted? The doubts quickly doused out the desire.

"Maybe not tonight," she said, not sounding sure.

"It's fine, Beth. I don't want to push you into anything. Another time maybe?"

"Maybe," she replied, putting her key into the door.

Andrew smiled, placing a quick kiss on her mouth before walking away. Beth wondered if Andrew finding 'maybe' a totally acceptable answer meant anything.

CHAPTER NINETEEN

18th of February 1893

Finally, I have received a reply from Mr Hardwick. It has been quite exhausting over the last few weeks, constantly keeping an eye out for the arrival of the post. I have not been the first there every day, which has left me quite anxious, but if I'd waited in the hall at all times, it would no doubt have made Lady Constance suspicious anyway, and that could have led to its own trouble. Although things seem much more settled between us and I'm sure that to outside eyes it appears we are as close as we have ever been, I think that anyone looking more closely would surely spot the tension. She questions almost every word I utter and every movement that I make. Are the many letters I write to Flora a sign I'm unhappy? Does the compliment I just gave her about her new hat mean I think she is too frivolous and that she is below my level of intellect? Did I want to go for a walk purely to escape her? The answer to the last one would be yes, but only because her behaviour is now driving me to feel this way.

I hadn't managed to be the first to the post today, but my letter was lying on the tray alongside some others when I reached the hall. The envelope was still sealed, and it does not appear it has been touched, which is a relief because I feel the contents would have pushed Lady Constance over the edge. To my mind, however, the contents are entirely pleasing, although they have left me in a quandary about what to do next. Mr Hardwick writes that he would be delighted if I was available to help with the day-to-day organisation of his business affairs. His wife has been keeping things under control, but she has many other concerns she would rather be dealing with. He says that there would be a place for me in their home for as long as I wanted. He also wrote that he has one partner and that they hope to expand their practice further. So this is my dilemma: do I pretend to myself that I have not read this and carry on waiting for Alex to speak, putting up with the vagaries of Lady Constance's moods along the way? Or do I try to persuade Alex that we should leave here together and start again? This letter shows me there are people willing to help us and that Alex's skills could be welcomed. Or do I simply inform the MacAirds that I am leaving, in the hope of forcing Alex's hand?

Would that be unfair to him? But is anything else fair to me?

5th of March 1893

Although I am certain Lady Constance could not have read my letter, her moods have been even more erratic than usual recently. The only thing that has prevented me from taking Mr Hardwick up on his offer is that Alex and I have managed to spend more time together. The weather, although cold, has remained dry, so we have walked together at some point almost every day. His kisses seem to render me powerless to make the decision to leave. I have talked to him several times about moving away. I have told him about Mr Hardwick and explained to him that we would not be alone if we left. But he is so sure that if we wait, we will eventually be able to be together here, and I know Ardmhor is where he truly wants to be. I haven't told him I am contemplating leaving alone. It doesn't feel right to place that amount of pressure on him. The problem is that I don't know if I can withstand the pressure of staying.

18th of March 1893

Today, Lady Constance suggested I move into the staff quarters. Although I can see where this came from, I don't really understand why it happened. I felt we were finally getting on much better. She has been less quick to anger recently, and I have spent a lot of time in her company, trying to join in with her interests and to show my gratitude to her. Maybe I've been trying too hard and have caused her to think my actions are insincere. This afternoon I had offered to help her with her hair, as Flora sometimes used to. We had been chatting about everything and nothing, and she described some of the balls she attended as a young girl in England. I expressed how wonderful they sounded. I was trying to please her with my response, as her descriptions made them sound like something she remembered most fondly, but I think she misunderstood my words. I think she interpreted them as a sign that Ardmhor wasn't enough for me, that I would rather be attending balls in England instead. Anyway, she suddenly snatched the brush from my hand and told me to leave her in peace. At dinner, she turned to Lord MacAird and said that perhaps it was time I moved into one of the servant rooms. She said it was clear I no longer wanted to be part of the family and that I would only be happy once I was in England. Her argument was that it would be better for me to be independent from the family until I could arrange my departure. I was speechless. I have never taken my place here for granted, but it had never crossed my mind to think she would turn me out into the staff quarters. It certainly confirms that she would never deem me suitable to marry Alex. Thankfully, Lord MacAird spoke up and said that it was not the time for discussing such matters. He said that I needed to speak to them if I was unhappy at Ardmhor, but that under no circumstances would it be suitable for him, as my guardian, to treat me the same as the staff.

Alex did not say a word. I have decided that I am going to write back to Mr Hardwick and accept his offer of employment. If Alex doesn't love me enough to stand up to his mother when my very position in the house is being threatened, how can I believe he loves me enough to tell her the truth?

CHAPTER
TWENTY

A shrill cry heralded a buzzard swooping above, and Beth looked up just in time to see the intricate pattern of its feathers before it soared too high for her eyes to follow. The sun had chosen that moment to reappear from behind the clouds, making the raindrops glisten on the grass. The volunteers were clearing away after a day of intermittent rain. A day that Beth had spent trying to think of anything but the outcome of her interview. She was also eager to get back to the diary. What she had read the previous night had left her feeling incredibly sad. She knew that reading more wouldn't bring about a happy ending, after all, she was already well aware that her great-great-grandmother spent the rest of her life married to someone other than Alexander, but she desperately needed to know what happened.

A buzzing sound interrupted her thoughts, and she realised her phone was vibrating in her pocket. The screen identified the caller as Lady Angela, and she anxiously swiped to accept.

"Hi Beth, I thought you'd just be packing away for the day, and I wondered if now would be a good time for you to pop up to the house?"

"Yes, of course, we're just about finished. Should I come straight across?"

"That'd be great. If you don't mind coming to the side entrance and letting yourself in, I'll just be in the old office."

Beth agreed and hung up the call. Was Lady Angela going to let her know about the job? Or had she simply found some more photos? Her stomach churned at the possibilities as she made her way across the lawn to the house.

"Don't look so worried!" Lady Angela said, looking up at Beth as she walked through the door to the office. "I wanted to talk to you about the interview yesterday. How do you feel it went?"

"I was quite pleased," Beth began cautiously. "I feel like I managed to express my ideas well." Then she hesitated, not wanting to dig herself into a hole.

"We didn't feel that you're right for any of the more casual roles we had advertised," said Lady Angela, filling the silence Beth had created. Beth's stomach lurched, but she forced herself to focus on the rest of Lady Angela's words. "We see you instead in a more long-term role. That's why I wanted to talk to you here. If you accept our proposal, this is where you'll be spending most of your time." Lady Angela looked up at Beth and smiled. "How does that sound?"

"So you're saying I've got a permanent job here?" Beth wanted definite confirmation and, for once, she didn't care if her lack of comprehension was obvious.

"We certainly are Beth," Lady Angela replied.

"Well, that sounds amazing!" Beth responded, relief and happiness coursing through her veins.

"Your outline of your ideas for the museum fitted exactly with what I want, and I just thought to myself, why are we still waiting? Duncan agreed we should be able to recoup the expenditure over time, as a museum will add so much to what we already offer visitors. So we were all in agreement that you should lead this, but I wanted to be the one to tell you."

Lady Angela went on to describe how they saw things working. In her interview, Beth had addressed her lack of formal museum qualifications and had stated that she was happy to undertake further training. The Ardmhor

Trust were proposing that she studied for a distance learning course, while also working around the estate. She would work as a guide in the house for the rest of the visitor season and then start work in the archive. They would hope to have a very limited museum, which would expand over time, ready to open for the start of the next season. It would be a tall order, but all Beth felt was excitement. She knew that panic would probably set in at some point, but for the moment she revelled in the feeling that everything was coming together.

She phoned her parents as soon as she stepped out of the house. They were overjoyed for her and immediately began making plans. They were supposed to be setting off the next day for their second Scottish holiday of the summer. The plan had been to collect Beth and bring her home on their way back. Now that she was going to be staying, they turned their thoughts to what extras she would need them to bring instead.

On reaching her room, Beth sat down to write her resignation from work and steeled herself to make the call to her Head of Department, in order to let him know that she really wouldn't be back. It all seemed slightly unreal, but by the time she joined the others for their evening meal, she had successfully undone most of the ties that bound her to her former life.

There were more offers of a trip to the pub,

this time to celebrate her appointment, but the reality of the changes taking place in her life were suddenly sinking in, and Beth decided she needed a bit of time alone. She set off towards the viewpoint, thinking how daft it was that she usually went there after dark. A viewpoint made a lot more sense when it was light enough to see the view, but that wasn't really why she'd been going—her trips out there had been about Alex rather than the pleasant outlook. Right then, though, she thought to herself, it might be better if Alex wasn't there. The events of the day were enough to deal with, without adding confusion about Alex's feelings into the mix.

It was the first time she'd been in the viewpoint outside of visiting hours, when it wasn't shrouded in darkness. Without the clamour of visitors, she could fully appreciate the magnificence of the view. The ground dropped away steeply in front of her, down to the broad expanse of the sea, before rising again in the shape of distant mountains where the land curved back round. Beth felt a shudder of excitement. This was no longer a view that she had to memorise to keep with her once she was back home. This was home, this was where she lived now.

"I thought it was you," said Alex's voice from behind her, "but I wasn't sure, as I didn't know if you actually existed in daylight."

"You've seen me in daylight plenty of times," Beth replied, smiling as she turned to see him approaching, her reservations about talking to him rapidly disappearing.

"True, but never to speak to. This feels like a special moment!"

"It's funny you should say that because it is. I found out today that I've got a permanent job here. I resigned from work this afternoon. So this is it, I'm staying!"

Alex took hold of her hands, and Beth felt her pulse quicken.

"I'm so pleased. I really feel you're supposed to be here," he said. Then he continued more quietly, "I'm sorry I didn't make it to the pub last night. I wanted to be there, but it just wasn't possible."

"It's fine," she replied, still conscious of her hands held within his and how right it felt for them to be there.

"No, it's not, but I suppose it is what it is. I just wanted you to know that if I could have been there with you, I would have."

Beth wondered what had stopped him, but something about the look in his eyes prevented her from asking directly.

"You know, if you ever want to talk, I'm always happy to listen," she offered.

"Thank you, but it's too late to do anything about it now. Tell me more about the job instead."

So Beth spent the next half hour talking about the details of her new job. At first Alex didn't let go of her hands, keeping his eyes on her all the time, but at some point, his arm slipped around her shoulders instead. Beth gradually found herself snuggled into him, her head resting comfortably against him as they chatted. The evening was a little chilly, but a warm glow spread through her. She felt as if she belonged on this bench with him. She didn't feel the pull to kiss him she'd felt with Andrew the night before. This feeling was somehow bigger than that, and now that she was staying, she knew there was no rush. They had as long as they needed for this thing between them, whatever it was, to move forward.

CHAPTER TWENTY-ONE

2nd of April 1893

I have been on tenterhooks ever since I wrote to Mr Hardwick saying that I would like to accept his offer. I've been anxiously waiting for the post, as I haven't wanted to cause another scene with Lady Constance, and, more importantly, I haven't known what to say to Alex. Aside from when I first realised the strength of my feelings for him, I have never hidden anything from Alex, and I didn't really hide anything then, as I became unable to string two words together in his company. At every other time, I have been able to speak my mind with him. Now, for the first time, I have actively concealed something from him, but I didn't want to tell him about my plans until everything was confirmed. I know that my leaving will break his heart, just as it will tear apart mine. But if we aren't to be together properly, I can't stay here.

Mr Hardwick's reply arrived this morning. He

is delighted to offer me a position helping with the administration of his office. He hopes I can be with them by the 17th of this month, which would give me a little over two weeks to organise myself. So now it is definite, and I have to break the news to Alex. That I have planned this without telling him is bound to add to his hurt. But this was the only method I could come up with where he would know this is completely my choice. He needs to feel I am certain of my decision, so that he is free to make his own. This way he will know that I am taken care of and that he is free to remain at Ardmhor if he chooses, but also that there will be a place for him in Manchester, if he feels able to pursue it.

4th of April 1893

I put off telling Alex until today. I just hadn't been able to find the words, and I still don't think I have conveyed my ideas and reasoning adequately. He wasn't angry with me, he just seemed broken and defeated. He said I must do what I feel is necessary and that he would never stand in my way, and then he walked off. I don't know if he even registered that my wish is not to leave Ardmhor alone, but for him to leave with me. Tomorrow, my only aim is to speak to Alex properly. I no longer need to worry whether I arouse Lady Constance's suspicions. I will tell both her and Lord MacAird of my plans soon, and if I have to be removed to the staff quarters until I leave, well, so be it. All that concerns me now is Alex and whether I can persuade him to join me.

5th of April 1893

I wonder if I am doing the right thing. It feels like my heart is shattering into a thousand pieces, but then what else can I do? I know Lady Constance does not see me as an equal, or as someone suitable to marry her son. And I know Alex will never stand up to his parents, no matter how much he loves me. I can't carry on living here, so near to Alex, yet so far away from him, constantly worrying about upsetting his mother. So although leaving may well be as painful as staying, it feels like my only choice. At least I feel Alex understands now. We talked for a long time, and I think he finally believes that I don't want to leave him. I just can't keep living like this. I think he still hoped we would eventually be able to tell his parents and that they would accept us, but now he seems to realise that would never happen. I told him about how happy my mother and father were when I was a child. Our life was nothing like his at Ardmhor, but we had a comfortable home and everything we could have wanted. I hope he will realise that we could have that, but I am trying not to force him. I know how much he loves this place, and I don't want him to resent me for making him leave, just as I might end up resenting him if I stay.

6th of April 1893

It is done. I have told Lord and Lady MacAird that I intend to leave, so there is no going back. As I expected, Lady Constance insisted straight away that it would not be suitable for me to remain living with the family. I assured her that my gratitude to them, and the affection I feel for her, has not changed. I told her that the motherly love she has shown me is something I will treasure for the rest of my life, but she would not even respond to me. Eventually, Lord MacAird asked me to leave them. A while later, he appeared outside my room, along with a maid. He asked her to move my belongings to one of the guest rooms, the one furthest from the family rooms. He said that he was sorry for the inconvenience, but that Lady Constance wanted to use Flora's old room for other purposes, so he needed to ask me to move. It seems he has stuck by his earlier statement that it would not be suitable for him to put me in one of the servant's rooms. This must be the compromise he had to make to appease Lady Constance. I asked whether I should still join the family for dinner, and he said perhaps it would be better if something was sent to my room. Maybe he's right, and this is for the best. I have already arranged my travel to Manchester, and it might make the next few days easier if I have little to do with Lady Constance.

9th of April 1893

It has been a strange few days. The life I have lived at Ardmhor House for almost two years is over, but I am still here, and my new life has not begun. Alex hasn't given a definite answer about leaving with me, but I think we both know that this is the end. What I'm finding hardest to cope with are the heightened emotions between us. Knowing our time together is limited has made us cling to each other all the more. We are less cautious now we have accepted that we aren't going to marry, for it no longer matters if his parents approve. I know Alex has not devoted the time to his work that he usually would. Instead of notes in the hidden compartment of the history book, there have been tiny objects. Small tokens that I know are to remind me of here after I leave. Today there was a heart-shaped pebble from the shore, worn smooth by the sea, and just small enough to hide in the palm of my hand.

11th of April 1893

My last day here. There were two things from Alex in the book today. One was a beautiful heart shaped locket, with a miniature photograph of each of us inside. He must have stolen a group picture from Flora's wedding out of the album, as I recognise the flowers in my hair. Wrapped around it, there was a note asking me to meet him at our clearing tonight. It says he has made a decision and that he hopes I'll be pleased. I don't want to get my hopes up, but he must mean he has decided to come with me. What else could I possibly be pleased about?

12th of April 1893

I am sitting on the train alone. I wonder if I'll even be able to read my handwriting when I look back at this. The train shakes so violently at times that it is hard to keep my pen on the page. But perhaps it is for the best if I can't read it again. I was so hopeful the last time I wrote in here. I really thought Alex was going to come with me. I didn't know then that I would experience the most wonderful moments of my life, and then the most devastating, before I opened it again. I am glad that it was raining when the cart took me away from Ardmhor, as it hid my tears. I feel as though I could have filled an entire ocean with the amount I have shed. I'm trying to think how I can explain everything that has happened.

My feelings were threatening to overwhelm me before I even met Alex at our clearing last night. Creeping out of the house after everyone else has retired for the evening always puts me on edge, and I knew it was either our last evening together, or that he was going to say he was coming with me. Whatever the outcome of our meeting, I knew my life was changing forever. Alex told me straight away that he wanted to join me in Manchester. He said that he had got things wrong. He had thought he loved Ardmhor too much to leave, but when he imagined being here without me, he realised he only loved Ardmhor because it was where I was. He said that realising this had made everything easy. If I was going to be in Manchester, then he would love Manchester. He said he didn't care what his mother and father made of it, that his heart had to be with mine, just like the locket.

We made plans between kisses. He was going to tell his father first thing in the morning, and we both agreed it would be better if I had left the house before then. He would meet me at the bottom of the drive, and we would leave together, getting a lift with the delivery cart to the station. I pointed out that his father might choose to cut him off, rather than accept the situation, but Alex said it didn't matter. He had been careful with his allowances and had enough money saved to enable us to get married and set up a simple home. So it seemed there were no longer any barriers. We had both made our choices, and our choices were each other.

It felt like I floated back to the house rather

than walked. Everything was in darkness, so we crept in, still holding hands. Then, I don't know what came over me, but after Alex kissed me goodnight, I didn't leave him to head up the main stairs while I made my way to the guest rooms. Instead, I took hold of his hand and pulled him after me. We were quite breathless as we shut the door of my room behind us. We knew it was completely improper for him to be in my bedroom, but it didn't feel that way. We had agreed our hearts had to be together, and it felt like this was right rather than wrong. Alex's kisses were gentle at first, even a little unsure. Breaking the rules doesn't come easily to him, and I have no doubt he was wrestling with his conscience. He prides himself on being a gentleman, whereas I have been secretly wishing desire might overpower his reason on many occasions. Once my responses made it clear to him I was not being forced into anything, he finally let go of his fears. The kisses weren't gentle anymore, but I don't mean it was something harsh or horrible, like some people describe the events of a wedding night. No, it was as wonderful as my dreams had suggested. As I lay next to Alex, watching the rise and fall of his chest, I felt almost weightless. The worries of the last few months had lifted, and everything was going to be alright.

When he finally left my room, we knew it was only a matter of hours until we would be together again, that this was just the start. I left the house before Lord MacAird and Lady Constance would be awake. I didn't want an awkward farewell. I placed a note for Lord MacAird in the dish on the table, thanking him for his kindness and hospitality. I also left a package for Lady Constance, containing the cameo brooch she had given me. It didn't feel right to keep something that had been passed through her family when I knew she no longer considered me part of it. It was cold and wet as I walked to the end of the drive, but I didn't really notice. The knowledge that Alex would soon be with me kept me warm. But then he didn't come. Time stretched out as I stood there in the rain and he didn't appear. The cold and damp finally reached me. I wondered at first if something had happened to him and I should rush back up to the house, but the household would all have been awake by then. Anything untoward would already have spread through the staff and been whispered to the delivery boy. As the cart drew to a halt next to me, I asked the boy if all was well at the house. It was clear from his response that he wasn't aware of anything out of the ordinary, so I had to go. I had already made my arrangements with the Hardwicks. There was no time to do anything else.

I know I must look a terrible mess after all the tears I have cried, and I seem to veer between hating Alex and then fearing for him as each second passes. I am so certain he meant what he said last night. So something must have stopped him from joining me. But what could have done that? I know that nothing would have stood in my way. Which makes me wonder if I could have been wrong all along? What if I've never really known Alex? What if the reason he could abandon his usual restraint last night was because he knew he'd never see me again? No, I know that isn't the case. It's easy for me to say nothing would have stopped me, when it's me that has been wanting to leave. As soon as I reach Manchester, I will write to him, and we will sort everything out. He said our hearts belong together, like the locket. I know he wouldn't say something he didn't mean.

CHAPTER
TWENTY-TWO

It was the last afternoon of the volunteer holiday, and the whole group watched the completion of the final task. As the senior members of the group, Mary and Bob were doing the honours. Mary was holding a small plaque, stating that the playground had been funded by the donations of clan members and built by volunteers. Bob was wielding hammer and nails, while joking that Mary might not come through the next few minutes with all her fingers intact. As the final nail went in, fortunately to the wooden post rather than Mary's hand, the group cheered.

The area in front of them bore no relation to the patch of overgrown land it had been three weeks ago. Now there was a miniature castle to crawl over and hide under, with a little slide to get down the other side. There was also a small assault course, for slightly bigger children, with nets to scramble across and big stumps to jump between. Tree bark surrounded the equipment to ensure soft landings, and tall grasses and colourful plants filled the borders. There were a couple of picnic benches, for weary parents, and the whole space looked across the already established older children's play area, out towards the sea.

Eilidh moved between the group, pouring fizz into plastic cups, and Beth looked at the people surrounding her. It was hard to imagine that they had all been strangers just a month ago, and it was even harder to imagine that they only had one more night together. Tomorrow, only Beth would remain here. That, she thought to herself, was going to be the real test. Would she still be feeling so happy once the others had gone? Fortunately, her parents were arriving in the morning, so that would give her a distraction. For now, though, she wanted to make the most of the celebrations.

The days had flown by since Beth found out she'd got the job at Ardmhor. She had been to look at the staff accommodation. It was much more basic than the coach house, but, for shared housing, it was surprisingly decent. There was a communal living area and kitchen, which looked clean and smelt nice, very different from the shared areas Beth had experienced at university. Also, the whole place was lovely and warm. For Beth, the icing on the cake was that each bedroom had its own small shower room. She felt she could cope with just about anything as long as she didn't have to share a loo.

As well as sorting out her accommodation, Beth had been busy completing the admin for her museum course. That, along with nightly trips to the pub, meant there had been no time to see Alex. But she was staying here now, so there was no need to rush their friendship. The volunteers, on the other hand, would be gone soon, and Beth wanted to focus on enjoying the time she had left with them.

Although she'd seen Andrew each time she'd been in the pub, Beth hadn't spent much time with him either. He'd been working, and the pub had been busy, so apart from him congratulating her on her new job, they'd only managed a few quick exchanges.

As her eyes roamed over the people surrounding her, some sat on picnic benches and others perched precariously on play equipment, Beth could hardly believe their time together was over. When she had arrived at Ardmhor, a month sounded like forever. She had imagined the time dragging and had thought she'd be desperate to leave. She'd not pictured making such good friends, and she certainly hadn't envisaged leaving her old life behind to stay here. It all seemed a bit surreal. She was watching Lady Angela, who was laughing with Mary and Bob, when Eilidh came over.

"Lady A really likes you, you know," Eilidh began, following Beth's gaze. "She was adamant she had to be the one to tell you about the job. I know you'll be panicking about whether you've done the right thing, but they're a great family to work for."

It occurred to Beth that she finally had her chance to do a bit of digging about Alex without seeming obvious.

"She does seem really lovely. Are the rest of the family as nice?"

"Well, Big Jim, that's what everyone calls Lord MacAird, is pretty similar to her. He's very involved in the estate. Normally you'd have met him by now, but he's been away."

"Why Big Jim? Is he very tall? Or maybe really..." Beth tailed off, realising she might sound rude.

"No, he's pretty average, I think." Eilidh paused for a second, looking confused. "Oh! I see what you mean! No, it's big as in older. There are so many people called James in the family that they all end up with a nickname. His son James is known as Jay, but he used to get called Tiny, because he was the tinier one of the two."

"I bet he loved that!"

"Well, he's gorgeous and has a body to die for, so I imagine it didn't bother him too much. Lady A always corrects people to use Jay instead nowadays, so it's pretty much died out."

"I suppose you know him quite well, with growing up here."

"No, not really. Strathglen is a way along the coast and although my dad's family have ties to Ardmhor, we didn't spend that much time here when I was growing up. Also, Jay and his brother are a few years older than me, and they went to boarding school. Plus, neither of them work for the estate, and it's only through work that I've got to know Lady A and Big Jim so well."

Beth would have loved to ask Eilidh more about what the brothers did; Alex was always evasive when the subject turned to him. However, Mary interrupted them by announcing there was only an hour until everyone was due at the pub, and Beth was soon busy collecting empty bottles and carrying them to the recycling bins.

The Ardmhor Hotel was bursting at the seams. It didn't take long for the volunteers, along with many of the regular staff, to fill the small pub. The only customers who weren't part of their group were those who propped up the bar each night. Fortunately, they didn't seem bothered as the noise level rose and events became increasingly raucous. Many toasts were made, but perhaps the most touching was from Steve, who raised a glass to new friends. His eyes never moved from Megan as he spoke of how lonely he had been and how the friendships he had made had changed his outlook on life. The emotion conveyed in the voice of such a private man resulted in more than a few tears.

The evening didn't end at the pub but continued back at the coach house. By the early hours, Beth was struggling to stay awake. Megan and Steve had long since disappeared, and even the hard-core Mary and Bob had said goodnight. Fraser looked like he'd be able to keep going until the sun came up, but Beth knew the time had come for her to call it a night. It had been an emotional day, and she was exhausted.

The next morning, Beth felt she was still riding an emotional rollercoaster. There had been a constant stream of farewells since breakfast, and not only was she sad to see her friends leaving, but she was also struggling with the practical side of the goodbyes. Finding the right words was difficult, and then there was the question of hugging or not. Now everyone was gone, and Beth's belongings were all packed up. New guests would arrive shortly to fill the rooms at the coach house, so she sat outside, with her case beside her, tired but excited as she waited for her parents.

Seeing their familiar car pulling into the car park gave her a fresh burst of energy, and she all but sprinted across to them, tugging at her mum's door before David had even turned the engine off. Within seconds, she was engulfed in hugs. It had been a long time since the three of them had spent an entire month apart.

"Right then," David said, opening the car boot. "Let's get this stuff moved to where it's going. Then we can relax for a bit before we need to set off back home."

Beth looked at them both sadly as she picked up a bag. "I wish you could stay."

As Jean and David had originally expected to be picking Beth up and heading straight home, they hadn't booked any accommodation, and at this point in the season, vacancies on Saturday nights were unheard of.

"So do we, sweetheart," replied Jean. "But we've got a few hours before we need to set off, so let's get you sorted, and then we can make the most of it."

It didn't take long to get Beth set up in her new room. Living in the staff block meant all the basics were covered, so she wouldn't need much until she found permanent accommodation of her own. Her parents had only brought another bag of clothes, some bits and pieces to help personalise her space, and her laptop, which she'd need for her course. Within half an hour, they had everything straight. Her room was nothing compared to the one she'd got used to over the previous month, but it was warm, clean, and cosy. There was a small double bed pushed up to the wall, with a little chest of drawers alongside. Against the other wall was a decent sized wardrobe, which was fortunate now her clothes supply had expanded, and a dressing table which she'd be able to use as a desk. While she no longer had a view of the sea, Beth had to admit the vista of trees trailing up the hill was still much more appealing than the suburban gardens and sheds she'd been able to see back home.

"I think you've done the right thing, Beth," Jean said, pulling her close. "You seem so at home and it's beautiful here. Maybe your dad and I should have been a bit more adventurous."

The three of them were strolling through the gardens. Beth had already shown her parents the playground that the volunteers had built, and they were on their way to the viewpoint. Beth wondered whether Alex would appear. She was torn between wanting him to be there and thinking it would be better if he wasn't. She hadn't mentioned him to her mum yet; Beth's inability to commit to relationships meant they had been few and far between, so now her mum got a bit over excited if one looked like a possibility. Therefore, Beth had taken to keeping quiet about anyone she liked, which then made it even harder to bring the subject up. As it was, the viewpoint was heaving with visitors, but there was no sign of Alex.

"So, do you think this is the clearing that Eliza mentioned in the diary?" Jean asked.

"Yes, I think so. It fits with the description, and I haven't found anywhere else that does."

"It's just so hard to imagine Granny Eliza being here," said Jean. "She was already well into her eighties when I was born, so I only remember her sat in her armchair. Don't get me wrong, she was still a big character, and she told the most amazing stories, but to me she only existed in that one room, and she never once mentioned this place."

"Maybe the ten years she spent here ended up seeming like nothing, against the 100 years she lived for?"

"Possibly, but she kept the diary, so it must have meant something. Maybe it just seemed too long ago by the time I was born. I wish I'd known though. I've got so many questions."

"We might find more answers in the diary," Beth offered.

"True, we might. But I don't think I'll ever be

able to imagine her sat here. Do you think she's the reason why we both love Ardmhor so much?"

"That's exactly what I think," Beth replied, squeezing her mum's hand. "I know it sounds silly, but I feel a bit like I'm supposed to be here, like we were supposed to come back."

"I don't think it sounds silly at all. It'd be sillier to assume we know everything about life, really."

"What are you two gossiping about?" asked David as he made his way back towards them from the other side of the viewpoint.

"Nothing much, just about our family connection." Beth replied, knowing her dad would tease them for getting carried away.

"Well, do you know what connection I feel, ladies? I feel a connection to a big piece of cake back at the café."

"We're looking in the house first," said Jean, laughing. "But then try to stop me."

It was another emotional farewell as Jean and David got back into the car an hour or so later. They promised to visit soon, and Beth intended to travel back at some point to collect her car, but despite knowing they weren't saying goodbye for too long, she felt bereft as they disappeared into the distance.

As she walked back to her room, it occurred

to her that for the first time since arriving at Ardmhor, she was at a loss as to what to do. There was no organised schedule of meals to fit her day around anymore. There was no group of people to suggest a quick trip to the Ardmhor Hotel or a wander down to the pier. It'll be fine by Monday, she told herself. Then her new job would start. Then she'd be busy, and things would feel normal again, but that didn't help her right now. Beth was the sort of person who usually welcomed a bit of time to herself. She had never been part of a big gang of constantly socialising friends. But over the last month, she'd got used to being a part of a group. Now that they were all gone, being alone seemed like she was being taunted. It felt as if something was trying to tell her she'd made a mistake and that a life here wouldn't really be any different to the one she'd left behind.

She knew Eilidh was spending a quiet night with Rich, and Beth wouldn't expect her to change her plans, but she did send off a quick text asking if she was free the next day. However, that didn't fill this evening. She could head round to the pub soon. Andrew would probably be working, so she could sit at the bar and chat with him. But she didn't feel brave enough to walk in alone right now. It would seem too different from walking in with all the others.

She reasoned with herself that this wasn't any

worse than a Saturday night back at home. Her best friend, Lucy, lived too far away to meet up regularly, so she'd often been at a loss for something to do. Their friendship had long been kept alive by emails, so at least that was one thing that wouldn't need to change. She opened up her emails and sent Lucy a quick message, giving an update on all the latest news. Lucy was the only person she'd told about Alex. She was much more sensible than Beth, so made an excellent person to go to for advice. Lucy had kindly said that Alex would be mad not to find Beth attractive. But she'd also pointed out that if he didn't fancy her, there wasn't anything she could do. Beth could see the truth in this. No one could help who they were attracted to, and no one could force an attraction they didn't feel. But she still had hope. As she pressed send, she realised what she wanted to do that evening; she wanted to see Alex. Maybe he didn't fancy her, but there was always that sense of belonging and connection when she was with him, and right now she really needed to feel like she belonged.

The last of the visitors had disappeared by the time she sat down at the viewpoint. It was so much more peaceful than it had been earlier. The waves gently rolling against the shore and the leaves rustling in the breeze were all she could hear now. It felt like a very different place, even though the view remained the same. She wondered if Alex wasn't at home today. After all, he hadn't appeared earlier, but a moment later he was there, slipping into the seat beside her.

"How are you bearing up?" Alex asked, taking hold of her hands and searching her face in the way that now seemed so familiar. "It must have been a bit of a strange day, with everyone leaving."

Then Beth did what she'd been trying to avoid all day and cried. She'd tried to hold the emotion in when she felt the tell-tale prickle of tears, but it had happened too many times already that day, and it was always kindness that got her in the end.

"I'm sorry, I'm being daft," she squeaked, before the tears took away her voice.

Alex didn't even reply, he just pulled her closer, wrapped his arms around her and held her to him, gently stroking her hair and murmuring shushes into her ear, the way a parent might comfort a small child. It was exactly what Beth needed, and her body relaxed into his. His arms were like a blanket, surrounding her with warmth and security, until eventually she was calm enough to speak.

"How do you always know I'm here?"

"Ah, I can't reveal my secrets. Let's just say I know."

"Really?" she lifted her head up to look at him properly. "You can sense when I'm here?"

"Well, that and you can see the path to

the viewpoint from nearly every room in the house. It's hard to do anything here and not get spotted."

"I suppose that's what made it so hard for Eliza and Alexander. Anyway, if you did have a sixth sense, it must be faulty because you missed me when I was out here earlier with my mum and dad."

"I saw you, actually. Your mum is really like you, isn't she? Apart from the hair colour. I'd love to have met them, but I didn't want to interrupt your time together, and you already know that I'm rarely around the grounds in the day, when it's busy."

"I see you about sometimes though."

"Yes, but I'm only ever toing and froing then. I can't settle somewhere for a chat when there are people everywhere."

"It is much lovelier here now than it was earlier," Beth sighed in agreement.

"Anyway, now you can speak again, tell me how you're feeling, and then tell me what else you've discovered about Eliza."

"Anything to avoid talking about you, eh?" she said gently.

Alex brushed it aside. "I've told you enough times already. I'm just hanging around, so there's nothing to tell."

"Fine, but next time we meet, I'm going to bring a set of questions, and I'm not telling you anything else about me until you answer them."

"Alright," he said laughing, holding his hands up in submission. "Now tell me your news."

So she told him how lost she was feeling now the others had left, and Alex reassured her, as she'd tried to reassure herself, that once she started her job, it'd feel different. Then she told him what else she had read about Eliza, from her last night with Alexander, to her leaving Ardmhor alone.

"She must have hated him," Alex said eventually. Although his arm was still around Beth's shoulders, he looked away.

"I don't think she did," Beth said. "She was upset and angry, but even then, she doesn't sound like she hates him. Her overriding instinct is that something must have stopped him from leaving."

"But she must have felt let down, like he didn't love her enough to leave?"

"I suppose there is a little doubt there. She does say that nothing could have stopped her from leaving, so she recognises that maybe his feelings weren't as strong. But she also says that it was her pushing to leave, when he'd never wanted that. So even though she feels let down, ultimately, she doesn't seem to doubt that he loves her. I think she realises it's not as simple as that."

"She was an amazing woman. It's hard to

remember sometimes that not everyone sees situations exactly as you would."

"In a way, it's like she feels a bit guilty. She knew it was as hard for him to leave as it would have been for her to stay. I think she was worried he might feel she didn't love him enough to stick to their original plan. That he might think if she'd really loved him, she'd have waited for the right time to tell his parents, so they could have made a life here."

"He would never have thought that," Alex stated with certainty.

"Yeah, but like you said, you can't assume everyone sees things the same as you do."

"That's very true. Was she alright though? Were things in Manchester as good as she hoped?"

"I haven't read much more yet, only a couple of entries from when she first arrived, but it sounds like it. Obviously, she'd have preferred it if Alexander was with her, but the Hardwick's sound very kind and welcoming, and she likes the other staff at the firm. I think she enjoys having a bit of purpose again. She's nothing like me, I reckon I'd have been perfectly happy just floating around at Ardmhor."

"I think you're more like her than you realise. You've refused to carry on being miserable at work, and you've given up a lot to make life better for yourself. That's exactly what Eliza did when she moved to Manchester."

"I suppose so. I hadn't really thought of it like that."

"Well, you need to keep remembering it now. So, what are your plans for the rest of the evening? Much as I'm enjoying sitting here, I think you might scratch yourself to death if you stay out any longer."

Beth had to admit the midges were getting a bit much. She'd been trying to pretend they weren't bothering her, as she didn't want to leave the comfort of Alex's arms, but the swarm was becoming increasingly difficult to ignore.

"You're right. I am going to have to go indoors. What about going to the pub?"

"Oh yes, you're bound to find some company there."

"I meant both of us, really. Is there a reason you never go?"

"I've had some good times at the Ardmhor Hotel in the past. I just can't go anymore."

"Why, what happened?"

"Nothing. Time just moves on and things change. It's not very exciting, really. I always hope that I'll be able to go again one day."

"But why not today? You're constantly trying to push me into facing my fears."

"I just can't, Beth."

"So tell me why."

"Maybe next time I see you. Why don't you put it on your list of questions?" he said with a small smile.

"Fine." Beth placed a kiss on his cheek, feeling colder as she removed herself from his arms. "But you know where I'll be, if you change your mind."

CHAPTER TWENTY-THREE

26th of April 1893

There was a funny incident at Mr Hardwick's offices today. A gentleman by the name of Mr Simon John had booked an appointment with Mr Burton, the junior partner. Anyway, I'd misunderstood when I wrote his name down and had filled in all the details for a Mr John Simon. Mr Burton called him the wrong name for most of his appointment before the confusion was cleared up. Fortunately, everyone saw the funny side of my mistake. I'd hate to make Mr Hardwick look foolish, especially as I know few are forward thinking enough to employ a woman in this sort of role. But the point of this story is that when Mr Hardwick recounted the situation to me later, his laughter bouncing off the walls as he spoke, I laughed too. I was wondering if I'd forgotten how to laugh.

The letter I sent off to Alex today was letter number fourteen. One posted almost every day since I left Ardmhor, but not a word in reply. I told him yet again that I love him, and I am sorry I had to leave. I told him I understand that something must have prevented him from joining me, and that I am not angry. I told him how much I wish there wasn't this distance between us. I also added a few more stories from the Hardwick home because I want him to feel part of this place too. After all, my dearest wish is still for him to join me here. My greatest worry is that he doesn't know about my letters and that he thinks I am angry with him. I know that Lady Constance might be withholding them. She's intercepted my post before, and I can't bear to think of him alone, feeling guilty. Of course, there are moments when I feel angry, when I want to reach out and shake him and scream at him that if he really loved me, he'd have come with me, but I know it isn't as simple as that. I know him so well, and after what happened between us before I left, I know what he'll be thinking. I know he'll be worrying in case I think he never intended to come, in case I think that he simply pretended in order to trick me. I don't think that at all. I know he meant what he said, and I know that something must have prevented him from leaving. If anything, I took advantage of him. Deep down I knew he would find it too hard to leave Ardmhor, but I wanted him anyway. I was more than happy to go along with the fantasy. I just wish I knew what had happened between him leaving my room and the time we were due to meet. If I knew, maybe I could help. But if Lady Constance is preventing my letters from reaching him, how will I ever make contact?

28th of April 1893

I have had an idea. I can contact Alex through Flora. I don't know why it didn't occur to me earlier. I have written to her explaining the situation, although I left out any details I thought Alex wouldn't want shared, and I tried to avoid anything that could read as criticism of Lady Constance. I don't want to place Flora in an awkward position. I only wish I had felt able to include her in our secret from the start. It has been very difficult to explain everything, and it must make much of what I have shared with her recently look false. Nevertheless, Flora isn't the type to hold grudges, and she has always loved a romantic drama, so I am hopeful she will want to help us.

This new plan has lifted my spirits greatly, and, for the first time, I felt like I could truly enjoy my evening with the Hardwick family. They are so welcoming, and their house really feels like a home. It is a very small space in comparison to Ardmhor House, but I envy the Hardwick children more than I have ever envied Flora, James, and Alex, for everyone feels cherished here. Mrs Hardwick has told me she and Mr Hardwick married around the same time as my parents, but they were not blessed with children for several more years. Apparently, they thought they would remain childless, and I became something of a pet to them, even staying with them when Mother accompanied Father on business trips. I suppose that explains why they have always tried to maintain contact with me, and it also explains why their own children are so treasured. It is as if their children are just allowed to be. There are no set expectations of them, and ideas are discussed here that would never be deemed acceptable at Ardmhor. This is how I feel life could have been for me, if Mother had not become ill. It is a lovely thing to feel part of, but until now I hadn't been able to let myself enjoy it. Knowing that Alex is still trapped at Ardmhor, drowning under the weight of everyone's expectations, including those placed on him by me, has made feel too guilty. Tonight, though, I felt I could let myself relax a little because maybe through Flora I can reach him, and maybe he can enjoy a different life too.

29th of April 1893

There is a lovely little park in front of the building where Mr Hardwick's offices are located. The weather hasn't been suitable to explore it until today. It seems it rains even more in Manchester than at Ardmhor, something I wouldn't have thought possible! Today, however, was beautiful and sunny, so I took the chance for a wander around. Mr Hardwick thinks it takes too long to return home to eat during the day, and he isn't keen to waste time eating at a club, so Mrs Hardwick arranges for a meal to be packed up for us to take to work. I think that if this weather continues, I shall start taking my lunch out to the park with me. There are lots of quiet benches to sit on, and there is a pond with ducks. Even though I was desperate to leave Ardmhor, I know it was a beautiful place. It is obvious that the view here does not compare with that from mine and Alex's clearing, but sitting out in the open made me feel a little closer to him. I so hope to hear from Flora soon, or even better than that, I hope I hear from Alex himself.

30th of April 1893

The weather held, and I kept to my plan, taking my lunch out into the fresh air. I didn't need to worry about whether Mr Hardwick thought it was acceptable, as on hearing my intention, he decided to join me. A while later, as we sat feeling warmed by the sun, congratulating ourselves on our excellent idea, we were surprised by the appearance of Mr Burton. He was just as surprised to see us and revealed that he tries to take a turn around the park every day. He invited us to join him, but Mr Hardwick said he needed to return to his work. However, he insisted I remain, so I strolled alongside Mr Burton for a while. He seems a very pleasant man, but I couldn't help comparing him to Alex. Mr Burton is taller. I needed to look up when speaking to him, whereas Alex and I are almost eye to eye. His colouring is slightly fairer, and I have to admit, his nose is more classically constructed. Although I have always loved Alex's nose, it really is too large for his face! Mr Burton was very interested in hearing about my work with Father at Ardmhor, and he told me about his own family. He lives with his widowed mother, and it would seem that her capable son is her pride and joy. It was nice to talk with someone closer to my own age. If only a letter would appear from Alex or Flora, then this would truly feel like a good day.

11th of May 1893

Today I received my longed for reply from Flora, but the contents were not as I had hoped. She wrote she is disappointed in me because she had believed us to be as close as sisters. She said that she had always shared her dreams with me and that the damage I have caused by not doing the same can never be repaired. She said my betrayal is made worse by the fact she had to discover it from her mother. It appears that

Lady Constance has already provided Flora with her own account of events—one which differs greatly from the truth. The story Flora has been told paints me as someone betraying the trust and hospitality of her family. She seems to have accepted that I led Alex to believe I was in love with him in order to win the security of marriage and an official place at Ardmhor. At the same time as this, I am supposed to have carried on several dalliances with estate workers. Then, upon the discovery of my inappropriate behaviour by Lady Constance, apparently, I ran away to Manchester, leaving Alex heartbroken.

No wonder Flora is disgusted with me. She must have seen my letter to her as an attempt to wheedle my way back into Alex's affections. And why should she believe me now, when it is clear that I have lied for so long? If only I had confided in her from the start, then she would always have been an ally. Alex and I were fools to think we could simply wait and that eventually things would work out. We should have seen that Flora, the only person who has ever successfully manipulated Lady Constance, could have helped us from the start. It is clear I won't be able to regain her trust now and that my only avenue of hope is closed off.

What scares me even more is what Lady Constance has said to Alex. Her outpourings to Flora suggest she is aware of our relationship, which must mean Alex told his parents he intended to leave. Did Lady Constance tell him the same stories she told Flora? Does he believe I was unfaithful to him? Is that why he remained at Ardmhor instead of leaving with me? And if that is the case, how will I ever be able to convince him of the truth? Part of me wants to think that Alex wouldn't believe her, but he has never had the inner strength that I have. He is always so fearful of making mistakes and looking foolish. I can't even feel angry at the lack of faith this would mean he had in me because I realise how differently our minds work. Alex sees obstacles, and I see solutions, and we can no more change that about ourselves than we can fly to the moon. The idea of him trapped in his office at Ardmhor, believing I never even cared and that I was laughing at him behind his back, sickens me to the core. And I can't think of a way to show him the truth. My ability to find solutions has failed me, and this feels truly hopeless.

12th of May 1893

My hopelessness eventually gave way to tears and despair. I am exhausted. I have used every scrap of energy trying to get through the day without crying. I wasn't totally successful, but I think that was a good thing in the end. I fulfilled my duties at work this morning but excused myself to the park to eat. I wanted to give vent to my anguish before the afternoon began. Anyway, as I sat sobbing in a quiet corner, I felt a hand on my shoulder. I quickly tried to pull myself together and turned round to see Mr Burton standing behind me. He did not seem repulsed by my display of hysteria, even though I was disgusted with myself for being so weak. Instead, he sat down next to me, pulled me towards him and comforted me as if I was a child. It didn't feel inappropriate to be in his arms, for some reason I felt safe. We have walked together in the park a few times since our first lunchtime stroll, so I know he is a kind man. He encouraged me to tell him what the matter was, and, somehow, I found myself confiding in him. I don't know what came over me because I told him everything that had happened with Alex, including the fact that I had let things develop further than I should. To my surprise, he did not offer any judgement, or seem shocked by my behaviour. He simply carried on soothing me, saying he understood how difficult relationships could be.

He told me he had been in love with a childhood friend, that they had made plans for a future together and that his every thought and deed had revolved around her, but one day she informed him of her intention to marry another. He still doesn't know what changed her mind. So although our stories are not the same, he said he could understand my frustration and sadness.

I still don't know how I can make things right with Alex, but at least with Mr Burton, William, I now have a friend to confide in.

CHAPTER TWENTY-FOUR

"So I don't know how they came to get married that quickly, but it seems my great-great-grandfather started out as someone to confide in. It looks like they had quite a lot in common, and it must have been lonely for Eliza when she first arrived in Manchester."

Beth was sitting in the back of Eilidh's car, leaning through the gap in the head restraints while they made their way along the road to Inveravain. Eilidh had invited Beth to join herself, Rich, and her parents for their monthly Sunday lunch at the Beinn View Hotel. Rich had been hearing the details of Eliza's diary from Eilidh and had been keen to hear what else Beth had discovered.

"I wonder if she ever managed to get back in touch with Alexander," Rich said.

"I don't know yet, but the fact she marries William means it doesn't look good," Beth replied sadly.

"I can't get over how cruel Lady Constance was. She must have known how much her lies would have hurt her son, not to mention how unfair it was to Eliza. I feel furious about it, and they're not even connected to me. How do you feel?" Eilidh caught Beth's eye in the rear-view mirror as she spoke.

"It's weird because in some ways it's like reading a book, where an injustice happens to a character and you're really hoping the author will resolve it in the way you want, but then I remember that I already know the outcome and that it's my relative it happened to. Then I feel a bit sad about it."

"I get that. I feel sad knowing it won't end the way I want, and I don't have the same personal involvement that you have. Anyway, not to change the subject, but while we're talking about romances, where are things up to with you and the lovely Andrew?"

"There are no things between me and Andrew," Beth said quickly as a tell-tale blush stole its way across her cheeks.

"That's not what I've heard!" Rich interjected. "A little bird told me he walked you home from the pub the other night."

"Nothing happened!" Beth protested, a little too strongly.

"Well, now I know that something definitely did!" Rich exclaimed triumphantly. "Andrew wouldn't give me any details either, even though he knows how much I love to gossip."

"He does, Beth, never trust this one with a secret," Eilidh confirmed with laughter in her voice.

"It's alright because there are no secrets to tell." Beth began. "Nothing really happened, and I haven't spoken to him properly since. I saw him at the pub yesterday, but it was packed, and he was busy all night. So that's all I can tell you. I like him, but I don't think either of us wants anything serious."

She wasn't prepared to reveal any more than that to Ardmhor's self-professed gossip king.

"That's pretty much what he said to me as well, so essentially the pair of you are useless for exciting information."

"I'm so sorry to have let you down, Richard," Beth replied in a mock serious tone.

"Apology accepted. Now get thinking of something interesting to tell me over lunch," he said as Eilidh pulled into the hotel carpark.

The Beinn View Hotel was situated just on the edge of the town of Inveravain. As the name suggested, it looked out across the sea, to the mountain known as 'The Beinn'. The hotel had once been a hunting lodge for a wealthy family, but it had been converted to its current use many years ago. The restaurant itself was housed in a modern extension, which had been built to take advantage of the views. It was busy with both visitors and locals alike, and Beth could see why: the food was delicious. Even though she was totally full, she couldn't resist trying to cram in the last few mouthfuls of sticky toffee pudding. Eilidh's parents had been just as welcoming as they had been the previous weekend and seemed genuinely delighted that Beth would be staying in the area.

"Now, I have a favour to ask of you, Beth," Alan announced as a waitress poured out coffees.

"To ask me?" Beth sounded surprised.

"Yes, you piqued my interest about that old house down by the Ardmhor Hotel, so I want you to be my excuse to have a good old nosy."

"You could just make an appointment to view it yourself, Alan," chided Claire.

"I know that, but there's no fun going alone, and I know neither of you will come with me," he said, gesturing to his wife and daughter. "So I'm asking Beth because she might actually want to buy it. Also, she's still at the stage where she'll feel she has to be polite and just agree to come!"

"Actually, I'd love to. It'd be really interesting to get a look at where my great-great-grandmother lived, and I'd be too scared to go by myself."

"Well, that's good, because I've already arranged with the agent to collect the keys. I'll pick you up after you finish work on Tuesday."

Beth smiled as the others laughed at Alan's excitement over his plan coming together. She hoped it wouldn't end up feeling awkward. It was one thing getting on with Alan when the rest of his family were around. Spending time alone together might feel a bit different.

Monday morning found Beth ready for her first shift as an Ardmhor employee an hour earlier than necessary. After getting back from Inveravain the night before, she'd phoned her mum and filled her in on the latest contents of the diary. Then she'd got herself settled for an early night. She had sat up in bed with a copy of the Ardmhor House guidebook, expecting to find sleep evasive, but to her surprise it had come easily, and she'd slept soundly until her alarm went off. The only problem was she'd been so keen to be on time that she'd hugely overestimated how long it would take to shower and eat breakfast. So there she was, in her brand-new uniform of black trousers and Ardmhor branded polo shirt and fleece, with nowhere to be for the next hour. She examined her reflection in the mirror again. She had been relieved to find the trousers were long enough—the embarrassment of her school trousers flapping around above her ankles was something that would never leave her. Although the navy fleece wasn't something she'd have chosen to wear, it was surprisingly flattering, highlighting the blue of her eyes and setting off the red of her hair. The hand on the clock had only moved on two minutes since she had last checked it, and she pondered how to fill this spare hour. She didn't dare start reading the diary again, in case she got too engrossed and made herself late, and it seemed a bit early to disturb her mum with a phone call, so she decided to go for a stroll in the grounds instead.

She headed upwards from the staff accommodation, into the woods, rather than down towards the house. The morning was overcast, with the sky full of dull grey clouds, yet the temperature was mild. There was barely any breeze, so Beth moved swiftly to avoid the pockets of midges hanging in the still air. A path led through the trees which soared above her, their branches meeting far over her head, like a spectacular living cathedral. Every so often, a plaque highlighted an unusual species. These were the legacy of a previous Lord MacAird who, keen to impress his visitors, had gathered exotic specimens from far-flung places. After a while, Beth turned onto a path signposted as leading to the house. She paused on a bench at the side of a series of ponds. They had been built into the slope of the hill, and each one trickled water into the next. Beth watched as a dragonfly flitted between the plants and was surprised at how calm she felt. The gentle sound of the water running between the ponds had a soporific effect. She had expected to be far more anxious about her first official day of work. A display board said the ponds had been added to the gardens about 30 years earlier. As she walked towards the house, Beth wondered what else had changed since Eliza's daily strolls around the grounds.

By the time 6 o'clock on Tuesday arrived, Beth was feeling pretty pleased with herself. She had completed her first two days as a guide at Ardmhor House, and she felt she had acquitted herself well. There had been a couple of questions from visitors that she had needed to pass over to one of the more experienced guides, but she had noted their answers and borrowed copies of the room guides to study, and she was confident she would soon be able to deal with any enquiries alone. The history of the house was fascinating. The wing of Ardmhor that opened to visitors had been built in the mid-nineteenth century, at the height of the

Clearances on the estate. At the moment, the guidebooks and display boards made no mention of this. That this addition to the house had been financed by violent evictions, where people were forcibly removed from land they had occupied for generations, was currently being ignored. Beth was unsure how she would tackle this issue in the new museum, but she was determined to make sure the story was told, and that the injustice carried out against those tenants was recognised.

As she stood in front of the coach house, waiting for Eilidh's dad to collect her, Beth was so lost in thought she didn't notice his van pull up until he wound down the window and called her name.

"Beth? Are you alright?"

"Sorry Alan, I was miles away. Between learning the history of the house and thinking about the museum, my mind's all over the place."

"I can imagine, and now I'm going to add a bit more to the mix by making you think about another house."

"No, I'm really excited to see this," she said, climbing into the passenger seat.

Only a minute later, Alan was parking the van at the side of the factor's house. As they picked their way through the overgrown shrubs to the front door, he explained that although the estate agents advised viewing with caution, the concern was mainly about broken glass and debris in the building. As long as they exercised caution on the upper floor, where leaks from the roof had caused some timbers to rot, they would be safe enough. However, Beth was happy to accept the hard hat that Alan handed to her.

The key turned easily in the lock, and it needed surprisingly little force to open the heavy front door. They stepped cautiously into the hallway, the dank air filling their noses as their eyes adjusted to the gloom. There were doorways to both sides of them, with another one directly ahead. To the side of that, a staircase ran up to the next floor. Alan led the way through the door to their left. It was a little brighter than the hallway, due to the enormous bay window, but the tangle of plants fighting to get in through the broken glass stole much of the light. The room was empty apart from a pile of rubbish in the corner, but an imposing fireplace hinted at how it must have appeared in better days. Making their way back out and through the doorway to the side of the stairs, they found a room lined with bookcases. Despite the gaping hole in the external door at the rear of the room, the shelving was remarkably intact.

"This would have been the factor's study," Alan explained. "The separate access meant that people visiting on business wouldn't need to come into the main part of the house."

"I suppose Eliza must have spent a lot of time in here then," said Beth, gazing around at the empty fireplace, the dusty bookcases, and the tiled floor, trying to picture it as a living place, instead of this decaying shell.

The door at the other side of the hall led to a room that stretched from the front to the back of the house. The bay window at the front and another window at the back made it brighter than the other rooms they had entered. At the back of the room was a very basic kitchen, which looked as if it had been added in the 1970s. The olive green and orange surfaces were probably just at the point of becoming fashionable again, but they were hopelessly at odds with the beautiful, tiled fireplace which occupied the other end of the wall.

"Shall we brave upstairs?" asked Alan.

"If you're sure it's safe."

"Just stick close by, but there shouldn't be any problems."

Beth tried to relax as she tentatively followed Alan up the stairs. She was expecting them to collapse at any moment, but they held firm beneath her feet. The window at the top of the stairs was thick with dirt, but Beth could just make out the road at the side of the house and the shore beyond that. Two doors faced each other at the top of the stairs. Alan opened the door to their left, and they peered into a room running the full width of the house, with a window at each end. It was much brighter than downstairs, as the plants hadn't yet blocked the windows. There were two fireplaces along the side wall, suggesting the room had once been divided, and the floor was just bare boards. It was less oppressive than the hemmed in darkness of downstairs, and Beth started to see the house a little differently. The door across the hall led into a smaller bedroom, which had just the one window. Part of the ceiling had collapsed, leaving a heap of wood and plaster on the floor, but a small cast iron fireplace still stood undisturbed towards the end of the far wall. This might have been Eliza's room, thought Beth, trying to ignore the mess and picture the space with furniture and a cheery fire in the grate. The last door on the landing led into a huge bathroom. The fact that it was a shrine to avocado suggested it could have been fitted at the same time as the kitchen, but Alan pointed out that a different suite could have been installed earlier than that. After all, this was a much grander house than most in the area.

Another set of stairs led from the end of the landing to the attic space. Alan tested them carefully before the pair of them made their way up. Once again, they found a landing with a door on either side. Although the ceiling sloped, there was still enough headroom for them to stand comfortably. They didn't step into either of the rooms, being conscious of the hole in the floor of one of them, but they could see both were largely the same, lit by roof lights and stuffed with all sorts of junk. Most of the light came from gaps in the roof rather than the roof lights themselves, such was the level of grime that had built up on them.

"So, what do you think?" Alan asked as they made their way back outside. "Can you picture yourself living here?"

"I don't think I could afford to. It'd cost a fortune to make it liveable, wouldn't it?"

"Well, that depends, really. Come and have a look at this," he said, leading her around the side of the house. "What you'd want to do, if you had the money, would be to open up here." Alan gestured to the window at the back of the kitchen. "Then you'd add an extension where we're standing. You could have the front of it entirely in glass, and it would look out across a little garden, straight to the sea. You'd have your dining area and a bit of seating in it and then the sitting room at the front of the house would just be a snug for the evenings. At the moment, the house doesn't really take advantage of the views, but an extension like that would change it completely. Now that would cost a bob or two. But if you were just to repair the roof and replace the windows, make good any damage from the elements and then fit a new kitchen and bathroom, I don't think it would be that bad. And although it's an old building, I don't think you'd have any issues with planning permission as it's already been messed about with."

"Would you want to buy it?" asked Beth.

"I don't think there would be much profit in it if I was to develop it in the way I'd want to. But it'd be worth spending the money if you were going to make this a home. So if you did have the money, would you want to live here?"

"I can't imagine having the money, but I think I can picture it finished. At first, I didn't like it. It felt dark and spooky, but once we went upstairs and it was a bit brighter, it felt really different. I think it could be beautiful. There are still so many original features."

"True, and it's also conveniently close to a decent pub. Come on, let's get a drink and chat about it a bit more."

They left the van outside the house and wandered along the road to the Ardmhor Hotel.

"Hi Alan, Hi Beth," Andrew nodded to them as they came in the door. "No Eilidh with you?"

"Not today. I've just been making Beth tour the old factor's house with me."

"Thinking of it as a project for you, Alan?" Andrew asked as he poured their drinks.

"It's not really right for me. I was more interested in whether it could work for Beth."

Andrew's eyebrows shot up. "I know it's cheap, but surely it'd cost a fortune to do up. You can't afford something like that, can you, Beth?"

"I doubt it, but Alan's trying to convince me. I think it'll just be a nice dream though."

They made their way over to a table and discussed things in a bit more detail. Buying the house wouldn't be an issue. Alan thought the price would come down, as it had been for sale for quite some time with no interest. Also, Beth was in the fortunate position of having a good amount of savings. The problem was whether she could afford to make it liveable. Although she knew she could have obtained a fairly large mortgage on her old salary, her new wage was less than half that amount. Alan offered lots of convincing advice making it sound plausible, but it still seemed hard to believe.

"I just think that as you're in such a lucky position, with all those savings, it'd make sense to buy somewhere. You could even rent a room out to help you pay for it. It gives me sleepless nights sometimes, thinking about the amount of money Eilidh is throwing away on rent. But she won't accept any help with a deposit, so there's not a lot we can do."

"I promise you that I'll really think about it. I love the idea. I just can't believe it'd actually be doable."

If she'd thought her mind was busy when she'd been waiting for Alan to pick her up, it was whirring twice as fast by the time he dropped her back at the entrance to Ardmhor House. Living in staff accommodation meant she could easily leave if things didn't work out. Committing to buying somewhere would be on a whole different level. Also, she really couldn't believe that something on the scale of the factor's house, needing the amount of work it did, would be viable. However, Alan had been convincing enough to inspire her to email the mortgage advisor that she'd spoken to before, back when she'd started looking at houses at home. As she pottered around making herself a big bowl of pasta, Beth reasoned that there couldn't be any harm in finding out what sort of mortgage she could get on her new salary.

There was still at least an hour of daylight left, so she decided to make a trip down to the viewpoint. It had been a couple of days since she'd last seen Alex, and she had more of the diary to fill him in on. She hadn't yet told him of the role Lady Constance played in keeping Eliza and Alexander apart, or how Eliza's relationship with her future husband had started.

Within moments of sitting down, Alex appeared alongside her.

"I'll never get over how you do that," Beth said, laughing. "You literally appear as if from nowhere whenever I get here."

"Not every time," Alex corrected. "Anyway, as I've told you before, I spend a lot of time hanging around, so I've nothing better to do than keep an eye out for you."

"What do you do?" said Beth, finally feeling bold enough to ask.

"Oh, nothing much, nothing as interesting as hearing about the diary anyway," Alex replied, deftly changing the subject.

"Are you warm enough?" he asked, moving along the bench closer to her.

It was actually quite a mild evening, but Beth wasn't about to pass up on the chance to snuggle into him.

"I am a bit chilly," she lied, moving into his arms, forgetting he'd avoided her questions yet again.

"So, what else have you read in the diary?" Alex asked, ensuring the conversation moved on.

"Well, Eliza was writing to Alexander every day, but she didn't get any replies, so she wrote to Flora, asking her to help. But then she got a reply from Flora, basically saying she wanted no more to do with her. It sounds as if Lady Constance told Flora that Eliza had been using Alexander, in order to get herself a good social position, whilst also playing around with several of the estate workers. Of course, because Eliza had never confided in Flora, she felt really let down and believed her mother's version of events. It all sounds like a total mess. Eliza can't think of a way to reach Alexander, and she's turned to William Burton, my great-great-grandfather, who was the other partner in Mr Hardwick's law firm, for some comfort. I don't know how they come to end up married though. At the moment, it sounds like she's still totally in love with Alexander."

Alex had been completely still as he listened to her speak and remained so, staring off into space. It was a while before he spoke.

"I imagine Alexander must have suspected his mother of intercepting the post. After all, she had already opened Eliza's letters. But it's upsetting to think of her involving Flora."

"I know. It's horrible how Lady Constance used her children. She can't have cared much for her son, to let him get so badly hurt."

"She could have just had a strange way of showing her love."

"I suppose so," Beth conceded. "But Eliza is distraught by the idea of Alexander thinking that she'd never cared for him. I feel so angry with Lady Constance because she's stopping things from working out the way I want them to."

"I suppose we need to remember that without Lady Constance interfering, your family wouldn't be as it is today. If Eliza had ended up back at Ardmhor, it's unlikely you'd exist. It is upsetting to hear what she did, and I'm not surprised Eliza felt she needed to turn to someone else, but I think it helps to concentrate on the good that came out of it. It's a really sad story, and I know the people involved will have lots of regrets, but your existence makes it worthwhile."

His voice was heavy with emotion, and Beth turned to look at him properly. He was so close to her, his dark eyes searching hers. She moved nearer, never breaking his gaze, but as her lips met his, something changed. Alex leapt away from her as if he had been scalded.

"I'm so sorry Beth. I can't do this," he muttered, jumping up and hurrying away.

CHAPTER TWENTY-FIVE

13th of May 1893

As I was struggling to sleep last night, a terrible thought occurred to me. It is now a month since I left Ardmhor, but my courses have not arrived. I've been so busy settling in and so distracted thinking about Alex that it hadn't crossed my mind. I know what it can mean when the blood doesn't appear. I've heard plenty of talk that the lack of the monthly visitor is a sign a baby is on the way. I know that Effie, one of the Ardmhor kitchen maids, left unexpectedly to get married, and then she had a baby just six months later. Morag, Flora's maid, said that the baby hadn't really been born early, as Effie was saying. Morag said that Effie only got married because she already knew a baby was on the way. I was shocked at the time because I'd thought men and women should only do the things that cause babies after they were married. I was quite disgusted by Effie and her behaviour. Now I see

I could be in the same position. How silly I was to think that what Alex and I did was different. I know that sometimes the bleeding stops for other reasons, but since mine began, it has happened every month without fail. It is only now, after that night with Alex, that it hasn't arrived. It can't be a coincidence.

I don't know what to do for the best. I desperately want to talk to Alex, but I don't know how to contact him. Everyone will be disgusted with me, just as I was disgusted with Effie. The Hardwicks are going to be so disappointed, and I'm sure they will want me to leave. How can they possibly keep me here if I am having a baby outside of marriage? I had thought that living without Alex was as bad as things could be, but I realise now that they could actually get much, much worse.

20th of May 1893

I feel as though I've been living in a sort of dream for the last week. Well, more of a nightmare, really. I've been lost in my thoughts, going through the motions of work and family life, while constantly wondering whether every sensation I feel is evidence of a child growing inside me. I know for definite that sickness is a sign of a new life to come, and I have been sick each day for the last three days. I think it is time to come up with a plan.

21st of May 1893

William found me crying in the park again today. He asked if I was upset because I had received more news about Alex. I told him I had heard nothing further and that it was another situation, one that I could not discuss, that had upset me. He sat down with me as he had before and said that although I did not need to tell him my worries, there was nothing I could say that he would be unwilling to hear. I told him he would no doubt feel differently if he heard the truth, but he insisted nothing could change his opinion of me. In the end, my desperation to talk to someone led me to take the risk. I had already alluded to the fact that Alex and I had been more to each other than an unmarried couple should be, so I suppose my confession was not as shocking as it might have been otherwise, but William barely seemed to register any hint of surprise. He was true to his word and did not rush to leave or cease our conversation. Instead, he talked about what could be done to resolve my problem.

He proposed I write to Alex to let him know the predicament I find myself in. I had been worried about Lady Constance discovering my situation, if she was indeed opening my letters. However, William reasoned that as she had cared for me in the past, the thought of a grandchild might soften her feelings and might bring her around to the idea of a marriage. He also pointed out that as her opinion of me is already so low, there really is nothing to lose by her finding out. From overhearing conversations between his mother and sisters, he knows quite a lot about the process of expecting babies, and he thinks it will be some time before anyone else need know what is happening. He thinks I can safely wait a couple of weeks, to see if there is a response from Alex, before taking any more action.

I feel a little ashamed having a conversation about something so intimate with a man I hardly know, but who else could I talk to? And overall, I do feel better for having shared my woes. My situation is as dire as it could be, but at least I feel a little less alone.

27th of May 1893

Today, it was William that shocked me. He said that if I did not hear from Alex by next week—he thought we should get married! I could not think of a response. He said that he did not expect me to give him an answer straight away, but he had been thinking it over at length and he believed this would be the best solution to my problem. He said that if we were to marry by the end of next month, enough time would have passed before the baby was born for people to have forgotten the exact dates. The child would be born to a respectable married couple, and there would be no reason for any questions. He said that he didn't want to discuss it any further today, he only wanted me to think about it.

He is right, it would solve all of my immediate problems, but surely it would be wrong for him to commit his entire life to mine, simply to spare me from disgrace. And if I accept, then it means giving up on Alex. If I commit to a life with William, I have to do just that. There can be no going back.

30th of May 1893

There is still no word from Alex, and I have done little but think about the answer I should give William. I asked him how he could sacrifice his chance of finding love in order to help me, and this time his answer didn't simply shock me—it left me stunned. He said he would not be giving up on anything because he had loved me from the moment we first walked together in the park. Although he hadn't expected events to take the turn they had, he said he knew he wanted to marry me. He said he felt sure he could love my child as his own, so there would be no sacrifice on his part. I told him I didn't know if I'd ever be able to return his feelings, but he said he wouldn't expect me to. His own experience of being abandoned by his first love means he realises I can't just transfer my affections from

Alex to him. He said he hoped that eventually I would grow to love him, but he accepted we might only ever be companions. His one condition, which he felt he needed to be honest about from the start, was that the child should never be told he wasn't their father. I honestly don't know what to think. I have sat here staring at Alex's picture in my locket, searching for the answers in his face, but the more I think, the more uncertain I become. In a strange way, I feel lucky that such a decent man is offering to help me, with absolutely no pressure on me to return his affections. But just a short while ago, I was expecting to be married to someone else, and I still love Alex with all my heart. If it wasn't for this life growing inside me, I wouldn't even be considering a different marriage proposal. But the existence of this child, Alex's child, can't be denied, and I have to be sensible to protect both of us. If Alex had said he no longer loved me, this decision would be so much easier. I know I could build a life with William, and perhaps in time we could both be happy. But Alex hasn't said he doesn't want me. I am certain that if he knew the situation I was facing, he would finally be willing to face the wrath of his parents and make things right. I wish I had a way to contact him. It feels wrong to accept William's offer without Alex's knowledge. It is as if I am handing the life that should be his to someone else.

CHAPTER TWENTY-SIX

Beth lifted her phone from the bedside table and checked the time again. It was two in the morning, five minutes since she'd last looked. Sleep seemed like an impossibility. Her mind was too busy churning over the events of the day. She could not work Alex out. In the moments before he'd walked away, she had honestly believed he felt the same as her, that the force moving her to kiss him was something mutual working between them. When he'd left so abruptly, she'd sat rooted to the spot, watching his figure shrink into the distance. She was still unsure what his words had meant. What was the real reason he had shied away from their kiss? He'd said he couldn't. Was that because he wasn't attracted to her in that way, or because something else was stopping him? Was he still involved in the relationship that had left him so damaged, even though he'd said it was a long time ago? All she knew for definite was that she felt rejected, and she felt embarrassed that she had mistaken their connection for something else.

On top of all the angst about Alex, the factor's house was also keeping her awake. Would it be foolish to commit herself to an ambitious project like that? Or would it be more foolish to ignore the opportunity and hand over thousands in rent instead? Was it even a viable proposition? Or was she wasting her time worrying over a pipe dream?

And now, after trying to clear her mind by reading Eliza's diary, there was another revelation rocking her world. She couldn't know for definite yet, but it was just possible that her connection to Ardmhor wasn't only that Eliza had lived there. If what she now suspected was true, her connection was an actual flesh and blood one, linking her directly to the MacAird family. Beth knew that her great-grandmother, Granny JoJo, was Eliza's first child, and until now she'd believed her to be the child of Eliza and William. But the diary was suggesting Eliza's first child actually belonged to Alexander MacAird. Nothing was certain yet. It was possible that the pregnancy forcing Eliza into marriage hadn't worked out. Beth didn't know Granny JoJo's date of birth, so maybe she was indeed the product of Eliza and William's marriage. But if Granny JoJo had been born less than nine months after their wedding, then she was Alexander's child, which meant Beth herself was also a direct descendant of the MacAird family. She needed to read more of the diary and get her mum to check the dates, but two in the morning wasn't really the time for doing either of those things. Not when she was still trying to prove herself in her new job.

Then, another thought occurred to her: did Alex already know about this shared heritage? Was that why he thought they couldn't have a relationship? Surely not, she reasoned. Firstly, how could he know? There seemed to be no records of Eliza herself at Ardmhor, so it was highly unlikely there was any mention of her children. Secondly, even if he knew, the connection was so far back they must only be very distantly related. Beth knew the current Lord MacAird and his family were descended from James, the eldest of the three MacAird children during Eliza's time at Ardmhor, whereas if Beth was indeed related, her connection came through Alexander, the younger brother. A quick internet search told her that would make them fourth cousins, or perhaps fourth cousins once removed; she didn't know whether the generations in Alex's family ran the same as in hers. It seemed that, on average, people could have over a thousand fourth cousins, which would make it a pretty distant link to be worried about, especially as the website said that many fourth cousins were no more genetically related than random strangers might be. No, Alex's rejection had to come from something else. The most obvious reason being that he just wasn't attracted to her.

For once, Beth didn't notice the scent of the flowerbeds as she took the path through the formal garden towards the house, nor did she see the magnificence of the view as she made her way through the entrance to begin her shift. Instead, her eyes itched from the lack of sleep, and she struggled to stifle a yawn. She'd fired off a quick text to her mum asking for confirmation of Granny JoJo's date of birth, and she'd have chance to read more of the diary later, so, hopefully, by the time she climbed into bed tonight, she'd know whether she was a distant part of the MacAird family or not. But before then, she had to get through her day at work. Even more worryingly, she had the first online tutorial for her museum studies course that evening. She hoped she'd be able to do everything justice with so little sleep.

To her surprise, work went really well. For the first time, she didn't have to hand over a single enquiry to anyone else, so she was feeling pretty confident as she logged into her first tutorial. However, by the time she logged off, some of that positivity was waning. It wasn't that she'd struggled with the knowledge. There hadn't been much actual learning, as the initial tutorial was more of an introduction to the course. What had worried her was the scale of the task ahead. It seemed there was so much ground to cover. Beth felt overwhelmed at the thought of completing work experience placements, essays, and a dissertation, all alongside working at Ardmhor. The other people on the course all seemed to have relevant experience already, and Beth's doubting inner voice instantly leapt to the fore, telling her she wasn't up to the job.

She felt a little better as she opened an encouraging email from Megan. Beth smiled as she typed out a quick reply. When she had first met Megan, she'd instantly written her off as a brash, image obsessed American. It showed how wrong first impressions could be because, in reality, Megan was thoughtful and sensitive, with an uncanny ability to pass on advice and encouragement when it was most needed. Megan's email prompted her to scroll through the latest comments on the volunteer group chat. Fraser had set it up in the week before they departed Ardmhor. Bob and Mary were taking things easy for the week, Olivia and Fraser were enjoying meeting each other's families, and Megan and Steve were preparing for an actual holiday together. It was hard to believe it was less than a week since they had all left. How Beth wished they were still there.

Feeling nostalgic for the past few weeks, she let herself out of the staff house and set off through the gardens, towards the sea. Her feet were making their way along the path to the viewpoint before she'd reached a conscious decision about where to go. The wind had picked up, and she drew her coat closer around her, watching the white horses on the tops of the waves. It occurred to her she had no idea what she wanted to say to Alex, assuming he even turned up. He might be as embarrassed as her by the way she had misinterpreted things. She had just started to accept he wouldn't be coming when she heard the scrunch of gravel on the path. She didn't turn round, not wanting to be disappointed if it was someone else approaching, but also not knowing how to begin if it was him. Within the space of a moment, he was beside her, taking hold of her hand, and she decided honesty was the best policy.

"I'm sorry if I made things awkward between us last night. I just felt really close to you, and I thought you wanted it too…"

"Beth," he interrupted softly.

"No, let me finish please," Beth said over him, needing to say her piece. She started again, hesitating at first as she got over her embarrassment. "I really like you. I've never felt this way about anyone before, and you always seem to understand me. You've known what I'm thinking before I've known, and you've pushed me to do things I'd normally have been too scared to consider. I've wanted to kiss you since the first night I met you, so I'm not sorry I tried, but I am sorry if I've spoilt things between us."

"Oh Beth, you couldn't do that. I just wish I could explain properly. You are so much more than you think. Moving up here, changing your entire life, it's so impressive. You think you're nothing like Eliza, but to me you seem so similar: taking risks for what you want, not being willing to settle for an unhappy existence...."

"But you're not attracted to me? You don't see me in that way?"

"No, I mean... Oh, I don't know how to explain it. Spending time with you has made me feel things that I never thought I'd feel again, but I can't be with you like that. I know I'm not the man for you."

"What do you mean, Alex?" Beth asked in exasperation. "How can you know who the right person for me is? Surely I get to decide that? So what you're really saying is you know that I'm not the woman for you. Is it about the relationship that went wrong? Are you still in love with her?"

Alex sighed. "I think I'll always be in love

with her, Beth. I'm sorry, but that's the truth. You remind me of her so much, but you're not her. And that's not saying that she's better than you. You are so very special, but we can never be together, not in the way you want. I don't know," he stopped and shook his head, gathering his thoughts before continuing. "The connection between us is so strange that I lost sight of reality for a bit, but as I've said, we can't be together."

"I still don't understand. If you're in love with her, why don't you tell her? Can't you work things out? And if it's too late for that, why can't we give things a go, if you like me too?"

"It's just not possible, Beth, for me and her, or for us. I wish I could explain better, but I can't."

"If you just tell me what happened, maybe I could help? Or at least I could understand."

"You can't, no one can, and I don't want to talk about it anymore." He sat silently, looking into the distance, deliberately not meeting her eye. Beth wondered whether she ought to leave, but just as she started to move, he continued. "I don't want to lose you though. I'd like more than anything for us to continue being friends. The time we've spent together has been so precious to me. I hope you can believe that."

Somehow, Beth knew he was telling the truth. Maybe he wasn't ready for a relationship and maybe he never would be, but she knew there was something special between them, and she would hate for that to end. They sat quietly for a while, Beth trying to adjust her perception of him to friendship rather than romance, struggling to see if that could ever be possible.

"I had my first tutorial today for the museum studies course," she began, trying to move the conversation onto safer ground. "It made me a bit nervous."

"Why? What happened?" "Nothing happened. It's just that everyone else seemed more experienced. I'm not sure I can do it."

"This is when you need to channel your inner Eliza. You're just as capable as all those other people. There isn't something different about them that makes them able to do things. They're just ordinary people giving something a try. If you always think others have got some special gift that makes them successful, a gift that you missed out on, well, then you'll never try anything, and then you really will miss out."

"But I think some things are easier for others. I don't think everyone worries as much as I do."

"And that's probably true, and it's not fair that things are much easier for some people. But even if things are harder for you, they're still possible. Some people might think you have things easy. After all, you're the one with enough money saved up to buy a house and give up your job, and you're the one making a start in your dream career."

"I suppose so. I hadn't really thought of it like that."

"You see, think like Eliza, not like Alexander. You need to make plans, rather than seeing problems."

"Which Alexander do I need to avoid being like?" Beth asked. "Not that it makes much difference. Neither of you seem particularly big on facing your fears."

"Well done," Alex replied with a rueful smile. "Slightly cutting comments sound much more like Eliza's style."

Beth smiled, pleased she'd managed to lighten the atmosphere. "Cutting comments aside, being like Eliza instead of Alexander, might be harder than it seems. I read some more of the diary last night, and it appears I might be just as connected to him as I am to her."

"Really? What do you mean?"

"Eliza was pregnant when she arrived in Manchester. It seems that the night she spent with Alexander had consequences, and that's why she ends up getting married so quickly. I haven't read it all yet, but if the pregnancy works out and Eliza's first child actually belongs to Alexander, that means he's my great-great-grandfather. Which also means that we are something like fourth cousins. Isn't that amazing?"

Alex was silent for a while before he spoke.

"Well, it means I'm right. I've been saying since we met that you belong at Ardmhor, but I have to admit, you saying we're related does feel strange."

"I don't know for definite yet, but it's an exciting thought."

"Well, I'm proud to be related to you."

"If you are," Beth corrected.

"I don't care. I'm proud of you anyway. I just hope I haven't disappointed you too much. I honestly believe you belong here, and I know that the right man will appear soon"

"I am disappointed. I'd be lying if I said I wasn't, but I'm not disappointed in you. I know you can't help how you feel. I just wish you'd trust me with whatever happened to you."

"It's not about trust, Beth, I just can't tell you."

"I know you can't yet, but there's still time. I'm not planning on leaving. You know, Eliza said something in her diary that reminded me of you. She said that if she married William without Alexander knowing about the baby, it would be like she was giving the life Alexander was supposed to have to someone else. It's almost the same thing that you said to me, when I was hesitating over applying for the job here. You said if I didn't try things, I'd miss out on the life I was supposed to have. It was great advice. Maybe you should take it yourself. It seems as if Alexander did miss out on the life he should have had with Eliza. Maybe you're missing out on the life you should be leading because you won't open up to anyone."

"I wish it was that simple."

"But maybe it is," Beth replied. "Maybe we both make things a lot more complicated than they need to be."

CHAPTER TWENTY-SEVEN

7th of June 1893

I have written two further letters to Alex, but I have received no reply. I even wrote to Flora again, although I did not mention my current situation. However, it has been to no avail. The only other avenue to explore is travelling back to Ardmhor. It will take me at least four days to make the journey, and it will use every penny of my savings, but I have to exhaust all options before I give up on Alex. William has offered to accompany me, but I feel that this is something I have to do alone. Mr Hardwick did not ask any questions when I said that an emergency meant I needed to return to Ardmhor. He is such a kind man that he simply said I should take as long as I needed. So I will set out on my journey tomorrow. I feel incredibly anxious, as I know I shall not be welcomed at Ardmhor, but I can't see another way.

13th of June 1893

It was a harrowing journey, where I felt constantly nauseous, but at least on the way, the thought of seeing Alex bolstered my spirits. The journey back to Manchester was just unbearable, worse even than when I first left Ardmhor. The trains ran with no delays on my outward journey, and I arrived in Inveravain slightly earlier than I'd expected. It felt strange walking towards the house. I had not expected to be back there so soon after my departure, and everything seemed different. I wonder if it is the new life growing inside me which is changing the way I view the world. Mrs Birch, the housekeeper, opened the door and informed me that none of the family were present. She had always been kind to me in the past, but there was something cold in the way she looked at me now. Had she been told the same stories Flora had about me? Did she believe them? Or was she just following instructions and protecting her position? Either way, I did not believe her. I rang the bell several times more, only to receive the same answer. My desperation then led me to take the undignified step of trying the other doors to the house, all of which were locked. I then shouted Alex's name outside his window. This resulted in Mr Harper, the butler, being sent out to inform me the police would be called if I did not desist. It crossed my mind that if the police were called, they might intercede and get word to Alex, but they would speak to Lord MacAird first, and if Lady Constance has persuaded him I am to be kept from Alex, the police would have got me nowhere apart from in trouble. I quietened down, but I remained on the lawn, and no police arrived. I suppose my presence back at Ardmhor would have been embarrassing enough for Lady Constance. No wonder she didn't really want the police involved as well. I stayed there, watching the door until it was time to make my way back to the station. I know Alex can't have been there. If he had heard me, I am sure nothing would have been able to keep him away. But now I have no plans left. I don't know where Alex is, and I have no way of reaching him. I think I ran out of tears on that terrible return journey. It seems that now I must be strong and sensible for our child, and I think that the only way to do that is to marry William.

29th of June 1893

I am a married woman. I am Mrs William Burton. Elizabeth Burton! However, I must admit that when I used to think of my wedding day, I did not imagine being married to one man and still in love with another. William is such a good man. I know that for him, today has been a happy day. I kept catching glimpses of pure pride on his face as we said our vows and sat for a wedding portrait afterwards. But he knew it was not the same for me, and he has been so careful to be sensitive to my feelings. When we were at the photographer's studio, William was asked to stand with his hand on my shoulder. As he did so, he gave me the smallest of squeezes, just a gentle reminder he knew this wasn't easy for me. I wonder how we will look in the picture, our faces serious as we hold the pose, and me with that enormous arrangement of flowers in front of me, in case anyone should see the tiny swelling of my stomach. We are to live in Williams' family home. His mother had long been considering a move to live with one of his sisters. Once she knew that her precious son would no longer need her, she felt she could leave without worry. So the smart house, on the quiet street where William grew up, is now our home. William had already showed me our separate bedrooms, making it clear he had no expectations of our relationship developing. Although I wish so much that my wedding night was different, that it was filled with joy as mine and Alex's dreams finally came true, I am also aware that I am lucky. I am married to the most decent of men, and I know that both my child and I will be safe and loved. I hope that over time I will also grow to be happy. If I had met William before Alex, I feel I could have loved him. Perhaps there is still a chance for that? I think William deserves that. But then I feel so guilty. Despite my love for Alex, I'm already moving on. My need to find solutions means I've given his child, and our future, to someone else, whereas Alex might still be dreaming of ways for us to be together. Maybe I don't deserve happiness again.

CHAPTER
TWENTY-EIGHT

I t was Saturday morning, and Beth was sitting with copies of marriage and birth certificates in her hands. William and Eliza's wedding certificate made perfect sense, agreeing with the date in Eliza's diary of the 29th of June 1893. However, the birth certificate for Eliza's first child was more confusing. The dates tied with the child belonging to Alexander, with the date of birth recorded as the 20th of January 1894, just seven months after Eliza and William's wedding. It was the name that made no sense. Beth had always known her great-grandmother as Granny JoJo, but the name on the birth certificate was Alexandrina. This brought up several questions. The name JoJo bore no relation to the name Alexandrina, so did this mean her great-grandmother wasn't Eliza's first child after all? And in that case, what had happened to Alexandrina? There had never been any mention of an older sibling to Granny JoJo. Also, why would William have agreed to the child bearing the name of Eliza's first love? Surely it would have been a daily reminder that the child wasn't actually his? Despite only having been aware of her possible blood link to the MacAirds for a few days, Beth realised she would be incredibly sad to find it didn't exist. She dialled her mum's number in search of answers.

"Oh, I see why you were confused," said Jean after Beth had reeled off her questions. "Alexandrina's married surname was Jones, so to me her name was always Granny Jones. Then when you were little, you couldn't say Jones properly, instead it sounded like you were saying JoJo and the name just stuck. It never occurred to me you didn't know her real name, but you were only about six when she died."

"So she really was Alexander's daughter? And we're actually part of the MacAird family?"

"It certainly seems that way. No wonder we feel at home at Ardmhor, eh?"

There was a hint of awe in Jean's voice. Neither of them could have predicted this turn of events when Beth had set off for Ardmhor at the start of the summer.

"I'm surprised William allowed that name choice though. It must have been hard living with such a constant reminder of Alexander."

"If you'd known Eliza, you'd realise William wouldn't have had much say in the matter," Jean replied, amusement clear in her voice. "Also, I suppose if William thought he could learn to love another man's child as his own, a name probably wasn't that big a deal. I don't think they really used her full name either. I only ever heard people call her Rina."

"I suppose Rina doesn't automatically make you think of Alexander."

"No, not at all. Maybe that's why I didn't connect the dots when you first started telling me the contents of the diary. Well, that and the fact I didn't realise Granny was born so soon after her parents got married. I suppose that was something they preferred to keep quiet. Really, when you think about it, it's no wonder Eliza didn't talk about Ardmhor. It must have been a can of worms she preferred to keep a lid on."

"I expect so," Beth agreed. "It's hard to imagine how different things would have been then. Eliza's story probably wouldn't play out in the same way if she was young now."

"True, but if her story was different, ours would be different, too. Maybe we'd have remained at Ardmhor, and you'd be Lady of the Manor, or maybe you'd be sick of the place and desperate to escape, or more likely, I suppose we just wouldn't exist."

"Who knows? I can't wait to tell Lady Angela about this. I think she's going to love the fact I'm working here and I'm a proper Ardmhor descendant."

"You don't think she'll think we want compensation or something?" Jean suddenly sounded worried.

"I think the fact Alexander was only a second son, and it's so far back, means the current family won't be too concerned," Beth reassured her, laughing at the fact her mum could sometimes worry as much as she did.

She was still smiling as she finished the call. She couldn't explain why it mattered so much to find she really was the great-great-granddaughter of both Eliza and Alexander, but it felt right to be connected to both of them. Alexander's dithering had seemed more familiar to her than Eliza's planning and action, and although many would argue character traits couldn't travel so far forward through time, it felt comforting to see herself reflected in the cautious young man from Eliza's diary. Maybe it wasn't that she was a bit pathetic. Perhaps worrying and waiting was just a part of who she was, something she needed to learn to embrace and work with instead of feeling bitter about. And regardless of anything else, Ardmhor truly was a part of her. Her own flesh and blood had built this place and lived here for centuries. Her time here over the summer had felt like a homecoming, but she could never have guessed then that a homecoming was actually what it was.

A knock on her bedroom door startled her out of her thoughts.

"Beth, are you in there? It's Andrew."

Surprised to hear his voice outside her room, Beth quickly checked her appearance in the mirror. She was pleased to see her curls had for once chosen to arrange themselves in glossy ringlets, rather than frizzing wildly, and, although she knew they were technically sun damage, she liked the scattering of freckles across her nose and cheeks. She opened the door to find Andrew smiling, a rucksack on his back.

"I know you're not on the rota to work today, so I'm hoping you've not got any other plans because I've got a day off, some news, and a bag full of food."

"Well, that sounds like an offer I can't refuse. Just give me a minute to get sorted."

A while later, Beth found herself following Andrew down a tiny path, which clung to the side of a narrow valley. The ground tumbled away to their left, down to a fast-flowing stream, while rowan and birch trees provided a canopy of leaves above them. The stream itself was a chain of miniature waterfalls, the water gurgling happily as it forced its way over each obstacle. Beth was concentrating on placing her feet carefully as they climbed over tree roots and squeezed between bracken. She did not want to end up in the stream, no matter how picturesque it looked.

"Where are we going?" she asked as they rounded yet another bend.

"You'll see soon enough," came Andrew's reply.

As he finished speaking, they stepped out of the trees, and the view opened up in front of them. They were standing a short way above a rocky cove, where the stream widened as it completed its journey to the sea. Great swathes of orange crocosmia marked the water's passage from hidden woodland to open shore. To either side of them, jagged cliffs rose skyward and vast slabs of rock lay scattered at improbable angles across the bay, creating rock pools in the hollows between them. Someone had strung a hammock between two perfectly placed birch trees, just where the path led onto the shore. The sun chose that moment to reappear from behind a cloud, turning the sea into a mix of turquoise and bright blue. It was a scene that looked as if it belonged somewhere much more tropical than the north of Scotland.

"Wow," was all Beth could find to say.

"I know," Andrew said, smiling. "I've been coming here since I was tiny, but it still takes my breath away."

"Have you always lived around here, then?"

"Yep, Ardmhor born and bred. I can't imagine living anywhere else."

"But you keep leaving?"

"Well, yes, but I keep coming back, too. I think it's because I've been spoilt growing up somewhere so beautiful. It's like I'm always trying to find somewhere else to top this, but after a while I realise I can't, so I come back. Until I get tempted to go again."

"Does everyone who grew up here feel the same?"

"Maybe, I don't really know. I mean, most people leave for a bit. Like my sister, she went away to university, but now she lives about an hour up the coast with her husband. Plenty of people leave because there aren't many jobs up here, but most of them end up coming back at some point. It's like we need to check out somewhere different, before realising we belong here."

"So, do you think you're at that point yet?"

"Not quite. That's what my news is about. Come on, let's sit down and sort the food out first."

Andrew's arm brushed against Beth's as they moved towards a flat slab of rock. She shivered remembering the last time they'd been alone together. Stop it, she thought to herself. Only the other day she'd been devastated that Alex didn't share her feelings, yet here she was now, excitedly anticipating what might happen between her and Andrew.

"So, I've been offered a job at an activity centre in Mexico." Andrew began, once he'd unpacked their picnic from his bag. "It's mainly water-based stuff, which I've got some experience in, but I'll be able to get fully accredited while I'm there. It's a two-year contract, which is longer than I usually stay in one place, but I feel like I'm ready to settle down a bit."

"I'm not sure moving to Mexico is exactly settling down," said Beth, taking a bite of her sandwich."

"Possibly not, but if I like it, maybe I'll stay, and if I don't, I'll have the qualifications I need to come back home and set up some kind of activity business here."

"Gosh, well, that is proper forward planning. When would you be leaving?"

"Next week. It's quite a fast turnaround."

"Wow! That is quick. It sounds great though."

And to Beth, it really did sound great. From the moment he'd said he was going to Mexico, she'd felt the heat between them increase. If he was leaving, there was no need to worry about details like whether she preferred Alex. Like she'd said to him the last time they'd met, maybe they made things more complicated than necessary. She'd tried to learn from what Alex had said about waiting for someone who really valued her as a person, but he'd already made it clear that wasn't him. And she'd only ever been herself with Andrew. She hadn't done what Megan had accused her of when they'd first met. She hadn't put on an act to attract him. He liked her as she was, so what was the harm in having a bit of fun?

When they reached the staff accommodation block, just after the sun had set, Beth didn't hesitate when Andrew asked if he should come in. She'd known what her answer would be for hours. As she took his hand and led him into her room, she realised she was holding her breath, and as he gently tilted her face towards his, she felt the electricity building. When his kiss finally came, it was as delicious as she'd remembered. For once, she didn't let her mind engage, and she didn't analyse whether she was doing the right thing. She focused instead on the sensation of his mouth moving against hers, his breath against her neck, and his hands reaching for the warm skin beneath her jumper. Soon, she wasn't thinking at all, she was lost in the moment, melting under his touch.

It was only later, as they were drifting off to sleep, enjoying the warmth of skin against skin, that Beth felt the familiar unease surface. No matter how much she had enjoyed the last few hours, she couldn't shake the feeling that she'd got herself into a situation she needed to escape from. It was just as she'd been giving in to the confusion of sleep that Alex had appeared in her mind's eye. She'd seen herself turning to him, playing with the dark hair at the nape of his neck as she snuggled closer into his chest. But when she'd opened her eyes to drink in the sight of his beautiful face, it had been Andrew lying next to her instead, his chest rising and falling with the rhythm of his breath.

Beth tried to look at Andrew objectively. He was a very handsome man, with his softly curling hair and his piercing blue eyes. He was also a fair bit taller than her, something she'd always liked the idea of, wanting to feel petite for once. Beth was sure she should feel happy, but all she felt was a nagging sensation that something wasn't right. Sleep made Andrew look innocent and peaceful, whereas Beth felt guilty. She knew she didn't want him in her bed. What was the matter with her? The last few hours had been great, in fact the whole day had, but now all she wanted was to get rid of him. It was Alex that she wanted lying next to her, and if it wasn't him, she didn't want anyone. She lay there for what felt like hours, trying not to disturb Andrew, willing her mind to switch off, but sleep remained just out of reach. Eventually, she slipped out of bed and stole her way over to the chair, reaching for the diary as she sat down.

CHAPTER TWENTY-NINE

20th of January 1894

My daughter was born today! How strange it feels to write those words. I can't quite comprehend that I am a mother, although my body certainly knows that something momentous has happened. I feel physically drained, and the discomfort is greater than I expected, but I also feel oddly elated. Every time I look at the tiny bundle in my arms, my heart seems to expand. I feel so much love for William today; he is besotted with his daughter and I know he sees her completely as his. He has looked after me so well, taking her from me as soon as she has fed, walking around with her, comforting her, and cooing at her, all so that I can rest.

Then he surpassed my expectations again. I had been thinking for a while that I would like to reflect Alex in the baby's name, that it was one small thing I could do to make him a part of their life. But I hadn't mentioned the idea to William. It seemed as if it would be asking too much of him. Anyway, as we sat together in the first hours after the birth, with the baby sleeping in his arms, he said he had been thinking about names, and if I agreed, he would like to call her Alexandra. Although he still wanted her to be brought up believing she was his own flesh and blood, he said he couldn't ignore the fact that everything good in his life was something that should have belonged to Alex, so he wanted him to be acknowledged. I immediately burst into tears, and William thought he had upset me by reawakening the old wounds. I had to reassure him that was not the case and that my tears were actually born of happiness. It constantly amazes me how similarly our minds work. I suggested we use Alexandrina, the Scottish version of the name. I've always thought Rina sounded pretty.

I still miss Alex, and I treasure the memories of our time together. It was a pure and genuine love that we shared, strengthened perhaps by growing up in the same place and both feeling that we didn't quite fit, albeit for different reasons. I will never be able to leave his memory behind. I will only have to look at my child to be reminded of what we shared, but I have to admit that I no longer want to change the outcome of our story. I didn't expect to feel this way. On my wedding day just seven short months ago, I was still enveloped in my love for

Alex. I could not believe William would ever be more than a good friend to me, yet now the arms wrapped protectively around my child are the arms I want wrapped around me. My feelings for him have developed and deepened until my love for Alex seems like a first infatuation. My feelings for William are different; ours is a love between adults. It happened so gradually. At first, we would just sit together, talking in the evenings until my eyelids drooped—each in our own armchair. William is so keen to change the world we live in, to make it fairer, and his words began to broaden my horizons, challenging my views on so many things. Gradually, we sat closer, sharing the sofa instead. William started to take my hand when we were out of the house together, and it felt right to return the pressure of his fingers. Then one night, he kissed me before we made our way to our separate rooms. Finally, the day came when we didn't turn to our own rooms any longer. The only shadow on my happiness is my guilt. What right do I have to be so happy, with my beautiful daughter and my loving husband, when I have no idea how Alex is faring? I feel like a fraud because I said I would always love him, but instead I have so swiftly moved on. I can justify my actions. I had little choice. However, it is harder to justify my happiness. I am going to write to Alex again today, to tell him about the birth of his daughter and also to return his locket. I have already written that I am secure and cared for with William, but now I need to admit to Alex that our hearts no longer belong together, that mine lives with someone else. I feel complete today, a little broken in body perhaps, but complete in heart. I sincerely hope that Alex will find that same feeling. I pray he already has, but I need him to know he is free to do so, no matter how guilty that admission makes me feel.

20th of January 1895

This diary feels long abandoned. From the moment of my marriage to William, my desire to write in it waned, and since Rina's birth, I have barely thought of its existence. Perhaps it is because it feels bound up with Eliza from Ardmhor, Alex's Eliza, and that is no longer who I am. Now I am a wife and mother, with another child on the way. I am writing in here today because I sent another letter to Alex, the first since the day of Rina's birth. I told him about Rina as she reaches her first birthday, what she looks like, what she enjoys, and all the little traits of her personality. I asked William what he thought first. He is, after all, the only father she will ever know, and his decisions regarding her life are as valid as mine, but he was full of encouragement and suggested we should do so every year. I know he shares my sense of guilt that we are overrun with happiness, and although I can now accept our happiness wasn't stolen from Alex, it is, none the less, a happiness that could have been his, if circumstances had been different.

27th of January 1895

A strange thing happened today. It was bright despite the cold, and Rina and I were in the front garden, awaiting William's return from work. I felt an odd sensation that we were being watched, but no one seemed to be around. As William came down the path and Rina toddled over to him on her chubby little legs, squealing with excitement, I felt the new life inside me kicking, as if it too was overjoyed by the knowledge its father was nearby. I put William's hand on my stomach as he greeted me with a kiss, to see if he could also feel it. It was then, as we turned to head into the house, that the strange thing occurred. I could have sworn that I saw Alex at the end of our street. I think I blinked in surprise, and when I looked again, there was no sign of him. Was he really there? Did he finally receive one of my letters and come to see his child? But if he did, why did he not approach us? I've made it clear that we would never prevent him from meeting his daughter, even though we still want her to believe she is William's child. Maybe I was mistaken. Perhaps it was just a manifestation of my guilt in such a perfect moment. But after speaking to William, I am going to take up his suggestion and write to Alex again, just to make clear that we would never stand in the way of him seeing Rina.

10th of February 1895

I received an unexpected letter today, the contents of which I can't quite bring myself to accept. I recognised Lady Constance's handwriting on the envelope straight away, and my heart beat faster as I opened it. I knew she would not have a happy reason for writing to me, and I was correct. With no preamble, she said that Alex was dead, and she had opened my letter while dealing with his correspondence. It took some time for me to register the meaning of that short word, casually tucked within the sentence, but as it finally sank in, I sank to the floor. Alex couldn't be dead. He couldn't have left this world without me knowing. Eventually, I was able to pick up the letter and read the rest of its contents. She said that Alex had died at the start of the month, from a fever brought on by infection. Therefore, she said it was impossible that I could have seen him in Manchester because by that point he was already ill at Ardmhor. She also said that he had long ago told her he wanted nothing to do with me, or the child I was trying to claim was his. She said that I was welcome to visit his grave in the family plot at Ardmhor church, but I should not contact her again, as no matter what claim I thought I might have over Alex's estate, nothing would be forthcoming to me, or to my bastard child. My mind has not known where to settle since reading her words. Is it even true? Can Alex really be gone? Or is this another one of her ploys to rid me from his life? If he is dead, had he really known of Rina but wanted nothing to do with her? Had he believed his mother's stories that I had been involved with other men? Had he hated me ever since I left? I suppose I have long since come to terms with the idea that he might hate me. After all, I have broken the promises we made to each other and fallen in love with someone else. But that he is no longer alive, that he is lying in the cold earth, never to find his own happiness, that is something I don't want to accept.

12th of April 1895

It is two years since I left Ardmhor, and I have just returned from there again. However, this time, although the journey back to Manchester was sad, my loving husband and the chatter of my squirming daughter comforted me. Rina couldn't get over the ever-changing sights flying past the window. We travelled to Ardmhor because William thought I would not be able to move on until I knew the truth. I fear I have been very difficult to live with since receiving Lady

Constance's letter. I couldn't grieve for Alex, as I couldn't really believe he was dead. But I could take no pleasure in life because another part of me was fixated on the idea he was gone, and if that was the case, how could I possibly be happy? So we travelled to Ardmhor, and I saw Alex's grave with my own eyes. It still didn't feel real. I couldn't believe he lay under that ground, but the words on the headstone were real enough. I ran my fingers over that unyielding stone, tracing his name and the short years he spent on this earth, and they told me all I needed to know. I couldn't feel his presence there, I didn't feel a closeness to him, and I can only hope that means his spirit is somewhere else, somewhere that he is happy. I'll never know for certain whether I saw Alex in Manchester that day; there seemed little point going to Ardmhor House to hear more lies from Lady Constance. But regardless of what she claims, I feel sure I saw him. Maybe he was there. It's possible he came to Manchester and then became ill on his return to Ardmhor, but why would he have left without speaking to us? Or perhaps what I saw was his spirit looking in on us as it left this world for another? I don't have any answers. All I know for definite is that he truly is gone. There is nothing I can do for Alex now, except to make sure his daughter gets to experience the things he loved, books, poetry, and the beauty of nature. I want to make sure that our expectations never become too much for her to bear. At the very least, I hope we will give her the strength to shoulder that weight without it overwhelming her, as it did with Alex. I don't intend to write in this diary again. I want to keep it as a record of who I once was, of who we were, but Elizabeth Ruth Turner, who loved Alex MacAird of Ardmhor, is long gone now, and Eliza Burton of Manchester, wife of William and almost mother of two children, is a very different person.

CHAPTER
THIRTY

T he faint light of dawn was showing by the time Beth looked up from the diary. She wiped away the tears that ran down her face. She wasn't sure why she was so upset. Unless she'd been expecting the world's oldest man to suddenly be revealed living in an Inveravain nursing home, it shouldn't have been a shock to her that Alexander was dead. But she hadn't expected his life to be so short. He hadn't even reached the age she was now, and he'd never met his daughter. That there definitely wouldn't be a surprise twist, giving her the happy ending she'd dreamed of, was harder to accept than she'd imagined.

She looked across at Andrew, still sleeping peacefully in her bed, and knew without a doubt that she didn't want to be there when he woke up. Gathering up her clothes, she dressed quietly in the bathroom. Then she scribbled a brief note before creeping out of the door. She knew it was cowardly, leaving a scrap of paper telling Andrew that she'd see him around, but she needed to be out of that room.

It was cold as she made her way out of the grounds and along the road to the churchyard. She felt compelled to find Alexander's grave, to make this man who was her own flesh and blood into a real person, rather than a character in a book. The sun hadn't yet breached the horizon, so although the sea showed its brightness, the warmth of its rays couldn't be felt. Beth shivered a little, pulling up the hood of her coat for extra warmth.

Her mind was whirring again, going over all the things that were bothering her: why could she never just relax and enjoy things, why wasn't Alex interested in her, should she be attempting to buy the factor's house? A reply had come through from the financial advisor, letting her know she would have no difficulty accessing a mortgage, so there was nothing to stop her, but was she even doing the right thing being here? Sure, she'd been unhappy before, but this was so far from home, and she barely knew anyone. With Alex refusing to open up to her and Andrew leaving, it only really left Eilidh, and she already had a life of her own. Maybe she was making a big mistake.

The white painted church, with its tall arched windows, gradually came into view through the trees. The MacAird family graves stood in a walled plot to the side of the building. Beth cautiously unlatched the gate and made her way in, aware of the presence of all these people, all these generations of her own family, somewhere beneath her feet. She read the name of one MacAird after another, wondering what her connection to each person was. She stumbled over a section of uneven ground and felt a chill pass through her, making her hair stand on end. It was so quiet, and the reality of being alone, surrounded by so much death, unsettled her. There was a mixture of simple gravestones and elaborate monuments within the plot, and she steeled herself to keep going, deciding to explore those most ornate graves first. Some were from earlier times than Alexander and others were more recent. Many graves bore the name Alexander MacAird, and each time she saw it written in stone her pulse quickened, but none were the right Alexander. Eventually, she found the place she was looking for. It was the name 'Lady Constance MacAird' that first alerted her to it, telling her that Alexander had to be nearby. His grave stood just to the side of that of his mother and father. Beth had thought they might have been buried in one grave, as many of the families seemed to be, but she noticed that James and Flora did not appear to be buried here at all, so maybe that had never been the intention. The inscription was simple, 'Here lies Alexander MacAird, beloved son of Lord James and Lady Constance MacAird, 1870-1895'.

She knelt down and ran her fingers across the letters engraved in the stone, imagining Eliza in the same place, reaching out in the same way.

"Hello, I'm Beth, your great-great-granddaughter," she said out loud, immediately feeling a little silly.

She'd never thought to visit Eliza's grave before, even though she'd always known which cemetery she was buried in, and she'd certainly never felt the need to introduce herself. But this was different, she reasoned. That was before she'd read the diary and felt such a personal connection to the people within it. Knowing that Alexander, that cautious young man she had related to so easily, was actually lying somewhere beneath her was disconcerting. As disconcerting as the anger she suddenly felt towards Lady Constance, how dare she describe Alexander as her beloved son after what she had done to him? And then it occurred to her it wasn't just Alexander she was descended from; Lady Constance was a part of her genetic mix too, probably most of these people were. It was a strange sensation, simultaneously grounding her, connecting her to this very place, but also unsettling her, changing what she had previously thought about her place in the world. If the grass, trees, and plants growing around her were being enriched by the remains of her ancestors, did that mean she was as much a part of Ardmhor as someone born and bred here like Andrew? He'd said that people tended to leave and then return. So far, she'd spent her life elsewhere, but now she too had returned, even though she hadn't known that was what she was doing at the time. Perhaps she really did belong here, after all.

Beth pulled her coat tighter around her. Clouds had pushed their way across the sky, preventing the sun from breaking through, so although the level of light had grown since she'd left her room, the chill in the air hadn't diminished. As she noticed her teeth gently chattering, she pulled herself back to standing and made her way out of the churchyard. She checked the time quickly as she made her way back along the road to the house. Although it was Sunday, the house and grounds were open every day during the tourist season, and she was scheduled to work. She felt like she'd been out for hours, but in reality, it was still very early. With a good while before her shift started, Beth ambled along the path leading to the viewpoint. She didn't want to arrive back at her room too soon. She was really hoping Andrew would have left first.

She didn't expect anyone in Ardmhor House to be awake to observe her progress, so she was surprised to hear Alex's voice within minutes of sitting down.

"You're up early. Couldn't you sleep?"

"Something like that. I finished Eliza's diary and then I went to the churchyard."

"Oh," Alex stiffened slightly, but he didn't offer anything else in response. Instead, he sat looking at her, waiting for her to add more.

"Alexander is definitely my great-great-grandfather, but he died. I mean, I know he'd have been dead by now, but he was only twenty-five. He never spoke to Eliza again after she moved to Manchester and he never met his daughter, my great-grandmother. Reading about it made me cry, and then I wanted to see his grave. I think I wanted to make him real. I've sort of seen him and Eliza as characters in a book, the fact that they actually lived and that I'm related to both of them, is hard to take in."

"And did it help? Did seeing the grave make him real?"

"Sort of. I mean, seeing that whole churchyard full of people related to me made me feel like I really do belong here, that I'm not just a visitor on an extended holiday. But I didn't feel closer to Alexander. He's still only real in the diary. I couldn't imagine him being there in the ground."

"I think that's how it is. I don't think anyone really is in their grave. I think they are in the places they loved, or with the people that they cared for and that cared for them."

"I hope so. I just feel so sad for him. Eliza ended up happy, whereas it seems Alexander was still here alone. He never escaped like she did. He just stayed here doing what his parents wanted, and then he was gone."

Alex got up and wandered to the far side of the viewpoint. He looked off into the distance, over the sea and the hills, not seeming to know what to say. Eventually, Beth walked over to him, taking hold of his hand.

"What are you thinking about?"

"Alexander wouldn't want you to feel sorry for him. Remember, it was never him that wanted to escape Ardmhor. That was part of the problem. Also, he isn't really gone. You exist because he existed, and you're here talking about him now, so that means he's still here. I'm sure he'd have had regrets. Regrets that he wasn't brave enough to leave the security of this place, and regrets that he missed out on what could have been. But I think he'd want you to use those regrets to help you, rather than feeling sad for him. He'd want you to use them as a reminder to take every opportunity that comes your way, so that you don't end up with regrets of your own. In fact, I know that's what he'd think, and I know that he'd be proud of the fact you're already doing it."

"It's a lovely thought, but I'm not sure I believe people are aware of anything after they're gone."

"I didn't either, but the longer I've been around, the more I realise things aren't as straightforward as life and death. Connections are stronger and more complicated than that."

Beth looked at him closely. His expression was wistful, and dots started to connect in her mind. Was it something much more serious than a simple breakup that had left him unable to move on? Was that why he was so adamant his relationship couldn't be repaired? She was wondering how she could broach the subject sensitively when Alex spoke again.

"I sound like a proper old man, don't I? Here, help me to a seat," he joked, rubbing his back and taking exaggerated hobbling steps back to the bench. "So, is the diary the only reason you're up early?"

"No, I'm escaping my room, or rather, what's in my room."

"Now, that does sound interesting."

"You're probably going to think I've not paid attention to anything you've said, but I slept with Andrew last night. Then I just had this feeling, like I didn't want him in my room anymore. So I basically ran away to avoid talking to him."

"Right, so have you decided you don't like

him? Is that what the problem is?"

Beth hesitated. "I do like him, but I don't like him as much as I like you." She looked down at her feet. "That's why I think you and Megan will be disappointed in me. I like Andrew, but that's as far as it goes, so I'm basically still throwing myself at anyone who's interested, rather than waiting for someone special."

"Oh Beth, that isn't what I meant, and I'm sure Megan didn't either. I'm so sorry if I've made you feel bad about yourself. It seemed you only thought you were worth something if a man liked you, whereas I wanted you to see your own opinion of yourself is all that matters. From what you've told me about Megan, it sounds like she was just trying to encourage you to do the same: to be yourself and know that's good enough."

"And I have been myself with Andrew. I haven't even been trying to impress him."

"So why do you think Megan would be disappointed in you?"

"Because I know he's not what I really want, so I should be able to just be happy on my own."

"The thing is though, Beth, some people take years to meet the right person. I don't think anyone would expect them to spend every moment alone until that happens. Just because you don't think something's going to last forever doesn't automatically mean it's wrong."

"But I know I'd rather have been with you,"

Beth said again, blushing.

Alex moved closer, putting his arm around her shoulders, giving her a gentle squeeze. "That can't happen, though, so as long as Andrew isn't expecting a lifelong commitment from you, I can't see a problem with two people enjoying each other's company."

"But I thought you were both encouraging me to be really sure of what I wanted, rather than making a play for anyone that's interested?"

"Yes, but that doesn't mean never having fun, or never connecting to anyone unless you're certain it's forever—and it sounds like you wanted this at the time. Sometimes you have to take opportunities as they present themselves, sometimes you won't know if they're what you really want until you accept them. You need to stop worrying about making mistakes. That's what stopped me taking chances that I should have, and I've had to live with the regret. Believe me, that is a much worse outcome than looking silly, or even than having to start all over again."

"So, what do you think I should do now?"

"Maybe apologise for running off? I know if I was Andrew, I wouldn't be feeling great right now."

Beth couldn't help thinking that she wouldn't have been running off if it had been Alex in her bed, but she took his point.

"I'd better get going," she said after a minute.

"I have to get ready for work. Thank you for chatting though. It's helped me to put things into perspective. Maybe you should try opening up a bit. It might help you as well."

Alex gave her hand a gentle squeeze as she got up.

"I really wish things could have been different between us," he whispered.

Beth gave him a tight smile, but she didn't reply. It was the first time since they'd met that she hadn't been able to believe him. As far as she could see, the only person stopping things from happening between them was him. If he really wanted things to be different, well, then they would be, so his words couldn't be true.

CHAPTER
THIRTY-ONE

All was quiet as Beth entered the staff accommodation block. She hadn't really got to know the other people living there yet, instead she'd taken the easy option of retreating to her room with the excuse of studying for her course. That would need to change, she told herself sternly. She had to make friends if she was going to commit to building a life here. As she turned the handle on her door, she was torn between hoping Andrew would still be there, so she could get her apologies out of the way, and hoping he'd be gone, so she could put it off. The door opened to reveal an empty room with a neatly made bed, and Beth was happy enough with the outcome.

It was the second time she'd worked a day

at the house with barely any sleep, and this time she wasn't pulling it off so well. She kept losing her train of thought mid-sentence, and it was noticeable enough for Kath to pack her off to lunch early. The huge cheese toastie and the injection of caffeine helped her get through the afternoon, but by the time her shift ended, all she wanted was sleep. Leaving the house, Beth automatically pulled out her phone, checking for any messages. She felt herself deflate when she saw a text from Andrew.

'You could have woken me,' he'd written. 'I hope I'm wrong in feeling you wanted to escape. I'm working tonight. Call in for a chat?'

It was the last thing she wanted to do, but she knew Alex had been right about Andrew. She hadn't behaved well that morning, and she needed to make things right. With a sigh, she made her way back to her room, not to collapse into bed as she so desperately wanted, but to get changed and head out to the pub.

"So what was the disappearing act about?" Andrew asked as he handed over her pint of cider.

"I'm sorry." Beth's face scrunched up involuntarily. "I had a really lovely time, but I just panicked this morning. It all seemed a bit too much."

"I'm moving to Mexico the day after tomorrow!" Andrew replied, amusement clear in his voice. "Exactly how serious did you think things were going to get? Did you think I'd been looking up quickie marriages while you were in the loo?"

"Well, no."

"So what had you so worried then?"

"I don't know," Beth sighed, feeling even more ridiculous now and knowing she'd never be able to explain. "I'm just rubbish at relationships."

"Well, that's alright then, because we've already established this isn't one. It's just two people having a good time before one of them disappears for a couple of years."

"So you're not annoyed with me?"

"Of course not. I had a great time yesterday. I was just worried about you, but now I know you're alright, I can relax and enjoy the memories." He winked at her, causing a blush to creep across her face, until it almost matched her hair. "Anyway, being abandoned was probably good for me: I've done my fair bit of sneaking off in the past, and I have to admit, I didn't like it much when the shoe was on the other foot."

"I'm sure they'll have coped. You're not all that," Beth replied with a grin.

Andrew treated her to his best 'deeply hurt' face, before reaching over the bar and pulling her into a kiss, earning himself a telling off from his boss.

As the taxi taking Andrew to the station pulled away from the Ardmhor Hotel a couple of days later, Beth had a moment of clarity. Although another friend was leaving, she realised she was feeling optimistic. With Eilidh and Rich stood either side of her, and others waiting inside for her to join them, she finally felt like she was putting down roots. After she'd cleared things up with Andrew the other night, she had forced herself to sit in the communal area of the staff block, rather than rushing straight to her room. Of the five others that shared the accommodation, only three were about. Brad, who was originally from Australia but had been travelling the world for some time, was spending the summer working in the gardens. He was the only one of the housemates to have arrived at Ardmhor before Beth. The others had all been employed at the same time as her. Dieter, from Germany, and Louise, from London, were both working in the shop and ticket office, so had finished work for the day at the same time as Beth. The other two residents of the house were Camille and Hugo, who hailed from France and Spain, respectively. They were both employed in the café, which meant some late shifts on the four nights a week it served evening meals. With the aid of a shared bottle of wine, Beth actually enjoyed sitting and chatting, swapping stories about what had brought them to Ardmhor. She'd made the effort to spend time with both Camille and Hugo the next day as well, and all of them had accepted her invitation to join her at the pub on the night of Andrew's send off. Each of them, apart from Beth, would move on when the season ended, so it wasn't like they'd be able to provide her with a permanent social network, but as Alex had pointed out, not everything you invested time in had to last forever. Sometimes, you just had to make the most of things while you could.

As Beth walked home, surrounded by her housemates, she noticed a gigantic moon suspended in the clear sky. It looked so similar to that first night at Ardmhor, it almost took her breath away. It seemed so long ago now, the night she'd first met Alex, when he'd studied her so intently it was like he'd seen straight through her. Before she'd had chance to think, she'd made her excuses to the others, and her feet were following the familiar path to the viewpoint.

For the first time, she didn't need to wait for Alex to appear. She could already see the reassuring shape of him on the bench.

"I really need to talk to you, Beth," he said, before she'd had time to take a seat. "I've been thinking about what I said to you as you were leaving the other day, when I said that I wished things could be different between us. I could see in your eyes that you didn't believe me, and to be honest, why would you? It must be impossible for you to understand what I mean, and you're right—the only way you will be able to understand is if I tell you the truth."

Beth's heart rate increased. "You know you can trust me with anything, don't you?" she said, scooping his hands into her own and looking straight at him.

"I don't doubt that I can trust you, Beth. I just hope you'll be able to understand why I've kept this from you for so long."

She didn't reply, but kept her eyes focused on his instead, giving him time to continue.

"When I first met you, I was completely taken aback. You reminded me so much of her, but you were different as well. You said things she would never have said, and you worried about silly things, things that would have concerned me in the past. I was overjoyed at the connection I felt to you, and I couldn't understand why I had been given such an unexpected gift. Then I realised it wasn't that you were a gift to me. I was supposed to help you. I needed to tell you about my mistakes, so that you'd be able to avoid making them yourself."

"And you have, you've helped me loads. I'd never have applied for the job here without your encouragement, and I am so glad that I did."

"But you still don't know the truth, Beth. I knew that once you understood who I really was, you wouldn't be able to see me in the same way, and I didn't want our time together to end. I still don't, but I realise now that it has to. There is a reason we found each other. I was supposed to help you learn from my mistakes, and you were supposed to help me accept the choices I made in the past. You were to help me finally move on. The problem is, I got too attached. I wanted the next stage of my journey to be here with you, but it can't be. You have a life to lead that doesn't involve me. So I finally need to be honest with you."

"Alex, will you please just trust me? There is nothing you could say that will change how I feel about you."

"I think this will, Beth, and I know for certain it will change how you see me. I need you to follow these instructions. The book that Eliza talked about in her diary, the one they hid their notes in, it's still there in the library. You need to ask Lady A to get it for you. It's to the left of the door on the third shelf up, tucked right next to the door frame so it's almost out of sight. The back cover is slightly thicker than the front, and if you push down on the top of it, it will slide out at the bottom, revealing the compartment. Can you remember that? You might need to make a note."

"I can remember, but I'll make a note on my phone in case. Wouldn't it be easier for you to get it yourself though?"

"You said I could trust you, Beth, and you're going to need to trust me. Everything you need to know is hidden in that compartment."

"But why can't you just tell me?"

"Because I don't think I could. Please trust me and ask Lady A for the book. It will all make sense then. I just hope you can forgive me once you've read everything."

He was so intense that Beth suddenly felt fearful.

"You're scaring me. I don't see what can be so bad."

"I'm sorry, that's not my intention. I just know this is the last time you'll see me like this, and I wish it wasn't."

He got up then, pulling Beth to her feet and drawing her into a hug. He hugged her so tightly and for so long that she felt he was trying to absorb her. Eventually, he pulled away, straightening himself up and looking deep into her eyes.

"I want to say promise me you'll be happy, but I realise no one can promise that, so promise me you'll be kind to yourself instead."

Alex stopped speaking, simply drinking her in, never once breaking contact with her eyes. They were rooted to the spot, and an eternity passed in the briefest of moments, until Alex freed himself with a small shake of his head.

"Right, well, I suppose this is it. Goodbye, Beth."

He turned to go, his face sad and resigned.

"It's only goodnight, I hope," Beth replied quietly.

Alex had already walked a short distance up the path, but then he turned and softly called back to her, "Beth, I know there is someone for you, someone not that far away, and I know that when you meet him, you will have no doubt."

And then he was gone.

CHAPTER
THIRTY-TWO

The first thing Beth did the next morning was to text Lady Angela and ask her to look for Alex and Eliza's secret book. Angela replied within minutes, excited that the book might still be in the house and intrigued by how Beth knew. With only half an hour before her shift was due to start, Beth replied quickly, saying that she'd fill her in on the details when she saw her later.

The morning seemed to drag on endlessly. At one point, Beth wondered whether her watch had stopped working. She found it hard to concentrate on giving visitors an introduction to the room she was hosting and struggled to retrieve the facts necessary to answer their questions. Her mind only seemed to have room for Alex and what his secret might be. His manner had been so odd the previous night. He was always intense, but this had been on a different level. He was so certain that once she knew his story, she'd never want to see him again. Whereas she honestly couldn't imagine anything bad enough to change her feelings. The finality of his goodbye had scared her. Partly because of the possibility she had got him wrong. Maybe he had done something terrible, and she'd spent all those dark nights falling in love with a monster. But mainly, it had scared her because she couldn't imagine her life without him in it. No, she told herself, that wouldn't be the case. They would be sitting at the viewpoint as usual by the time evening came around. Alex had only ever been gentle and caring. He had challenged her at times, but she couldn't bring herself to believe he was capable of doing anything that could seriously repulse her.

She allowed herself to imagine a new scenario instead: Alex waiting distraught at the viewpoint, herself walking towards him. Her hair would be perfect, and her photoshoot worthy dress would float gently around her legs. As the sun set dramatically in front of them, the temperature would have risen by at least fifteen degrees, and all midges would have mysteriously disappeared. Alex would turn, startled by her approach, and amazed by her acceptance of him. He would walk towards her, taking her hands in his. There would be no barriers between them. Now that she knew everything, there'd be nothing to stand in the way of his passion for her. He'd stare into her eyes and then he'd.... "

"Beth, are you alright?" Lady Angela's voice brought her back down to earth with a bump. "I've got the book. Why don't you come to the old office as soon as your shift finishes? Then you can fill me in on everything."

"Great," Beth replied, a little too brightly, embarrassed by her daydream.

"Are you sure you're alright? You look a bit flushed. Do you think you might be coming down with something?"

"No, I'm fine, honestly. I'll see you later."

She couldn't bring herself to give the truthful answer! She hadn't thought it possible, but after Angela left, time seemed to creep forward even more slowly. Beth found herself willing the visitors to leave so she could finally discover the answers to her questions.

"Oh Beth, thank goodness you're here! Hasn't today seemed long?"

Lady Angela greeted her from the large desk in the centre of the office. The book was in front of her, and she didn't wait for a response before continuing.

"I've been so desperate to know what's inside. I've literally been counting the minutes."

Beth sat down next to her, looking at the book where it lay on the desk. It was an average sized, if fairly chunky, hard backed book. The black cover had faded slightly with age, and the words 'History of the MacAird Clan' were embossed in gold on the spine. It didn't look special. No one glancing at it would guess the secrets it held.

"I know," Beth said. "I feel like I've done nothing but watch the clock all day."

"I don't know why it surprised me the book was still here. Nothing ever seems to get thrown away, but I wouldn't have been able to find it without your instructions. It was so tucked into the edge of the shelf it was practically hidden."

"I still don't see why Alex couldn't just get it himself though."

"Well, I suppose we'll find out soon enough. Did you find out anything else of interest when you finished the diary?"

"Oh blimey, yes. I'd totally forgotten with all the intrigue over the secret book, and I'd been really excited about telling you. So, I've told you before that I'm descended from Eliza's first child, who we'd thought belonged to Eliza and her husband William. Well, we've now found out that she wasn't William's child after all. Her father was actually Alexander. I mean, this is what the diary says, and the dates fit. They even named the baby after him, but there isn't anything official because the birth certificate names William as the father. So if it is true, which I think it is, it means Alexander is my great-great-grandfather. Which would mean I'm not just connected to Ardmhor because Eliza lived here—I'm connected because the MacAirds are my ancestors too."

"Gosh, Beth, that's amazing, and to think you've found this out since you got the job here. It makes me feel it was all meant to be. It'll be such a great story for when we open the museum: that the person in charge of telling our story has found out it's their story too. I just love it."

Angela reached over, pulling Beth into a hug. "Welcome home!"

"Thank you. I really am starting to feel that I belong here."

"You'd belong here even if there wasn't a family connection, but I'm glad you're finally feeling it. Right, shall we get on with what we've been dying to do all day? Were there any instructions for the secret compartment?"

"Yes," Beth said, picking the book up and turning it over.

As Alex had told her, the back cover was thicker than the front. It was obvious when you looked, but you'd never have noticed when it was on the shelf. There was a slight ridge all around the top, so Beth pushed down gently on the area within the ridge. At first, it didn't seem as if anything was going to happen, so Beth increased the pressure slightly, and then she felt it move. A very thin drawer now revealed itself at the bottom of the book, and Beth gently pulled it open. A yellowed piece of paper was folded inside. With trembling hands, she carefully unfolded it and smoothed it out on the table in front of them.

"My dearest Eliza," she read out loud, and then she stopped. "I don't understand. This is to Eliza, but Alex said it would explain everything about him."

"Well, it might," said Lady Angela, sounding a little confused. "We won't know until we read it, will we? Now come on, I've been waiting all day for this."

So Beth looked back at the paper and began reading again.

CHAPTER THIRTY-THREE

My dearest Eliza,

There is so much I want to tell you, and I don't really know where to begin. I think I will start by telling you where I am. At the moment, I am on a train, travelling towards the Scottish border, and the reason for that is I have been to see you. I have been to your home in Manchester, and I saw you stood outside. You looked so beautiful and content that my heart soared. I saw our daughter too. Our daughter! After you left, I didn't imagine I would ever get to write such words. Oh, what a joy she is to behold, with her chubby legs and her mass of curls. It took every ounce of strength I possess not to run to you both, but there was a reason I didn't. It was because I also saw your husband. I know he must be a good man from what you have written in your letters. I trust your judgment, Eliza (well, perhaps leaving aside the mistaken trust you placed in me), so I was not reluctant to approach because I feared his reaction: I knew I had his permission to visit. It wasn't so much the fact he was there that held me back: it was the fact that he exists. Seeing him made him real and seeing how you and that beautiful child responded to him made me question whether I had a right to encroach on your life. You both lit up when you saw him walking towards the house. I don't think I've ever seen a better depiction of love. Then, when you placed his hand on your stomach, I saw what I hadn't at first noticed. Your family was expanding into one in which I definitely had no right to a place. I didn't want to intrude on that happiness by even the smallest measure. You deserve the love that I could see surrounding you and I would never want to harm that, so I left. I don't feel I'm being cowardly this time. On the contrary, this feels like the bravest and most difficult action I've ever taken, but I know it is the right one. However, I want to explain everything, so you can understand why I didn't leave Ardmhor with you. I want you to be free from any doubt or worry about me.

The night before you left Ardmhor was the most wonderful of my life. I want you to know I don't regret anything that happened between us, especially now I have seen the incredible child we created. But although it was wonderful, I was also a little afraid: afraid of how easy it had been to throw away all of my self-control. Just as I was finishing gathering my things together, Mother appeared in my room. As you know, I'd hoped only to deal with Father before leaving. Mother's volatility seeming a much more daunting prospect. However, she surprised me in several ways. She was very calm and in control as she spoke. She informed me she had known of our relationship for some time, and although she felt it totally unsuitable, she hadn't been too concerned, as she'd been confident it would soon run its course. I contradicted her. I told her we were very serious, and we intended to marry. However, she stopped me, telling me I was not aware of the full story. It is here I wish I had acted differently. I wish I had told her to stop, told her I had no interest in anything she had to say. Unfortunately, I can't change the past. So, ever the dutiful son, not wanting to upset anyone, I allowed her to continue.

She told me she had not been concerned because she knew I wasn't the only man you were involved with. She said you had carried on dalliances with at least two members of staff and those were only the incidents of which she was aware. In her version of events, that was why she had been so angry with you and so keen to remove you from the household. I argued with her that there was no way this could be true, that it wasn't within your nature, but she told me I was a silly boy blinded by love. She told me she knew of these relationships for certain because you yourself had confessed them to Flora, who had then relayed the information to her. I still did not believe her, and I said to her that even if it was true, I didn't care, that I knew that then, at that moment, I was the only man you cared for, but she hadn't finished. At that point, she actually laughed at me. She said she knew what had taken place between us the previous night and if I believed that proved I was your true love, I was a greater fool than she'd thought. According to her, the only thing my actions proved were that I was not the right man for you. How could I hope to protect you when I could not even behave decently around you? She argued that you were of a different background to me and that it would be impossible for you to live the life of a lady without a strong man to guide you. My behaviour, she said, had only proved I could never be that man. How could I possibly guide you when I was too weak to control myself? She said that if I truly loved you, then I had to let you go. I had to let you make a fresh start where you wanted to be, with a man more suitable for you. She was certain that if you remained with me, I would not be enough.

I want you to know I never believed her accusations against you. Even with the fears that have always plagued me, I knew deep down there was no truth in her claims. But I am ashamed to admit I had enough doubt in myself to allow her words to destroy our plans. I never believed you'd been unfaithful to me, but I was too easily convinced that I wasn't good enough for you, that you needed more. I suppose perhaps she was right. If I had been a stronger person, her words couldn't have taken hold. So no great calamity was responsible for my failure to meet you, just a few words from my mother that easily hit their target and proved my love for you was not as strong as my self-doubt. It is the greatest regret of my life that I did not ignore her words and run down the drive to be with you. But I am at least comforted by the knowledge that my weakness has not permanently harmed you and that you have indeed found a more suitable man.

I feel terrible for what you must have suffered when you first left. You must have thought I did not care for you at all when you received no word from me. I have no excuse for not writing. I knew where the Hardwicks lived. There was nothing stopping me from explaining to you what had happened, but I foolishly allowed myself to be led by Mother again, yet another example of my weakness. She told me it would be better for you if I left you alone, pointing out that you had not written to me and arguing I should respect your wishes not to make contact. I know it should have occurred to me she was not being honest, that she was acting from motivations other than your happiness, but I had become so accepting of my uselessness that I allowed myself to be convinced. Had I known of your letters, I would have acted differently. Even the weakest version of me would never have left you to carry our child alone, but that still doesn't excuse my behaviour. I should have acted differently. I shouldn't have given up.

The only reason I came to know of our daughter is because Mother became ill, and the fever prevented her from leaving her bed. It just so happened that I was by the front door when the man arrived delivering the post. I offered to take it from him, but he refused. He apologised and explained he was under strict instructions to hand all post directly to Lady Constance. When I explained she was bedridden and said I would take it straight to her, he relented and handed it over. I hadn't really thought anything of the conversation, but as I made my way up the stairs, intending to do exactly as I had said, I noticed what looked like your writing on one of the envelopes. When I examined it more closely, I saw that it was indeed your hand, and it was addressed to me.

The letter I read from you filled me with equal amounts of joy and horror. Joy to hear of this wonderful child who bore my name and shared my colouring. Horror that you had faced all of this alone. It was clear this was not the first letter you had written to me, so I set out to find the others. With Mother incapacitated, there was no one to stop me searching her desk. I had known of the secret compartment within it since childhood explorations with James and Flora, so the missing letters would always have been easy to discover had I only thought to look. My heart ached as I read them. Knowing that you had understood the situation correctly, yet still loved me, was hard to bear. Your love for me was so much more than I had ever deserved. Although my heart broke for what might have been, I was almost relieved when I read the letter enclosing the locket. Knowing that you were happy and loved, even though I had let you down so badly, was at least some comfort. The generosity of your husband, in allowing the child he would raise to have my name, told me he was a much better man than I could ever hope to be.

That you were willing for me to meet my daughter, after all the ways I had let you down, amazed me. Finally, I found the courage I had always lacked. I hid the letters away in my room to keep them safe, tucked the locket into our book, along with the picture of us that I have always kept there, and headed straight to the station. However, as you have already read, once I saw you, I decided that the braver course of action was to let you go. My mother's behaviour was completely wrong, and I don't know whether I will ever be able to forgive her. However, it isn't entirely her fault that I'm not married to you, raising our daughter with you, or living a life with you. I have to accept responsibility for the fact I wasn't brave enough.

So perhaps in a way Mother was right: I wasn't the man for you. You would never have been happy remaining at Ardmhor, and I had never really wanted to leave. Perhaps in a different place, in a different time, our love could have survived, but seeing the contentment on your face as you welcomed your husband home, I know you are with the right man now.

So be happy, Eliza. I will always love you, but I know it is time to move on. Please don't feel any guilt over your happiness. I am in the place I am supposed to be. In fact, I am almost back at Inveravain. It has taken me many stops and starts to express myself adequately. Ardmhor is where I belong and where I am happy to stay. Hopefully, I too will have another chance at love. Maybe I can persuade Mother to throw another of her matchmaking parties! I won't be able to post this straight away. It will have to spend a little time tucked away in our book because I have neither stamp nor envelope to hand, and I don't have the energy to do anything other than head straight to Ardmhor once we reach Inveravain. That's another reason why staying away from you was the correct decision. If this malaise is a sign of the illness mother has been suffering from, I am grateful I cannot have passed it on to you or your family, especially given your current condition. I would ask, if you don't mind, that you continue to inform me of Alexandrina's progress. I am not selfless enough to forgo all knowledge of her. But I promise you, Eliza, you have nothing to fear from me. She is William's child now, and I will have no involvement in her life. Don't have any regrets, I feel I carry enough for both of us. But alongside them, I carry my memories of our love, and I will never regret that.

All my love,

Alex.

CHAPTER THIRTY-FOUR

Both Beth and Lady Angela were in tears by the time they reached the end of the letter. They busied themselves finding tissues to make sure they didn't damage Alexander's precious words.

"He loved her so much," Angela said between sniffs. "The fact he just wanted her to be happy, even though she'd moved on, tells me his love was much stronger than he gave himself credit for. It's just heart-breaking that she never got to see this."

"But I think she knew all this, even without seeing the letter. She was convinced she'd seen him in Manchester, and she always believed it was Lady Constance that kept them apart."

"Oh, if I could get my hands on that woman,

she'd know about it," Angela interrupted. "How she could mess with her son's emotions like that is beyond me."

"I know. I can't understand her either. But Eliza definitely understood Alexander. She didn't really blame him for not leaving with her. She knew how hard he found things, and she didn't want him to feel guilty and blame himself. It's just sad that they loved each other so much, but it still didn't work out."

"It sounds as if Eliza was truly happy though," said Lady Angela.

"Yes, Mum says that she always talked about William very fondly."

"I suppose Alexander could have been just as happy eventually, if he'd lived a bit longer."

"Yes, perhaps he could have been," Beth replied.

"It shows you can never know the right course of action. If Eliza hadn't been so keen to leave, maybe they could have been happy here, or maybe she'd have resented Alexander and their love would have disappeared anyway. And, of course, if she'd stayed here, your family could look very different. If Eliza had never left Scotland, you might not even exist. Even if Alexander had been brave enough to go with her, maybe he'd have regretted leaving Ardmhor instead. It's impossible to know."

"It's just a shame he didn't live long enough

to move on himself." Beth said, something troubling her she couldn't quite put her finger on.

"It really is. Twenty-five is no age at all."

They sat for a while, musing over the contents of the letter, before Lady Angela finally broke the silence.

"There's something I don't understand. Before we started reading the letter, you seemed surprised it was to Eliza, but you said that Alexander had said it would explain everything. What did you mean? Wouldn't you have expected the letter to be to Eliza? Who else would Alexander have been explaining things to? Also, how did Alexander tell you where the book was? I'd assumed you'd got all this information from the diary, but Alexander wouldn't have been writing in there. I'm confused, Beth."

"Oh, I see. I never really explained properly, did I? And I still don't actually know how the letter explains anything. The location of the book wasn't in the diary, and I didn't mean that Alexander had told me where to look. It was Alex that said the book would explain everything and gave me the instructions, you know, your Alex."

"*My* Alex?" Lady Angela now looked totally confused.

"Yes, *your* Alex, your son. I mean, that's weird too. I don't know why he couldn't just tell me what was going on, and I have no idea why he wanted me to read about it with you, but he said the contents of the book would explain everything, and I didn't really question it. I just wanted to know what had been bothering him so much, but the book hasn't told me that anyway."

"I'm still confused, how do you know my son?" asked Angela.

"Because I've met him since coming here," replied Beth, thinking that should be obvious.

"But that's not possible, Beth."

"Why not?" Beth asked, now as confused as Lady Angela.

"It's not possible because my Alexander isn't here. He's been working in South America for the last year, and he won't be back until December."

"But I've been meeting him ever since I got here. Are you sure?"

"Of course I'm sure, love. I know he's there because Jim's with him at the moment. That's where Jim's been. He went to New York for a clan conference, and then he flew down to spend some time with Ali. Jim will be back this weekend, but Ali still has another couple of months out there."

"Ali?"

"Yes, that's the other reason I know you haven't been talking to my son. He only ever refers to himself as Ali."

"So who have I been talking to?"

"I don't know, Beth, and how could they have known about the book?"

They sat in silence again, both unsure what to think or do. Once again it was Angela who spoke first.

"I've just thought of something else: the locket is missing. Alexander said he put it in the book along with a photo of them. Is there anything else in there?"

Beth picked up the book and felt in the tiny drawer that protruded from it. When she pressed down, she realised that what had appeared to be the base of the drawer was actually the back of a photograph, and when she prised it out of the drawer, it revealed a gold locket hidden underneath. As Beth turned the photograph over, she gasped. At the bottom of the picture were the words - 'Eliza and Alexander on the front lawn'. Above those words, standing outside Ardmhor House, was her great-great-grandmother. She had flowers in her hair and a huge smile on her face, making her look so different from her wedding portrait, making her look much more like Beth. But it wasn't this recognition that had made Beth gasp. Eliza wasn't the only familiar sight in the photograph. What had really shocked Beth was the face of the man standing next to Eliza. It was the face of the man Beth had been talking to at the viewpoint. The man who'd told her the book would explain everything.

CHAPTER
THIRTY-FIVE

"It isn't possible," Beth kept repeating, turning the locket over and over in her hand.

She was still sitting in the old office, surrounded by the antique bookcases and cupboards, at the desk where Alexander himself must have gone about his work all those years ago. Lady Angela had placed a cup of hot tea in front of her, and although Beth didn't like tea, she was sipping it anyway, not noticing what it was. She'd looked at the photograph what felt like a thousand times now, as well as the image of Alexander within the locket, but the pictures hadn't changed. They still looked exactly like the man she'd been meeting, the man she thought she was in love with.

"It must just be someone who looks like him," she said after a while. "I mean, I look quite like Eliza in that picture."

"But you don't look exactly the same, Beth. Anyone could see the difference. That's not what you seem to be saying about this man. Right, so if we're assuming the man you've been talking to can't be the man in the photograph, who could he be?" Angela asked. "What else did he tell you about himself?"

"I don't know. When I think about it, he never really told me anything about himself. He had an almost English accent, just the odd Scottish hint here and there. He didn't actually say he lived in Ardmhor House, but it was definitely implied. Also, he said he had a brother called James. So everything fitted with him being your son. If I ever asked him about himself, or what he did, he'd make excuses—saying that he was just hanging about, or that there wasn't much to tell. The only thing I know about his life is that he has a lot of regrets about a failed relationship, and he had some sort of secret that he said the book would explain to me."

"I can see why you thought he was Ali, some of those details would fit, and Ali does have a look of the man in the photo. But I don't think he's ever had his heart broken, and he's quite an open book. He'd have happily told you about his job and anything else. Anyway, we know it can't be

Ali, and I also know there isn't anyone who looks like the man in that picture living on the estate at the moment. So I honestly don't know who he could be."

"Are you absolutely certain it couldn't be Ali? Could he have come home early without telling anyone?"

"What, and meet you for chats, but never actually come to the house or say hello to me? It's not really likely, is it? Anyway, I know for definite he's not here because Jim's out there with him at the moment."

"But I can't have been talking to my great-great-grandfather, who's been dead for over a hundred years. Things like that aren't possible, are they?"

Lady Angela hesitated before she next spoke.

"Look, I don't want to insult you, but I have to ask. You're certain you haven't imagined this, that you haven't got so caught up in the diary that you've somehow made Alexander seem real?"

"No!" Beth almost shouted. "The person I've been talking to is real. I've hugged him and touched him. He's definitely solid flesh and bone. Also, I first met him before I knew the diary existed, before I even knew Eliza had a connection to Ardmhor."

"I'm sorry. I'm only trying to understand. Let's just go over things again, see if we're missing something. Is there anything else you know about him?"

Beth trawled through all the details of their conversations in her mind, but there was so little he had told her about his life.

"He was very evasive about himself. We only ever met at the viewpoint and only when no one else was around. He told me he couldn't go to the Ardmhor Hotel, but he wouldn't explain why. Oh, and he told me I reminded him of the girl he was so heartbroken over."

"So you've only ever seen him at the viewpoint?"

"Well, I've only spoken to him there. Sometimes I've seen him in the distance elsewhere, but only ever in the grounds."

"Did you arrange to meet, or was it by chance?"

"He was always just there. Every time I went to the viewpoint after visitor hours, he would appear. I asked him how he seemed to know when I was out there, and he said that most of the windows of the house look at the path, so it was easy to spot me."

"He's right. You can see the path easily from the house, but only if you're next to the window. Even though you've obviously been to the viewpoint loads of times, I've never spotted you heading out there. Also, no one resembling the man in those pictures lives in Ardmhor House.

So how could the person you've been meeting have known you'd be there? It's a bit creepy, really."

"I suppose it is. When I thought he was your son, it seemed to make sense."

"Alright. So are you absolutely certain the man in the picture, who it says is Alexander, is the man you've been talking to?"

"I'm certain he looks exactly the same. But I don't see how it can be him."

"And the man you've been chatting to, who looks exactly like the picture, calls himself Alex?"

"Yes."

"Which is what Alexander tells Eliza she should call him, isn't it?"

"Yes," Beth replied again.

"And he said you look like his lost love, and we know you look like Eliza. And he told you the book contained the answers about him, and we found the truth about Alexander and Eliza in there."

"Well, yes," Beth agreed hesitantly, unsure where this was going.

"So basically, everything suggests the man you've been talking to is Alexander MacAird, who died in 1895. Alexander from the diary."

"But he can't be."

"Well, I know it doesn't seem likely, but as people say, if it looks like a duck and quacks like a duck, it probably is a duck. Maybe we need to accept that it is possible?"

Beth leaned back in her seat and looked at Lady Angela, considering her for a moment. As usual, she was wearing tall waterproof boots, with jeans and an Ardmhor fleece, her hair pulled back into a sensible ponytail. Everything about her seemed so practical and down to earth. Surely she couldn't believe that?

"When I first arrived here," Lady Angela continued, "a few of the older ladies liked to tell me folk tales about the area. They claimed Ardmhor was a 'thin' place, a place where the divide between worlds is thinner than usual, so there is less to separate the living and the dead. They had lots of ghost stories to tell."

Beth shivered slightly. Hearing the sensible Lady Angela talk about ghosts as if they could be real had made the hairs on her scalp creep up.

"But you didn't believe them, did you? You've never seen anything?"

"Well, I've never been certain I have, but I did have a strange thing happen when I first came here. It was when I was struggling to feel settled, and the funny thing is it happened at the viewpoint. It was after all the visitors had gone. I was sitting out there in tears, thinking I'd never fit in, when suddenly I heard a voice right next to me. I'd been sure the viewpoint was empty, and I hadn't heard anyone approach.

Anyway, this lovely young man was just sitting there beside me. He reassured me—telling me he knew I belonged here and that I was a part of the future of Ardmhor. I'd never seen him before, but he spoke about me with absolute certainty, and his manner made him seem older than he looked. Anyway, as I was searching through my pocket for another hanky, he just vanished. It was weird and, because of all the ladies' stories, I did wonder if maybe he'd been some sort of ghost, but I also told myself I hadn't noticed him arrive, so maybe I just didn't notice him leave. I never saw him again, anyway. He seemed a bit familiar at the time, and all the MacAird men have a slight look of each other. Looking at the photo, it could have been him, but it was so long ago I couldn't be sure."

Beth stood up, readying herself to leave. The idea she'd been meeting with some sort of resident ghost, who loitered around the viewpoint waiting to reassure young women, and who also happened to be her great-great-grandfather, was just too absurd to accept. Then a thought struck her.

"There is an obvious way to solve this. I could just go out there tonight and ask him who he is. Do you mind if I keep hold of the book and things for now?"

"Not at all, they're yours. You have the closest connection to them. I think I should come with you if you're going out there tonight though. If he is there, this man knows a lot about the house, and he's possibly been watching you. He could be really dodgy."

"Dodgier than a ghost?" Beth said with a laugh she didn't feel.

"Well, less spooky, but potentially more dangerous. Also, you realise he might not be there, don't you? You said he'd told you that you wouldn't see him in the same way anymore and that his goodbye seemed very final."

"Yes, but nothing I've read today has changed how I feel about the person I've been meeting. I've always felt totally safe with him and I still would. There's bound to be a logical explanation."

"I still think I should come with you."

"You can't, then I know he won't come. He's only ever out there when I'm alone."

Lady Angela regarded her for a minute, studying the determined look on her face.

"Alright then. But let me know when you set off and as soon as you get back to the staff block. If you need help, just phone me. I'll be waiting and I can be with you in minutes."

CHAPTER
THIRTY-SIX

I t was early evening, a good while before
sunset, when Beth made her way down
to the viewpoint. Although she'd told Lady
Angela nothing had changed about how she
felt, she had to admit now that wasn't true.
She couldn't bring herself to accept the idea
that Alex was some sort of supernatural entity.
Even saying to herself that she'd been meeting a
ghost sounded crazy. But she knew for definite
Alex wasn't Lady Angela's son, which meant that
whoever he was, he wasn't who she'd thought.
So it was a different kind of anticipation she was
feeling as she walked along the path. It wasn't
because she wanted an early night that she was
going out there before dark: it was because she
was afraid. She was either meeting a man that

no one else knew, who had misled her about who he was, and had apparently been watching her, or she was meeting a ghost. Neither option sounded good. So it turned out Alex had been right when he'd told her she wouldn't see him in the same way again. The contents of the book had changed things in the end.

She sat on the bench until the light faded, and her nerves failed her completely. The talk of ghosts had spooked her, and every branch breaking in the woods, every rustle from the trees, and particularly every mournful shriek from the birds making their way to roost, had her heart thumping. But there was no sign of Alex. And there was no sign of him the night after, or the night after that.

The mystery of who he was consumed her. She showed everybody the photo, but no one had seen anyone who looked like the man in the picture. She told her mum about how the diary had ended and finding Alexander's book and letter, but she didn't tell her about her meetings with a man who looked exactly like his photograph. It seemed too complicated and bizarre a story to explain over the phone. Although she'd told Lucy all about Alex in her emails, she struggled to tell her about this development— 'I think that crush I had was actually on my long dead great-great-grandfather'—seemed too surreal to type, so she just didn't mention him, thinking she'd have a proper explanation by the time they next met face to face. The only person she confided in about the many times she had met this unknown man and the way she had felt about him was Eilidh. But although Eilidh was sympathetic and concerned, she was as confused as Beth. She couldn't provide any answers about who he was, or where he had disappeared to.

The more she played her memories of their meetings over in her mind, the more things seemed to point to the conclusion that Alex was indeed who he had always claimed to be. He was Alexander MacAird of Ardmhor, just not the one she'd thought. He'd never lied. She had just fitted his words to her assumptions. He'd said he hadn't felt anything for a long time, and Beth had assumed he'd meant he hadn't felt romantic desire since his difficult break up, but what if he'd meant it more literally, that he hadn't felt *anything* since his death? When he'd said he couldn't go to the Ardmhor Hotel anymore, what if he'd meant he physically couldn't and that he was somehow tethered to the grounds of the house? And now she really thought about it, there were times he'd seemed to know details from the diary that she didn't think she'd mentioned. When she'd told him she'd discovered Alexander was her great-great-grandfather, he'd said it was strange to hear her say they were related. He'd been surprised that she knew, rather than surprised at the news.

He'd also spoken with such certainty about how Alexander would be proud of her and what he'd want her to take from his story. How could he have been so sure of those things from her brief descriptions of what the diary said? The way he spoke about Eliza had always sounded as if he really knew her, too. He'd told Beth often enough that she was like Eliza and that she reminded him of his lost love. It was just that she hadn't picked up on them being one and the same. If he somehow was the spirit of her great-great-grandfather, it would certainly explain why he'd said their relationship couldn't go any further. She'd never been able to tell whether Alex felt the sort of attraction to her that she felt to him, and when she really thought about it, he'd never said or done anything that would have been inappropriate in a platonic relationship. Any uncertainty over his feelings had been down to her wishful thinking, and the failed kiss had been entirely instigated by her. His reaction had shown nothing could have been further from his mind. Alex being some kind of supernatural being would also explain how he always seemed to sense her presence at the viewpoint. But accepting what all these little details suggested, when it was so far beyond the realms of what she'd thought possible, was difficult. And when she thought about where some of her Alex fantasies had taken her, it was also pretty creepy.

Over the next few weeks, as the season was

drawing to a close, Beth tried to throw herself into her work. Her first assignment for her course, about different perspectives on the role of museums, had received really positive feedback, and she was still enjoying guiding visitors around the house. She wondered if the novelty of telling the same stories every day would eventually wear off, but it didn't seem like it at the moment. The next hurdle would be a two-week placement at a museum in Edinburgh, but that was a little way off yet. She still visited the viewpoint at least once every day, she wasn't quite ready to give up on Alex being an actual person yet, but he never appeared, and gradually her mind adapted to the idea that he hadn't really been a part of this world. Occasionally, she'd hear a whisper on the wind that sounded like his voice, or she'd think she'd seen him in the distance, but either he disappeared, or it would turn out to be someone else. She made herself concentrate on building relationships with people she knew were real, making sure she branched out further than the group chat with the other volunteers, but she constantly thought about what her time with Alex had meant.

With just two weeks left before the house, shop, and café closed for the season, Beth was feeling a little anxious about what life might be like in the staff accommodation over the winter. After shutdown, most staff would stay on for a couple of weeks to help with the clear up, but then only a skeleton staff would remain to keep things ticking over. All the other occupants of the staff block would leave at that point, and Beth wasn't sure she could handle living by herself in such an isolated building, especially as she was still freaked out by the whole being in love with a ghost relative situation. Although she'd had a few chats with Eilidh's dad about the potential of the factor's house, she still wasn't sure if it was too much to take on, and even if she did go ahead, it would be months until she could contemplate living there.

She was sitting in the Ardmhor Hotel, nursing a pint of cider and waiting for Eilidh. She'd been eyeing the bar wistfully, wishing Andrew would suddenly reappear for some uncomplicated flirting, when Eilidh finally walked in and took the seat next to her, calling over to the barman to bring her a large white wine.

"I've got some news that you're either going to love or hate," she announced by way of a greeting.

"Come on then, don't keep me in suspense," said Beth, trying to be patient as Eilidh's drink was placed in front of her and she took a long, drawn-out sip.

"You're going to be getting some company in the staff block over the winter."

"Well, that's brilliant," Beth interrupted.

"But it's me and Rich, so I don't want you

feeling like a big old gooseberry."

"I don't get it. You've already got a flat."

"I know, but you've had so many chats with my dad about the merits of buying somewhere that I've finally decided to give in to his nagging and stop wasting so much money on rent. You know already that the estate only takes a small amount from wages in return for accommodation, so by moving into the staff block, I can save loads."

"What about Rich though? I thought the accommodation was for staff only?"

"It is, but because he'll be sharing with me, they're fine with him moving in as well. So what do you think?"

"I think it's great. I've been dreading being on my own there. As long as you don't mind me intruding on your couple time?"

"Well, you were there first, so technically we'd be intruding on your alone time, but it won't just be the three of us, so there's no need to worry. There's a girl called Sarah who works in the main estate office. I don't think you've met her, but she's lovely. Anyway, she's been renting a room off someone which they need back, so she's going to be moving in as well."

Beth felt herself relax at the thought she wouldn't be alone on those dark winter nights, but she felt the tension return as she passed the viewpoint on her way back to her room. It took all of her courage to sit down on the bench. Although she concentrated on how safe Alex had made her feel, she couldn't trick her mind into calming down, and within minutes, she scurried away, rushing towards the security of lights and people. Eliza's locket was around her neck, and she felt for where it rested at her throat, running her finger across the smooth gold. Before she'd found it, the last person to touch the locket had been Alexander himself. Beth wondered if Alex was disappointed that she'd struggled to accept his explanation of the truth. And now that she finally was accepting it, she didn't know what scared her more—the thought of seeing him, or the thought that he was gone from her life forever.

CHAPTER THIRTY-SEVEN

Beth was standing amongst dozens of individually sized and labelled boxes in a museum hall full of echoes. The few staff present didn't absorb the sounds in the same way a crowd of visitors did. They were busy preparing the contents of a temporary exhibition for their journey home, and it was a painstaking process with no room for error. Under the watchful eye of her supervisor and a representative of the museum that had made the loan, Beth picked up a small porcelain bowl and checked it carefully against the condition reports. These reports had been made before the artefacts began their journey and had been checked again on arrival at the museum to make sure nothing had changed. Once Beth was satisfied that everything was still as stated in the reports and her observers were satisfied her inspection was correct, the object needed to be gently placed back into its specially commissioned container. The process required intense concentration and would need to be repeated for each artefact. Beth felt the weight of responsibility on her and was surprised to find she was relishing it.

She was halfway through her placement in the museum in central Edinburgh and could honestly say she was loving every minute. She had expected to feel a bit of a spare part, observing the regular staff as they went about their work. Memories of herself at fifteen, completing her school's compulsory two-week work experience placement, had not filled her with confidence. She remembered spending most of the time being unsure what was expected of her, and she'd been left embarrassed when her supervisor commented on her lack of initiative. This placement, however, could not have been more different. The programme was so well structured that she had been busy from the moment she'd arrived. It was fascinating to see some of the theory she had been learning put into practise, from how the collections were curated, to the different ways in which visitors responded to the same exhibits. She was particularly interested in the way the museum communicated oral history. From what Lady Angela had told her, there were still many stories and traditions in the area surrounding Ardmhor that were being passed on through families mainly as spoken word, and she was really keen to make these a part of the Ardmhor museum when it opened.

It had been so intense she'd had little time to explore the city. All she had managed was a quick wander up to the castle and around Princes Street Gardens in her lunch breaks, but she intended to put that right this weekend. Her parents had arranged to travel up and spend her days off with her, and she already had a packed itinerary planned.

The Beth that greeted Jean and David from the train on Saturday morning was giddy with excitement. When she had last seen them in August, just before she began her official employment at Ardmhor, she had expected to travel home after a few weeks to collect her car and some other belongings, but somehow the time to make the trip had never materialised. This was the longest Beth could remember going without seeing them, and she threw herself into their arms as if she hadn't seen them for years.

By the time they settled themselves into the window seats of a cosy Italian restaurant, with the lights of Edinburgh shining before them, they were all a little exhausted. They had tried to cram in as much of what the city had to offer as possible, but there was still so much they hadn't seen. They had marvelled at the views from Calton Hill, spotting the castle, Holyrood Palace, and the Scottish Parliament buildings. They'd strolled between the different structures and posed for photos by the columns of the National Monument. It had been inspired by the Parthenon, and they wondered just how imposing it would have looked if it had been completed. Then, the views from Calton Hill had been eclipsed as they walked round Arthur's Seat, their legs aching as they reached the top of the ancient volcano. Later on, they'd ambled up the Royal Mile, mooching around the shops and exploring the outside of the castle. All of this was accompanied by much chatter and discussion as they caught up on each other's news. Beth could see why the city was so popular with tourists. Although they'd been on the go all day, they had barely scratched the surface. However, the crowds had come as a shock after three months at Ardmhor. Much as she was enjoying the change of pace, Beth suspected city life was no longer for her. She often found herself thinking of the open space of Ardmhor and yearning for the tang of the sea air.

"So you really feel Ardmhor is permanent, then?" enquired David as they tucked into steaming bowls of pasta.

"I do. I've been missing it while I've been here. I feel like I've finally found where I'm meant to be."

"That's fantastic, love," Jean reached out and stroked her hand. "We're so pleased you're happy, even if we are missing you a little."

"Only a little?" Beth joked, but she knew exactly what they meant. The distance from her family was the only fly in the ointment.

"I was thinking about the fact you haven't been able to collect your car yet," began David. "Seeing as you're already part way home, why don't you get the train back down to us when you finish here next Friday? Then you can pack up some more stuff and take it back to Ardmhor in your car."

"It's a good idea, Dad, but I'm not sure I fancy driving all that way on the motorway, especially as I haven't driven for over three months."

"Knowing how you are about driving, I'd thought you might say that. So how about if I drive us all back up there in your car, then me and your mum can stay over for the night and get the train back the next day? I've heard it's a lovely scenic run."

"That'd be amazing," Beth replied, feeling lucky to have so much support from her parents.

Her mind suddenly flitted to Alex. If he really had been the Alexander of the diary, which was the only explanation she had now, he certainly hadn't been so fortunate. It had taken a lot to accept that Alex hadn't been 'real', but she knew he hadn't been a figment of her imagination. After all, she'd known nothing of Alexander MacAird when they'd first met. But accepting he wasn't real hadn't pushed him from her mind. On the contrary, she thought of him constantly, pondering on what he'd tried to teach her, doing her best to be brave and open to opportunities. However, she did try to push away his parting words—that the person for her wasn't far away. She so much wanted them to be true that she couldn't allow herself to dwell on them. She couldn't see how anyone she'd met at Ardmhor could be right for her, so she was trying to become happy with herself instead. If the right person did come along, she wanted them to be a pleasant bonus, rather than the key to her happiness.

Waking up in her old bedroom the following Saturday morning, being startled by the security light as a cat ran across the garden, Beth felt a sense of relief that this wasn't permanent. It had been nice to see familiar sights as her dad drove her home from the station the previous night, and it had been heaven to tuck into her mum's shepherd's pie, but she realised this wasn't home anymore. It was familiar, and it was comforting, but in a short space of time Ardmhor had become where she belonged.

The journey back wasn't as scenic as the one they'd made together in July. They'd set off early, long before it became light, in order to make the most of the day. Then, once daylight had arrived cloud covered the tops of the hills, stunting their height and hiding their majesty, but nothing could hide Beth's excitement. She now knew for certain that she wanted to put down roots at Ardmhor, and she had arranged for Alan to meet them at the factor's house, so that she could show her parents the place she was considering buying.

"This fireplace is lovely, and look at the detail on that ceiling rose," gushed Jean, taking in the features of the factor's house. "I'm trying to imagine Eliza here, but I still find it hard to picture her anywhere other than in her armchair."

They'd already unpacked the rest of Beth's belongings and had a quick drink with Lady Angela in the private apartment at Ardmhor House. She'd been lying in wait for their car to arrive, after texting Beth for updates on their journey. Beth had been embarrassed and delighted in equal measure while Lady Angela sang her praises to her parents. Jean had really taken to Angela, who'd made a fuss of the family connection, getting out photo albums to point out shared facial features she'd spotted. Angela had even gone as far as dragging Jim over to the window, so they could better see what she referred to as the 'Ardmhor nose'. When Beth had mentioned her worries about lacking the experience needed to oversee the opening of the museum, Angela had told her not to be daft and said that her appointment fitted the Ardmhor ethos of developing their own staff. Then Jim had made them laugh by pointing out, somewhat more pragmatically, that finances wouldn't have allowed for anything else.

After spending at least an hour looking around the factor's house and discussing in detail how much work it would need to make it liveable, David and Jean seemed convinced that buying it was a sensible idea. Jean had been charmed by the original features and the family connection, and David was excited by the potential. Perhaps it was just being there with her family, but Beth found the house much more welcoming on this second viewing. Last time she'd been there she'd been able to picture it renovated, but this time, as she wandered around the rooms, she could really see herself living there.

It was almost dark as they left the house and walked down the road to the Ardmhor Hotel.

David and Jean had booked a room there for the night, so Beth had arranged for Eilidh, Rich, and Eilidh's parents to join them for dinner. Beth was keen for her parents to meet more of the friends she had made at Ardmhor, so they'd be reassured that she wasn't alone. As always, the food was excellent, and conversation flowed easily. Eilidh and Rich shared their plans to save up and buy somewhere themselves, and then later, Jean and David, and Alan and Claire, swapped tales of how they'd met and of their first homes together. Beth surveyed the little group happily. She didn't even mind that she hadn't got a love story of her own to add to the conversation. All she could think about was how good it felt to be home.

CHAPTER
THIRTY-EIGHT

I t was a crisp day in early December when Beth walked out of the solicitors in Inveravain clutching the keys to the factor's house—or her house as it was now. She crossed the road and pushed open the shiny green door of her favourite café, intending to treat herself to a celebratory cake. She couldn't believe that she was finally the owner of her own home. Admittedly, it was a house that no one would choose to live in at present, but eventually it was going to be beautiful, and it was all hers. It seemed her luck really was in because the best table in the house, with the sunny window seat overlooking the harbour, had just come free. So she ordered a slice of three-layered caramel cake, along with a hot chocolate, and settled herself in.

The buying process had been surprisingly hassle free, and Beth felt proud that she'd managed it alone, without relying on the help of her parents. As the factor's house was being sold by the Ardmhor Trust, she'd had the advantage of being able to discuss the purchase with Duncan Matthews, the estate manager, before asking her solicitor to make a formal offer. This meant she'd already known what the Trust would accept, and as no one else had noted their interest in the property, there had been no drawn-out negotiations. The conveyancing process hadn't thrown up any unexpected issues either, so they had proceeded quickly to settlement. Beth was amazed that just six weeks after making her offer, her name was being added to the land register as the official owner.

Her phone buzzed, and she saw several new messages in the volunteer group chat, each of them wishing her luck and asking if she'd got the keys yet. She typed a quick response and looked out over the boats bobbing in the harbour, noticing a fresh dusting of snow on the tops of the hills. She felt she really was living the life she was meant to have. With the season over and the house closed for the winter by the time Beth returned from Edinburgh, she could now spend two days a week concentrating on her course. The other three days were spent sifting through the archives and planning the Ardmhor museum. The intention was still to have one section ready to open when the next season began. Eilidh had been co-opted into helping with the cataloguing of artefacts one day a week, and Lady Angela usually volunteered to help on that day as well. Beth was enjoying it so much she could finally understand those people who said their work didn't feel like work. She was loving sharing the accommodation block with Eilidh, Rich, and Sarah as well. They'd started taking it in turns to cook and often shared a bottle of wine rather than trekking to the pub in the cold. Now that it was December, Rich had insisted on putting up Christmas decorations. The girls had pretended they weren't that bothered, in order to get him to do the bulk of the work. They'd sat there drinking mulled wine and listening to Christmas tunes, then they'd swooped in to take over the fun final touches.

Since finding out that her parents would travel up to her for Christmas, Beth had been getting increasingly excited. She had been expecting to make the long journey back to England to celebrate with them, so the fact that they were going to rent a house near Ardmhor instead was a huge bonus. The house they had chosen was also fully accessible for her grandmother, so the whole family could be together. Beth smiled at the thought of showing her gran the places the diary referred to and the house she now owned. Christmas songs were tinkling away in the background of the café, so

Beth decided to embrace the festive feeling fully and make a start on searching for Christmas presents before driving back to Ardmhor.

Returning to the car park and loading her purchases into the boot, Beth felt even more pleased with herself. For her gran, she'd chosen a miniature pottery version of the colourful buildings that lined Inveravain harbour. Beth knew she'd love to add it to the collection in her display cabinet. Then she'd bought a necklace, with a pendant made of broken sea crockery, for her mum. The tiny ceramic fragments still revealed their blue and white patterns, but unknown amounts of time being swirled up and down the beach had smoothed their edges. What they might once have been, who they had belonged to, and how they had found themselves at the bottom of the sea fascinated Beth. Her dad was always trickier to buy for, but she'd seen a book about the building of Scottish lighthouses in the cavernous bookshop on the corner of the high street. The practicalities of building these enormous structures in treacherous locations had always intrigued David, so Beth hoped it was something he'd enjoy.

She had a definite sense of everything coming together. If only Alex's parting words about the right man not being far away would prove true as well. Then everything really would be perfect. However, as she pulled out onto the coast road, enjoying the sight of the sun glistening on the sea, she reminded herself that she didn't need a man to complete her. She was going to make her life complete by herself, and it already felt like she was doing a pretty good job of it.

As she left work a few days later, Beth was still feeling good. If the first stage of the museum was going to be ready when the new season began, they would need to start preparing the space in January. The rooms they would be using had been the café and shop before they'd moved to the coach house. All traces of their previous existence had long since been removed, but they would need repainting and possibly new flooring. They would also need display cases and boards building, and this was the part Beth had been finding hard. It was difficult to know what she would need before she knew exactly what the contents would be. She had decided a while ago that the initial stage of the museum should focus on the house and its occupants. Then the later stages would expand to cover wider local history and the MacAird clan across the world. The idea was to use photographs of the house today, alongside old photographs from the family albums, to show how past occupants had lived at Ardmhor. They intended to focus on the parts of the house that were now private and that the visitors didn't get to see. They were also going to highlight previous residents of the house that had made an impact outside of Ardmhor. Beth wanted to showcase items belonging to each of them as a way of getting visitors to engage with their stories. Once she had started researching, it hadn't taken long to find plenty of potential candidates. The MacAirds had been very influential people and had been involved in many important events both nationally and internationally. The problem had been discovering if they had enough artefacts belonging to each person to do their stories justice. For the past few weeks, Eilidh, Lady Angela, and Beth had devoted their time to the search, and today Beth felt like she finally had everything she needed. Lady Angela had found a dressing table set which was engraved with the initials of a MacAird daughter who'd been a strident member of the suffrage movement. They'd also found a corset showing the tiny waist she was expected to create each day. The plan was to display these alongside the writing chest she had used to compose missives demanding equality for women. Beth hoped they would illustrate the difference between the world women had been expected to inhabit and the one they were fighting to be part of. They had uncovered hundreds of artefacts for display, but amongst them all, Beth was particularly fond of an intricate set of building blocks. The detail on them was far beyond that of the usual child's toy, allowing the little builder to create turrets, sash windows, and all sorts of unexpected features. Beth knew they would help transport visitors to the world of the early nineteenth century MacAird who'd played with them as a child, before going on to design some of Scotland's most iconic buildings. Although there was still a long way to go preparing everything, Beth was relieved that she now knew exactly what she wanted to achieve.

As she walked further away from the house, the light changed. It had been dull all day, but a patch of sun now broke through the cloud. It made the white paint of the oldest section of the house glow against the forbidding cloud that lay behind it. The sky had an unusual colour to it. They rarely got any snow here down by the sea, even though it regularly graced the tops of the hills, but that was what the colour reminded Beth of, the pinkish hue of snow clouds. Beth found her feet making their way to the viewpoint. She'd been going there less and less, partly because darkness came early now, and partly because she'd finally come to accept that Alex wouldn't be there.

It was just as she rounded the corner, where the path opened up to reveal the benches, that she saw him. It was unmistakeably him. He had his back to her, but she would have recognised his height and the set of his shoulders anywhere. A ray of sunlight was shining on his unruly hair, and as he turned slightly, she could see the familiar profile of what she now knew to be the Ardmhor nose. Beth froze, scared to approach him. After all this time looking for him wherever she went, hearing his words on the wind and not knowing whether they had been spoken aloud or just in her head, she couldn't bear the thought that she might scare him away. But conversely, her feet were already preparing to run to him, they were desperate to shorten the distance between them, and her arms were ready to encircle him and never let go. And that's what happened. Within seconds, she was next to him, her arms squeezing him tight. Her face was buried against his neck as she told him he should never leave again. She was so overwhelmed by his presence it took her a moment to register that he was speaking as well.

Well, I'm not going to complain about such a great welcome, but do I know you?"

Beth pulled away with the speed of someone escaping a burning building and looked at him again. Yes, he had Alex's height and build, but now that she looked properly, his hair had more of a curl to it than Alex's. Also, although he had that same large Ardmhor nose, it didn't have the prominence that Alex's had, instead it sat more comfortably amongst the rest of his features.

She could see clearly now that the man stood in front of her was incredibly like Alex, but he was definitely not him. She felt her face turning pink. The thought was also running through her mind that he was unreasonably good looking. She could hear Alex's words as if he was next to her, 'Beth, I know there is someone for you, someone not that far away, and I know that when you meet him, you will have no doubt.' It was so clear she couldn't believe this other man wasn't hearing it too.

"I'm Ali," he said, having realised she wasn't going to answer. "Is there any chance of me finding out who you are?"

"I'm so sorry, I thought you were someone else," she finally stammered. Her heart was beating twice as fast as normal, not just out of embarrassment, but because this was actually him. This was Ali, the man she'd thought she'd met on her first night at Ardmhor.

"I'd sort of worked that bit out," he said with a smile. Beth noticed his eyes were slightly darker than Alex's, with a mischievous twinkle of their own. "So, do you have a name? Or do you prefer to remain a mystery?"

"I'm Beth," she said, her voice approaching normal at last. "I work here, setting up the new museum."

"Oh, so you're Beth," he said slowly, looking at her closely. "My mum's told me a lot about you."

"That sounds ominous," she replied, desperately hoping everything he'd heard had been good.

She tried to focus on his words rather than Alex's, which were looping round her brain, 'when you meet him, you will have no doubt'. Get a grip, she told herself. The last time she'd felt an instant attraction, it had turned out to be to a ghost, a ghost who also happened to be her great-great-grandfather. She needed to slow down here.

"Not at all," Ali replied. "My mum's just so excited about the museum. It's what she's wanted for ages, so she's thrilled to have someone to share her vision. She thinks you're incredibly talented, and then obviously the family connections have been the icing on the cake. If you haven't noticed yet, she loves that sort of thing."

"I have noticed, but it's a very distant family link." Beth replied. She felt it was important to make that clear. "So your mum said you've been in South America. What were you doing there?"

She already had a rough idea from Lady Angela, but she needed to take the attention off her. The sensation of a whole kaleidoscope of butterflies fluttering round her stomach was unsettling. They chatted for quite some time, with Ali explaining about his year volunteering with a charity in South America. He had been following the family tradition of working in finance in London, but he had increasingly found himself questioning the inequalities he saw around him, until he realised he could no longer continue to work there and live with himself. The work in South America had been the total opposite, and now he was ready for something new. He wanted to improve opportunities for young people in the Ardmhor area. The lack of employment forced many to move away, and he was hoping to use the estate to rectify that. He just needed to get everyone, especially the Ardmhor Trust, on board. Beth told him about the plans for the museum, and Ali was fascinated by tales of interesting ancestors he'd never been aware of. Darkness had long since surrounded them when Ali asked who she had expected him to be.

"Has your mum told you about the diary and how I came to find out I was descended from the MacAirds?"

"Yes, for a while I didn't hear about much else from her."

"And did she tell you about Alex?"

"Well, yes, he's the guy in the diary, isn't he? Your great-great-grandfather."

"That's right, but did she tell you anything else about him?"

"I don't think so, like what?" He sounded curious, and his eyes were twinkling again.

"Ah, well, that is a story for another time," Beth said, wondering how she'd ever explain her relationship with Alex when she still didn't really understand it herself.

"I'm glad you've said that because I was wondering if it was too forward to ask to see you again, but now you've already said that we have to."

Beth laughed. "Well, I reckon seeing each other again would be pretty inevitable, what with you living in Ardmhor House and me working there!"

"Yes, but..." he hesitated, suddenly more serious. "I meant properly see you, like a date. This probably sounds silly, seeing as we've only just met, but I don't want to stop talking to you. I've already agreed to meet some old friends in Inveravain tonight, but can I see you tomorrow?"

The butterflies in Beth's stomach took flight again, and she struggled to stop herself grinning like a Cheshire cat. Lady Angela hadn't been wrong when she'd described Ali as an open book. He might look like Alex, but his directness was in total contrast.

"I'd love to," she replied, trying to keep her face under control. "But can we go somewhere a bit warmer? I'm freezing!"

"I know. Somehow, I hadn't noticed how cold it was getting. How about the Ardmhor Hotel? Shall we meet there at seven?"

"That sounds great," Beth replied.

She was relieved to discover that Ali could make plans beyond the viewpoint, but she carefully held back from saying so. That was definitely too bizarre a conversation for a first meeting. She was expecting Ali to disappear towards the house and leave her sitting on the bench, just as Alex always had, so she was surprised when he took hold of her hand. She startled, as if a jolt of electricity had passed through her.

"I'm sorry," said Ali, dropping her hand. "I didn't mean to make you jump; I should have asked first. I was hoping to walk you home. Would that be alright with you?" he added, sounding less confident.

"That'd be nice, if you're sure you've got time before meeting your friends."

"Definitely," he smiled, taking her hand again and pulling her to her feet.

They walked hand in hand to the door of the staff house, then they lingered for a moment, both seeming unsure what to do next. Ali looked at her, and Beth could recognise the same feeling of intensity she'd felt when Alex used to gaze into her eyes. This was different though. It wasn't just a connection she could feel, although that was definitely there, she could see an attraction in Ali's eyes as well. He leaned in and kissed her briefly on the mouth. His lips only brushed hers for a fleeting second, but it was enough. Beth felt as if she'd turned to liquid, barely managing to respond to his 'see you tomorrow' as he turned to go.

As she watched Ali walk away, feeling the absence of his hands around hers, the first delicate flakes of snow descended from the sky. By the time he disappeared from sight, it was as if she was inside a giant snow globe. Thick white flakes swirled around her, and she couldn't help feeling she'd been shaken. Maybe Alex had felt something a little like this when he'd first seen her at the viewpoint. Ali was so familiar, so like Alex, yet completely different. Had Alex thought she was Eliza before realising she was a very different person? Maybe she'd seemed even more familiar to Alex. After all, she wasn't only descended from Eliza, and while it was Eliza's looks she shared, it was Alex's personality that had come to the fore. Had Alex somehow known that she was meant to meet Ali? Was that what his parting words had been trying to tell her? She wasn't sure she believed in love at first sight, or the idea of there being one special person meant for you, but as she stood there, looking at the picture postcard world the snow was creating, hearing Alex's words in her head, she knew one thing for certain—she couldn't wait to see Ali again.

CHAPTER
THIRTY-NINE

Four years later....

Beth was nursing a mocktail as she wandered around the museum, stopping to chat to guests and ensuring everyone had a drink. She paused for a moment in front of a display, marvelling that this was all down to her. Well, she knew she couldn't have done it without the support of Angela, Eilidh, and the countless others who'd contributed, but she had led them. This museum was her creation. She'd come a long way from the girl who was too scared to ask Angela to let her see the archives. It was strange to think that just a few years earlier the name Ardmhor meant nothing to her. If pushed, it might have sparked a vague memory of a childhood holiday, but now it made up her world. She paused by a colourful arrangement of roses to straighten a stray flower. The volunteer group had sent them up as a surprise that morning. Beth thanked her lucky stars for the other members of the group. Even though four years had passed since the volunteer holiday, they were still in regular touch, supporting each other constantly. They were one reason she'd always be grateful for her time as a teacher. Without that job, she wouldn't have been overwhelmed by marking. Then she wouldn't have been procrastinating by reading her mum's magazine, and she'd never have seen the advert for the volunteer holiday. The holiday she'd been so dismissive of. The same holiday that had changed the course of her life.

The museum had gradually taken shape over the last few years and had become a major draw for visitors. It had expanded from that first section, which detailed the lives of notable Ardmhor residents. There were now several rooms looking at the clearances as well. One room covered the reasons behind them and dealt with the uncomfortable truth that much of the MacAird fortune had come through the suffering of others. Another section looked at the brutality of the clearances, and an immersive exhibit gave visitors an idea of the terrible conditions many of those forced from their homes experienced when they were transported overseas. Another room looked at their destinations. Several evictees had gone on to important roles in the communities they established, and elements of Scottish customs still thrived in the places they had travelled to. The descendants of others had gradually made their way back to Ardmhor, and their stories were told in the museum as well. Other sections looked at Ardmhor's role in the wider timeline of Scottish history, from the establishment of the clan system to the present day. There was also a section covering the local legends and superstitions that Beth had been so keen to include. They had needed to employ several more members of staff, but even with the extra costs, the museum was proving a valuable addition to the estate.

They didn't close over the winter as the house did. Although there were fewer visitors after the main season, the museum was kept busy working with schools and people wanting to research local history. Beth particularly enjoyed the work with schools. When she told stories from her museum, she finally felt like she shone as a teacher. Each day, as she walked the short distance from the factor's house to the museum, she reminded herself how lucky she was. The dread and anxiety she'd felt each morning had been replaced with a pleasant anticipation of what the day might bring. There were still things that challenged her, but she no longer felt the fear of being revealed as a failure. She knew what she was capable of, and she knew she had people to rely on if things got too tough.

She scanned the room and located her parents chatting with Eilidh, Rich, and Andrew. Eilidh was proudly showing off her engagement ring. They hadn't set a date for the wedding yet, sorting out their house was still their number one priority, but they hoped it'd be within the next year or two. Andrew had been back in Ardmhor for a while now. He had followed through on his plan of opening an activity centre, and it was becoming increasingly successful as its reputation spread. Beth was so pleased her parents had travelled up for this evening. They had been unfailing in their support since she'd decided to remain at Ardmhor and were now in the middle of some significant life changes themselves. They'd sadly lost Beth's grandmother two years ago, but it had been her wish for them to use the money she'd left to buy a house near Beth. Her gran had made the journey up to Ardmhor several times before her death and had fallen in love with the area in the same way Beth had. Then, last summer, the house they had holidayed in when Beth was a child came on the market, and they were lucky enough to buy it. It was in the middle of renovations at the moment, but their intention was to sell their home in England and move in permanently as soon as David retired. Once again Beth wondered at how despairing she'd been that summer before she set off for Ardmhor, feeling like she'd plod along miserably forever, yet less than five years later everything was falling into place so beautifully.

She realised she had come to a stop in front of her favourite exhibit. It told the story of Alexander MacAird and his love, Eliza. The diary, Alex's letter, the book with its secret compartment, and the locket were all displayed in a case beneath the information board. Beth's favourite part was right at the bottom of the board, where there was an explanation of how the items came into the museum's possession. It delighted visitors to read that Beth had moved to Ardmhor with no idea of any connection to the estate, before gradually discovering she was part of the clan. But what always got the most comments were the two enlarged pictures displayed side by side. The first one showed Eliza and Alex, relaxed and smiling, on the lawn in front of Ardmhor House. The second picture mirrored the first, another smiling couple on the lawn. However, this photograph was much more recent. Instead of showing Eliza and Alex, it showed Beth and Ali moments after they'd exchanged their marriage vows. Visitors couldn't get enough of the two strikingly similar couples and the delayed happy ending—when an Alexander MacAird finally married his Elizabeth.

Beth felt a hand on her waist and smiled as Ali

hugged her close to him. She wore a new locket around her neck now: one that Ali had given her on the anniversary of their first date. That first date had proved that Ali existed outside of the Ardmhor grounds, and it had also been the night when Beth felt certain Alex had been right: just as he'd said, the man for her hadn't been far away—he was the man she'd thought she'd been talking to all along. As her relationship with Ali had deepened, she'd waited for the familiar feeling to surface, the feeling that something wasn't right and that she was making a mistake, but it never came. Alex had been right about that, too. Now that she'd finally met the right man, she really didn't have any doubt. Ali impressed her every day. He had convinced the Ardmhor Trust to reconfigure parts of the estate, putting more land into the hands of the community, and forestry schemes and a renewable energy project were already providing new jobs. It had also been Ali's idea to open the café and museum all year round, so only the house took a winter break. Although there were fewer visitors, they still turned a profit, which could then be ploughed back into the other projects, and it meant more year-round employment in the area. Beth loved that they lived in the factor's house together, she knew it had been Alex and Eliza's dream to set up their home there, and although they hadn't managed a room entirely lined with books yet, it felt as if the story had come full circle.

It really did feel as if Ali and her had been made for each other, and who was to say they hadn't? Her experience with Alex had taught her that not everything can be easily explained or understood.

Since meeting Ali, she'd given up looking for Alex, but he was never far from her mind. Whenever she doubted herself, she'd hear his voice telling her to try, to not just accept that something was beyond her. She knew he'd wanted her to avoid the mistakes he'd made. He'd wanted to ensure she didn't miss out on the life she was supposed to have, and Beth felt it really was down to him that she hadn't. If he hadn't challenged her that night, pushed her to be braver and made her reconsider applying for the job, she might still be back in England, plodding along full of dread. She still didn't know for certain what had happened with Alex. The idea she had spent weeks talking to a ghost remained hard to accept, and occasionally she'd wonder if perhaps she had imagined it— but believing that was equally impossible. Although she hadn't seen him again, his voice remained totally real. She hoped he was also on the next stage of his journey, that their time together sharing Eliza's diary had brought him the acceptance he needed. He'd told her once that the dead weren't in their graves; he'd said they were with the people they cared about or in the places they loved, so perhaps he was still close. Beth was sure that sometimes she'd seen a shock of recognition on a new staff member's face, when they'd read Alex's story and seen his photograph. So perhaps he was still out there, dispensing encouragement to the anxious of his beloved Ardmhor, but she hoped he had found peace as he did so.

The family connection seemed especially important tonight. The thought that without Alex, she might have made a different decision and missed all this was sobering. Not that Beth was drinking that evening; she'd been wandering around with mocktails because tonight's party was to mark the start of her maternity leave. She felt a kick and reached for Ali's hand, wanting him to feel it too. This sudden focus on her stomach had taken a bit of getting used to, but she could recognise that people were excited for her, and she had gradually adapted to the attention. They didn't know whether they were expecting a son or a daughter, but they knew for certain they would not be naming their child Alexander or Elizabeth. Their marriage might have represented the final chapter of Eliza and Alex's story, but their child represented a new beginning. They would write their own story and Beth and Ali wanted them to have their own name. What that story would be was a mystery. Would they love Ardmhor like Beth and Alex, always wanting to remain? Or would they be like Eliza, desperate to escape? Beth knew you couldn't predict the future or know how things would turn out. She could not have imagined the ways in which the holiday at Ardmhor would change her life. However, she recognised that it was impossible to change completely. She knew there would always be a part of her that was waiting for whatever came next. Looking round the room again, at the people she loved and the museum she had created, she felt another kick and saw the smile on Ali's face. This is everything I could want, she thought to herself. But even as the words took shape in her mind, it was already setting off again. She was acutely aware that she couldn't wait for the next chapter to begin.

Acknowledgements

Firstly, I'd like to thank you for reading this book. I have always wanted to write, but it took a long time to build the courage to have a go. It then took even longer to have something ready to share with others, and I am hugely grateful to every single person who takes the time to read my work. If you have enjoyed this book and are able to leave a rating or write a review, that would be fantastic!

Secondly, thank you to my family for putting up with me and my funny ways.

In particular, thanks to P, E, and R for letting me ignore you, trying to teach me grammar, and constantly encouraging me. I think I used up all my luck getting each one of you in my life, but you are worth never winning anything else!

Thank you to the Jeans, my amazing mum and mother-in-law, for reading my drafts and being so positive.

Thank you to my sisters, Rae and Bags, for all your feedback and ideas.

Thank you to Lindsey; I am possibly the most useless friend ever, but you've stuck with me for over a quarter of a century, and I couldn't be more grateful.

And finally, thank you Mum and Dad for giving me a love of Scotland and giving all these characters places to go!

BOOKS BY THIS AUTHOR

The Holiday At Ardmhor

Always, Ardmhor

What Was Hidden At Ardmhor

Printed in Great Britain
by Amazon